INVISIBLE
BY DAY

Debbie,

Best Wishes,

Teri Fink

A Novel by
Teri Fink

INVISIBLE BY DAY
Second Expanded Edition
Copyright © 2018 Teri Fink

SECOND EDITION SOFTCOVER
ISBN: 1622530829
ISBN-13: 978-1-62253-082-3

Editor: Kimberly Goebel
Senior Editor: Lane Diamond
Interior Designer: Lane Diamond
Cover Graphic Designer: Dale Robert Pease

EVOLVED PUBLISHING™

www.EvolvedPub.com
Evolved Publishing LLC
Butler, Wisconsin, USA

Invisible by Day is a work of fiction. All names, characters, places, and incidents are the product of the author's imagination, or are used fictitiously. Any resemblance to actual events or persons, living or dead, is entirely coincidental.

Printed in Book Antiqua font.

PRAISE FOR *INVISIBLE BY DAY*

"Teri Fink's suspense driven novel offers readers captivating characters, involved in powerful relationships, within a dramatic historical setting. Every chapter leaves you hungry for the next."
~ *Cathie E. West, Author of "The Educator's Guide to Writing a Book: Practical Advice for Teachers and Leaders"*

"If you loved Downton Abbey, you'll devour *Invisible by Day*. Teri Fink recreates World War I era England with vivid details, but while she paints the era with love, she doesn't sentimentalize it. Instead, she captures much of the brutality, sexism and class warfare that defined the times. A detailed, sweeping novel that explores three of the most compelling facets of human life: love, war, and redemption. Readers will be marking their calendars for Teri Fink's next release."
~ *A.C. Fuller, Author of the "Alex Vane Media Thriller" Series*

"Often books are good because of the story. There are a few that are special because the words are beautiful and take you to another place and time. Those are harder to find. You have both! I loved it! I look forward to your next book!"
~ *Debbie Taylor*

"Teri Fink's first novel is a genuine page-turner, the kind of book you want to have on a long flight or a lazy few days on a beach. The people and events are completely believable, in part because of how well the author researched the time period and how stylishly she describes it. This book is suspenseful, fast-paced, and satisfying. If you're looking for entertainment, it would be hard to do any better than this. I recommend it most highly."
~ *L. F. Smith*

DEDICATION

For Don Fink.

TABLE OF CONTENTS

BACK-OF-THE-BOOK EXTRAS:
Book Club Guide
Interview with the Author
Acknowledgements
About the Author
What's Next from Teri Fink?
More from Evolved Publishing

Epigraph

For age is opportunity no less
Than youth itself, though in another dress,
And as the evening twilight fades away
The sky is filled with stars, invisible by day.
~ Henry Wadsworth Longfellow

Chapter 1 – London, April 1917

Kate started up the steep, narrow staircase, feet throbbing in her black lace-up boots. Her linen jacket and skirt hung limp on her willowy frame. When she reached the fifth floor and the door to her flat, she inserted the key into the lock and turned it, but the door wouldn't budge. She turned it the other way, and the lock clicked open.

Odd, but she was too tired to give it much thought.

She stepped inside, closed the door behind her, and walked slowly through the pitch black toward the kitchen. With her hand outstretched, she groped for the cord to switch on the single light bulb that hung overhead. Wartime blackout required all windows be covered at night.

She touched the edge of the kitchen table, orienting herself, reached up and pulled the cord. The light clicked on.

A man was sitting at the table, close enough to touch her.

She jumped backwards, and went weak-kneed with fear as his face came into focus.

He stared up at her, his suit rumpled, hair out of place. Two items sat before him on the table: a red purse and a plate.

Her vision widened to take in the flat. Drawers and cupboards yawned open, spilling out their contents. Clothes lay strewn across the bed and floor.

The man indicated the chair across the table with a gloved hand. "Please, sit down. You must be exhausted after your long day."

Kate wavered, then collapsed onto the chair.

He studied her for a long moment.

Wide-eyed, she stared back at him, struggling to keep her fear at bay.

He sat forward. "I believe you have something of mine. I want it back. *Now.*"

Kate answered, her voice sounding surprisingly casual, conversational even. "Whatever could I possibly have of yours?"

He exhaled, a brief, sarcastic hiss of air, and picked up the red purse, reached inside, and pulled out a small brown bottle. Removing the cork, he held the bottle over the plate, tipped it, and with one finger, tapped out cream-colored powder into a little hill.

With one gloved finger, he pushed the plate across the table until it sat directly in front of Kate. "For you."

She tried to look nonchalant, knowing the contents of those bottles all too well.

His lips twitched on one side. "I know you like it. It would be a shame to waste. In fact, I think you'll take all of it—tonight."

She knew how a modest portion of the powders affected her. The entire amount on the plate would put her into a sleep from which she would never awaken. "I don't think I can drink that much."

"Why don't you sniff it?" He inhaled noisily through his nose. "It's quicker to work, and far more potent that way."

They both knew it was enough to kill her regardless of how she took it.

Self-pity swept over her, and her lower lip trembled. To have gone through so much and have it end like this. Unthinkable.

"Will you answer a question first?" she asked, desperate to stall for time.

His eyebrows rose, gaze never leaving hers, and he nodded slightly.

She took a deep breath, and asked the question only he could answer. "Why did you kill him?"

No need to say the name; they both knew who she meant.

"Tell me," she persisted, trying to hold herself together. "What happened the night he died? I need to know. At least leave me with that."

He paused, shrugged. "If you wish."

Chapter 2 – London, September 1910

James Casey hurried along in the wet dark, coat collar pulled up against the lashing rain. He had worked late at the shipping office, past seven, and relished the thought of a hot cup of tea. He reached his apartment building and hurried up three flights of steps to his flat, his blond hair dripping as he unlocked the door and stepped inside. He shrugged out of his coat, shook off the raindrops, and hung it carefully on a spindly rack near the door. A narrow, neatly made bed, a wardrobe, and a kitchen table were all that furnished the room.

The small flat, the tired neighborhood — none of it discouraged him.

Things had worked out even better than he'd anticipated in London. He'd started his new job as office clerk and accountant at Lyman & Stonebeck, where the owner, Mark St. John, had hired him after a single interview, thanks in part to a letter of recommendation from the company he'd worked for in Glasgow. This new company, at triple the size of his old one, marked a step up. James worked directly under the office manager, Myron Bridger, a portly man who stood a full head below James. With caterpillar eyebrows and salt-and-pepper hair that frizzed into a halo, Mr. Bridger feigned a gruffness that didn't hold up to scrutiny.

The teakettle had worked itself up to a whistle when a knock sounded at the door. James lifted the kettle from the stove and pulled out his pocket watch: nearly 8:00.

Who on Earth could be knocking at this time of night?

He opened the door.

"Telegram." A rain-soaked delivery boy handed him an envelope and looked up expectantly.

"Oh, yes." James rummaged in his pocket for a coin and pressed it into the boy's hand.

He stepped back into his room, tore open the envelope, and scanned the contents. He experienced a mixture of emotions, sadness followed by a touch of excitement.

Inappropriate excitement, he scolded himself.

He stared at the message from Katie MacLaren.

> *Can you come home? My mum has died, and I need your help.*

He hesitated, stuffed the letter into his pocket, and began to pack his clothes for the trip back to Kirken, the village where he'd grown up. He would have to take a few days off—problematic this early in the new job—and would soon find out if Mr. Bridger truly possessed kindheartedness.

He had no choice but to ask. For Katie MacLaren, it was worth the risk.

Chapter 3

James almost didn't recognize her when she opened the front door to the small stone cottage. She looked thin and tired. Her skin, usually a creamy white, appeared nearly translucent.

"Katie." He took off his hat, squeezing it in his hand. "I'm so sorry."

"Thank you for coming, James. Please, come in." She led him inside.

The place smelled damp and musty.

Katie walked over and sat in front of the fireplace, holding her hands out to the sputtering flames. "She never was vital, you know," she said quietly. "Never had the bloom of spring in her cheeks, not since I can remember. She's had a bad cough for years, but it seems like when the weather turned cold this year, she got worse. She would sit for hours in front of this fire, coughing and complaining about the cold. Friday last week...."

She looked over her shoulder at James. "She simply didn't wake up."

He shifted uneasily on his feet.

Katie turned back to the fire. "Some of the women came and we laid her out right here in this room. They took her to the churchyard and buried her yesterday." She stood and turned away from him. "And the landlord said he didn't mean to be cruel or unkind, but with the rent long past due, I couldn't live here anymore."

"I'm sorry," he said.

"I thought," she struggled on, "that maybe you could help me find an employer in London. I've had enough of this village." She turned from the fire, staring at him full in the face. "Will you help me find work in London? Please, James?"

"Certainly, I'll help you."

She let out her breath, stepped past him to the kitchen, and picked up a battered suitcase. "Good, let's go to London."

"Now?" he asked, incredulous.

"Now."

"But... but there's still a fire in the fireplace."

"Yes, and I hope the whole place burns down. What would the landlord think of that?" She walked out the door, never giving a last look at the only home she'd ever known.

Their train pulled into London after dark. Windows, streetlights, and automobile headlights glowed through the rain, and Katie's heart pounded with excitement. More people crowded into the train station even at this hour than populated the whole of Kirken.

Here she could be anonymous. No one would know.

"We need to find a suitable place for you to spend the night," James said, carrying Katie's solitary bag as they made their way through the station.

"Don't you have a place?" Katie couldn't keep the surprise from her voice.

"I do, but that wouldn't be proper. I don't know many people here yet, and the only person I can think of who might be able to help is Mister Bridger, my supervisor at the company. The Bridger's youngest daughter recently married, so they may have a room until we can find someplace suitable."

When James had asked for time off, Mr. Bridger had begrudgingly given him three days, without pay, after hearing that a young woman from his village had just lost her mum and needed his help.

They walked miles to get to the Bridger's place, a tiny house on a street lined with identical houses packed tightly together. James stood on the Bridgers' doorstep, soaked by rain, and knocked, nervous and unsure of what to expect.

The door opened. "I'm sorry to bother you so late," James began as Mr. Bridger, shirt untucked and stocking-footed, stood gaping. "This is the young woman I told you about, Katie MacLaren."

"Kate, not Katie," she said as she stepped forward and extended a hand. "I'm not a child anymore." She glanced sidelong at James. "I'll be called Kate, now."

"Is this the girl?" A woman peeked around Mr. Bridger's shoulder.

"My wife," Mr. Bridger said. He had found his voice. "Edith."

Mrs. Bridger, a plump woman with scarlet cheeks and white hair, stepped around her husband. "The both of you, come in the house this minute. You'll catch your death out in this weather. Kate, you must be exhausted. A spot of tea and a biscuit should put some color back in your cheeks."

Over tea, Mrs. Bridger insisted that she stay with them indefinitely.

"Our daughters' bedroom just sits empty," she said, turning to James. "Don't you worry about your girl, Mister Casey. You go on home. She's in good hands."

Mrs. Bridger proved to be a gracious guardian, if a bit overwhelming. After a few days, a routine began to take shape. Kate helped with housekeeping and meals, but as a member of the household, not as a domestic servant.

James came by every night after work, often arriving with fresh meat from the butcher or bread from the baker, and he always stayed for dinner.

Filled with an intense curiosity to see and learn everything about the glorious city, Kate had asked James to take her exploring whenever he could make time. Propriety dictated that either Mr. or Mrs. Bridger or both accompany them, so this ill-matched foursome could often be found strolling through Kensington Gardens, or sightseeing in the city. One evening, they even attended a play at the Lyceum in the West End.

London bustled, thriving with more people than Kate had ever imagined could live in one place. She loved to walk along Piccadilly or The Mall, lost in the curious throng of people. During the day, she often coerced Mrs. Bridger to stroll along the Strand, where they watched all the ladies in luxurious satins and furs rushing off to who knows where—luncheons perhaps, or maybe long-overdue visits for tea with an elderly aunt.

She peered in the display windows at Harrods, astonished at the enormity of the place, let alone the array of clothing one could purchase on a whim. She dragged Mrs. Bridger into the store at least once a fortnight, where they wandered, Kate examining the latest fashions and committing them to memory. She hatched a plan to sew her own dresses to look just like them.

James, always attentive and full of shy fun, filled her evenings and every Sunday, his one day off. She'd wait impatiently for his arrival, if for nothing else than to talk with someone besides Mrs. Bridger for a while. Like an old shoe, being with James felt increasingly more comfortable.

Her new life in London suited her well, but Kate wanted more. She couldn't live with the Bridgers forever, and she began to plan how she might make an independent life for herself.

Chapter 4

Mark St. John turned his Mercedes Double Phaeton motorcar out of the bustling docks and drove away from the heart of London, until the road curved up a slight hill and businesses gave way to homes, and farther on a marble-and-stone mansion. He pulled into the drive and climbed out of the Mercedes, stopping to admire the gold trim and red leather interior of the open-topped automobile.

In his mid-thirties, he held the title 'Earl of Tunbridge'. Not usually one for extravagant purchases, automobiles were his one luxury. He wiped off a bit of imaginary dirt from the hood, and sighed.

Might as well get this over with.

The massive door opened before he reached the top step. "Hello, Bronson," he said to the white-haired, slender, and slightly stooped butler.

"Sir."

"You look as healthy as a horse."

"Thank you, sir. Lord McGregor is expecting you."

Mark followed Bronson through the foyer, footsteps echoing off marble floors, and into the library. Cherry-wood bookshelves lined one wall from floor to ceiling, filled with leather-bound books — all for show, Mark thought, doubting anyone had ever read any of them. A fire crackled in the fireplace.

Mark and Des had known each other all their lives, and had played together as children. Des had been a dark-haired rascal of a boy, slightly shorter in stature, and Mark, the taller, fair-haired thinker. They followed their fathers' footsteps to Trinity College, where Mark had excelled in business and languages — French and German. Des had studied literature, graduating by the skin of his teeth.

Their fathers, Rory McGregor and Elliot St. John, both gone now, had been inseparable friends throughout their lifetimes. They'd both attended Trinity College, Cambridge, where they rowed as members of the boat club and played cricket. They'd each married shortly after university, Rory to Phoebe Lyman and Elliot to Winifred Stonebeck, women from excellent families, titled, and of significant means. Together, Rory and Elliot purchased prime property along the Thames and founded a shipping firm, naming it Lyman & Stonebeck, their wives' maiden names, a gesture that endeared them to both spouses. Elliot also built a lavish country house in Royal Tunbridge Wells for his wife, naming it Stonebeck Hall. Rory and Elliot passed a great deal of their free time hunting fox, boar, and pheasant on the thousand-plus acres of the estate. The men had also spent a significant amount of time in London running their business, and where, Mark suspected, their love of the hunt encompassed more than woodland creatures.

"Mark, old man. Good to see you." Des walked into the library.

"Des." Mark nodded. "I've brought your copy of the quarterly reports."

"First things first. How about a drink? A brandy perhaps?"

"Nothing for me."

"I'm ready for one, myself." Des poured himself a drink and sat behind a huge mahogany desk.

Mark pulled a sheath of papers from his jacket. "Business is good," he began, handing the papers one at a time to Des, who glanced at each summarily.

"Splendid," Des remarked. "Excellent quarter."

"The man I hired in the autumn is working out quite well. James Casey is his name, and he's living up to my expectations and then some."

"Oh, yes," Des remarked, distracted. "The one from...."

"The University at Glasgow," Mark finished for him.

"Yes, that one." Des smiled.

"He's come up with some great ideas that have saved us a lot of time and money."

"And how does your Mister Bridger feel about that?" Des asked.

"Oh, he took the credit, but actually the two are getting along just fine."

Des took a long drink, eyeing Mark. "It's quite unseemly, you working at the business, you know. People talk. We're above all that, you and me. I know your mother is quite upset that you spend so much time there, like a common working man."

"I'm not above paying my debts, and keeping Stonebeck Hall up and running is a challenge these days."

"Debts aside, don't you get bored with all of that?"

"Not at all. I find it all quite fascinating. As a matter of fact, I know you have no interest in the business. I came here not only to bring you the report, but to make you a business offer."

Des stretched his legs out before him. "Let's not go through this again."

"I'd like to buy you out, Des. Name your price."

Des smiled. "I would love to take your money, old boy, but I simply can't afford to. Lyman & Stonebeck is far too lucrative a business. You know me — pay me one lump sum and it would be spent in six months. Besides that, I enjoy our business meetings. It's a good idea to stay in touch with old friends — you never know when you might need one."

"I'll keep that in mind," Mark said, disappointed but not surprised. "Now, if you'll excuse me, I have a full afternoon."

Des drained his brandy, stood, and the men shook hands.

"It's a standing offer," Mark said on his way out, "if you should ever change your mind."

Des gave a half bow, his gray eyes reflecting the flames of the fire.

Chapter 5

Kate awoke with a start Saturday morning, excited. Sun filtered through the lacy curtains she'd recently crafted and hung in the window of her small bedroom. The evening before, she'd convinced Mrs. Bridger that the change in weather—an entire week so far of rare, sunny spring days—simply begged for a picnic.

Before noon, the two of them had packed up a lunch and set off to the shipyard.

James and Mr. Bridger didn't need any convincing to take a long lunch break, and the foursome walked to nearby Battersea Park on the Thames. They spread their blankets on a grassy slope and set out steak-and-kidney pie, pickled yams, freshly baked bread, cheese, and apples the Bridgers had kept in the cellar over winter.

"You two made all this?" James cut an apple to share.

"This little missy has some fancy recipes up her sleeve," said Mrs. Bridger while chewing a generous forkful of pie.

"Missus Bridger is an excellent cook," said her husband. "But Kate has brought some new ideas into the kitchen."

Kate smiled.

"She should," James beamed. "She prepared the finest food in an important household for years."

Kate's smile collapsed and she picked at her meal.

James frowned. "Did I say something wrong?"

"No." Kate forced a smile. "Those days are gone, and best forgotten, that's all."

"That was thoughtless of me."

"No apology necessary, James. It's fine."

After eating, James and Kate took a rare walk by themselves. They strolled along the grassy slope that bordered the river. The green water sparkled in the afternoon sun.

"How are things at the business?" Kate asked. She envied his career, and was growing increasingly weary of Mrs. Bridger's constant prattle and talk among "us girls."

"Very well." He stopped abruptly, turned to face her and, grasping both her hands in his, studied her face with such intensity that she had to laugh.

"What is it?" she teased. "Am I wearing a portion of lunch on my nose?"

James smiled self-consciously, but gripped her hands a little tighter. "Kate, I know I have no right to hope or to expect you to...." The color rose in his face.

"Expect me to what?"

"Expect you to say yes. I was just hoping that... that maybe you would...."

"What are you talking about? That I would what?"

"Marry me," he whispered. "That maybe you would consent to marry me."

Kate looked at his tousled blond hair, his aquiline nose, and clear blue eyes. He wore sincerity and innocence like a simple garment, but he only *thought* he knew her. He held an illusion of her.

Her past had taught her to keep a secret.

With one hand, she reached up to smooth his hair. She had no choice, really, and although she had never admitted it to herself, she had known since her mother died that she would end up marrying James, or someone very much like him. What else could she do? She had tried to dream up a life where she could support herself, but the prospects were unlikely.

She touched her hand to his cheek, and took a deep breath. "I would be honored to be your wife."

Kate met the owner of the shipping company on a Sunday morning, three weeks before the wedding. Or rather, one of the owners: she had no idea which one. His name wasn't Lyman or Stonebeck, but St. John. Mark St. John, and he'd invited James and Kate to accompany him on an outing.

Mark picked them up at the Bridgers' house, and her first impression of him was a handsome man who seemed unaware of it. He exuded the self-confidence and ease of someone brought up in a life of plenty. She had been around his type before.

After introductions, he led them to his automobile parked out front. A few of the neighborhood boys had gathered around it, peering in at the leather seats and touching the shiny exterior of the Mercedes. James shooed the boys away and climbed into the back while Mark helped Kate step up to the passenger seat in front.

She was embarrassed to be trembling with excitement at her first automobile ride.

Then they were off. Driving through the streets felt like flying. Wind blew through her hair and houses blurred past as people stopped to stare.

Mark drove straight to Chelsea, a stylish area in central London, where he pulled up in front of a two-story brick house. The house formed the shape of a shallow U, with the front entrance sunk back at the base, and the two side wings jutting to the front on either side, framed by tall windows at the front.

Mark turned in his seat. "I live not too far from here, close enough to the business to be convenient. This is my uncle's home."

"Oh." Kate smoothed her windblown hair. "Are we to meet your uncle?"

"I'm afraid not." He gave an apologetic smile. "He died a few months ago."

"I'm so sorry," she said.

"As am I," said James.

Mark nodded. "Thank you. He was elderly and died peacefully in bed. What more can any of us ask? He had a very good life. Now let's have a look, shall we?"

He stepped out of the auto in one smooth motion, and moved around to open Kate's door, offering a hand. He then led them to the entrance, unlocked the door, and ushered them inside. They stood in a broad tiled foyer with oversized wood doors on either side. Directly ahead, a staircase climbed out of sight.

"Since my uncle is gone, the house sits empty," Mark said. "I inherited it, and I'm not interested in selling it, so why don't you two live here?"

Kate gasped.

James looked astonished, but recovered and quickly said, "We can't afford it."

"Nonsense," Mark argued. "I'll charge a reasonable rent, and you'll be doing me a favor. Can't just have the thing sitting here with no one living in it. It comes fully furnished, as you can see."

They followed him into a sitting room with gleaming wood floors and a brick fireplace, furnished with a divan, matching chairs, and tables.

"There are bedrooms upstairs, servants' quarters in the basement, and the kitchen is on this floor. Nothing fancy. My uncle enjoyed simplicity and practicality, and he traveled a great deal. He had a particular fondness for Egypt."

They followed him down a hall to a dining room with a table large enough to seat a dozen people, and through a door into a voluminous kitchen. Gleaming copper pots and pans hung over a butcher-block island, and the stove across from it was enormous.

Kate felt breathless. She ran her hand along the long countertop and turned to face both men. She walked to James and took his hand in hers, looking up at him, her mood earnest. "It's a grand house, James Casey, a house such as I never dreamed I would live in. And if we do live here, it will be because of you, because of your college education and your hard work. But if you decide that you can't accept Lord St. John's offer, so be it. We'll find a flat. We'll make do. It's your decision."

A slow blush crept up James's neck to his cheeks as he gazed down at his fiancée. At last, he sighed. "Well, I guess you'll be needing a house, now, won't you, when you're Missus Casey?"

Kate's breath caught in her throat, and she stood on her tiptoes and kissed his cheek.

"Quite right," Mark said, looking pleased. "By the way, a cook and a housekeeper come with the house. All of the others have found employment elsewhere. The cook's name is Lucy—she was the assistant to my uncle's cook. She's young and shows promise. Missus Ames is the housekeeper. She can be a bit stern, but she has a kind heart."

James began to protest, but Mark held up a hand. "It's a favor, really," he insisted. "I can't just let them go."

Kate smiled, squeezed James's hand, and turned to Mark. "Yes, help around the house is most welcome. Thank you. Now, if you gentlemen will excuse me, I would love to have a good look at this new home of ours."

The men watched her go, and Mark smiled. "I'm afraid you have no choice. She likes it."

"This is too generous of you."

Mark waved his hand, dismissing the notion. "Nonsense. By the by, you won't see me in the office for a week. I'm sailing to Nordenham to have a chat with the fellows at Norddeutscher Lloyd."

"I've heard of the company," James said. "It runs both freight and passenger ships."

"Right. It's an economically sound company. I want to look over their docks and facilities and learn from their success. Good chance to practice my German, too, which is getting rusty from lack of use. I'm relying on you and Mister Bridger to keep things running smoothly."

"You can count on me," James said.

Chapter 6 – London, June 1911

James and Kate married on June 25, 1911, exchanging vows at St. Bride's Church in London. Kate had no relatives to invite, but James invited his mum, who declined reluctantly. She hadn't been out of Kirken in over a decade, and couldn't face the travel. For best man, James invited the cousin who had helped him through college and hired him after graduation. Kate asked Mrs. Bridger to be matron of honor, a role she accepted happily.

Mark St. John insisted on hosting a gathering at the shipping office afterward, and several of the men from the company brought their wives. They had come to know and respect James in the year since he'd arrived, and... they'd never been known to pass up a free drink.

Kate sat straight-backed at her dressing table—a Hepplewhite with a matching chair. Oblivious to the pedigree of her furniture, her thoughts jumbled with panic.

At this very moment, James might be in the bedroom, waiting for her. Ever since she accepted his proposal, she had worried about this night—her wedding night—and now it was upon her. Tonight could be a disaster. Would he know that she had been with another man? If he did, what would happen? Would he care?

Her eyes widened as she picked up a brush and mechanically stroked her hair. Should she pretend to feel pain? And the sheets... would he look for that crimson sign of virginity on them in the morning? She set the brush down and tried to relax.

She stood, pulled off her dress and unlaced her petticoat, slid it down her legs and stepped out. From the wardrobe, she selected a silver-gray chemise, so light a silk it had no weight at all. She added a matching dressing gown and wrapped it around her, tied the sash at the waist, and walked back to the mirror. With her reflection staring back at her, she took a deep breath and walked into the bedroom.

James was nowhere to be seen. A canopied bed of spring-green linen damask filled the center of the room, surrounded by walls of soft-green wallpaper. Ties held gray-green drapes on either side of floor-to-ceiling windows. Kate walked to one of them and looked down on a lavish rose garden, paused there a moment, then walked to a door that separated this bedroom from another smaller bedroom. She knocked and, upon receiving no answer, opened the door. The room was decorated in a darker, masculine color, with its own fireplace, a table, chair, and bed. From what Mark had told them, she guessed that his uncle had slept in this bedroom, often referred to as a man's dressing room, but famed as the spot where husbands retired when they arrived home late, a bit worse for wear, or when the marriage was in trouble. A separate door to the hallway provided a discreet entrance and exit.

For now, the room sat empty. She turned back to her room, closed the door, and crawled into bed. Heart pounding in her ears, she pulled the covers to her chin, and waited for her new husband.

Downstairs, James paced the floor in the library. For the fifth time in the last hour, he walked over to the brandy bottle, uncapped it, and picked up a glass, and for the fifth time he recapped the bottle, replaced the unused glass, and resumed pacing. As Kate prepared for bed upstairs, a jumble of emotions coursed through him.

God, I want her.

He closed his eyes and trembled at the image of her slender neck and creamy skin, at the narrowness of her waist—and looked at the brandy bottle again.

No, I mustn't drink. I must keep my senses. I can't risk losing control and scaring her, or hurting her. I need all my faculties about me.

He had never made love to a woman.

Oh, he knew the procedure, having read about it from some dog-eared books that a fellow student at the university had lent him, and he had heard talk from some of the boys at school who bragged about their exploits. His studies and work consumed him, and he simply had never made time to socialize with women. Some women around the university had made their living from accommodating young men, but that sort of thing had never held any appeal for James. He hadn't consciously saved himself or any such thing, but now he found himself, on his wedding night, an inexperienced man.

More than anything, he wanted to make Kate happy, for everything to be perfect.

He walked out of the library and glanced up the stairs. Except for the ticking of the grandfather clock, the house was silent as a tomb. He started up slowly.

Kate turned to the sound of the bedroom door opening. James stood in the doorway, and she could hear his breathing. She wanted to say something, to chat as if they were an old married couple and this were the thousandth night they'd gone to bed together, not the first, but she couldn't utter a sound as she lay stiffly beneath the covers.

James walked straight past the bed and into the other bedroom.

Kate sat up, startled. Were they to spend their wedding night in separate rooms? Separate beds?

After a short while, he reappeared in the doorway, dressed in a nightshirt. Kate sank back beneath the covers as he walked toward her. He lifted the covers and lay down beside her, and for a few excruciating minutes, they each lay stiffly, afraid to move.

"Kate," James whispered at last. "Are you awake?"

"Yes."

He slipped his arm beneath her head and around her shoulders.

Kate hesitated, and then shifted her head into the hollow of his shoulder. Almost imperceptibly, he began to caress her, drawing circles on her arm. His hand slid gently from her arm to shoulder, down to the curve of her back, to the gentle rise of her buttocks. Her breasts ached beneath the cool silk fabric of her nightgown, and an urgent throbbing began between her thighs as his hands moved over her. She drew her head back, raising her face toward him. He quickly covered her mouth with his, pulling her even closer. She gently explored his mouth with her tongue, her hands moving over the rough surface of his nightshirt. He hesitated, and apprehension shot through Kate—fear of being too forward, raising suspicion.

A woman shouldn't respond too ardently, especially a bride on her wedding night.

She quieted herself, forcing stillness into her hips.

James turned toward her, his hand on her lower back pulling her into him.

She could feel the hardness between his thighs as his lips traveled from her mouth down her neck, and with his free hand, he drew her dressing gown off her shoulders. Kate lay listening to his breathing become more rapid as he fumbled with her chemise. She raised her hips as he pulled it up and over her head, and lay on her back, naked beneath the sheets.

James lifted his own nightshirt and rolled on top of her, his breath coming in ragged gasps as Kate lay beneath him, aching with desire yet afraid to move. Awkwardly, he separated her legs and pressed his body toward her. After several failed attempts, he entered her. A warm tingling enveloped Kate's body as he began to move within her, and then he arched, shuddering. After a few moments, he gently withdrew and collapsed by her side.

She lay staring at the canopy, her breasts and loins awash with desire.

After several minutes, James sighed and turned his head toward her. "I love you," he whispered.

Kate's eyes remained fixed on the canopy, grateful for the cover of darkness. Forcing herself to move, she drew the covers to her neck. "I love you too, James," she managed. "Good night."

She listened as his breathing grew steadily deeper, waiting until he slept, and then slipped out of bed. She fumbled in the dark, finding and donning her discarded gown, and walked barefoot across the cold floor to the window. She pressed her forehead to the cool glass. The moon hung full and bright in the night sky, casting a glow over the garden below. Rosebushes reached long tendrils upward toward her.

She glanced back to James's sleeping form. Her body ached with desire, but there had been no ugly scene, no accusations, no begging for forgiveness or tears of contrition. She passed her wedding-night test—an appropriate boudoir performance. Officially, now, she was Mrs. James Casey, mistress of the house.

Chapter 7

Kate peeked beneath the red-checkered cloth covering the basket, and mentally ticked off each item: chicken, scones, pickled herring, cheese, apples, and ale. She replaced the cloth, satisfied. She planned to surprise James at work. Lucy the cook, freckle-faced, red-haired, and eager to please, had prepared the feast.

The September air felt cool and damp. Kate had dressed carefully in an indigo-blue wool dress. An ivory lace collar overlaid the blue at the base of her throat. The dress flared from hip to ground, with only the toes of her high-buttoned boots peeking out.

During the months since her marriage, she had explored London relentlessly. She loved walking the Strand and Devereux Court with a stop in between for a cup of tea at Thomas Twining's teahouse. She wandered about old Ludgate Hill with its goldsmiths and diamond merchants, and Oxford Street with its pavement of inlaid flagstone. She inhaled the composite odor of horses and gasoline, as the two modes of transportation merged in the streets. She admired the laurel and yew hedges that outlined the property of grand homes and men's clubs that she passed.

And she shopped. She bought Manchester velvets, worsted damasks, and Italian silks. She loved the attention the willowy, dark-eyed shop girls lavished on her. "Garden silk, lady," they would beckon. "Very fine mantua silks. Geneva velvet."

She asked James for a sewing machine and he surprised her with a brand-new Singer. She began to design and sew her own dresses using the beautiful fabrics she purchased, sure no one could tell the difference between her creations and those from the finest dressmakers — or even the ready-made fashions from Harrods.

James tried to convince her that his salary, although not meager, couldn't support a wardrobe — even if she did all the sewing herself — competitive with society's high standards.

London society. Kate had learned a painful lesson about her place in society, and embarrassingly, her lesson had been learned glaringly in front of both Mrs. Ames and Lucy, not to mention James. It had started with a good idea: to have a tea party.

Mrs. Ames lowered herself with a slight groan onto the wooden kitchen chair, its slight concave seat worn smooth by countless occupants.

"My poor, aching feet."

She sighed as she relaxed into the chair at the servant's dining table. The wood table gleamed with beeswax rubbed into the grain, healing scratches from countless cutlery, bowls, and plates, and smoothing rings from hot tea cups.

"Fetch me a kidney pie and a cup of tea, dear," she called out to Lucy, who worked in the kitchen next door.

Sunlight streamed in through three small windows high on the kitchen wall, bathing the room with a golden glow. Located at the rear of the house, as far from the main dining room as architecture would allow, the kitchen's large stove took up the lion's share of the back wall, with polished marble counter tops on each side.

Lucy put the kettle on to boil and dropped tea leaves into a porcelain pot, then cut two wedges from the kidney pie, leftover from the Caseys' dinner the night before. She took one to Mrs. Ames and set another on the opposite side of the table for herself, then went back for forks.

"This table used to be crowded, back when I was your age and just started working for Lord. St. John." Mrs. Ames sighed again. "Now look at the place, just the two of us to take care of his Lordship's home all by ourselves, where there used to be eight."

The kettle worked itself up to a high pitch. Lucy wrapped a towel around the handle and poured the steaming water into the teapot. She set their teacups, milk, and sugar on a tray and carried it to the table, sitting opposite the older woman.

"I do miss his Lordship," said Mrs. Ames before forking a large bite of pie into her mouth.

"He was never here," said Lucy. "Always running around the world, that man. You liked him so much because we all did our jobs without his Lordship around, and got paid the same as if he were. Other girls I know had to stay up half the night taking care of their families, but not us. To bed early after a quiet evening of cards amongst ourselves."

She poured tea into each of their cups and took a bit of pie herself.

"What a pity that he had to go and die, God rest his soul." Mrs. Ames crossed herself and glanced skyward.

"And all the others went out and found positions in other houses, except you and me, Mrs. Ames."

The older woman's expression turned sour, and she took another large bite of pie.

"If his Lordship hadn't passed on," Lucy continued, "I'd still be the cook's helper instead of the cook. I'm sorry he's gone, but I like being cook. The missus asks what I think, wants to know if I have ideas about what might go well with chicken or lamb. She sends me to market with money to buy fresh vegetables that I get to pick out. No one ever asked me what I thought before. Everybody just told me what to do. Mr. and Mrs. Casey talk to me like I'm a real person, not just someone to order around."

"That's all well and good for you," Mrs. Ames said, "but surely his Lordship would be rolling over in his grave this very minute if he knew what his nephew has done, letting the likes of the Caseys live in his grand home."

"I hear them talk," Lucy argued. "Mr. Casey's got an important job, works side-by-side with Lord St. John, they say."

"I do like Mr. Casey," said Mrs. Ames, "He's such a nice man, soft spoken and well mannered. Still, I don't know what the young Lord St. John was thinking, letting them live here for rent. And another thing...." She was working up a good head of steam. "I think it's odd that Lord St. John works at the company. It's just not right for a man of his station. His father founded Lyman and Stonebeck, but he didn't spend his days working there, I'll tell you that, because I seen it with my own two eyes."

The sound of footsteps approaching the kitchen put a stop to the conversation.

"Good Lord," said Mrs. Ames under her breath. "What's she doing coming in here instead of ringing for us?"

Kate peeked through the kitchen door. "May I come in?"

Mrs. Ames and Lucy stood, the wood chairs scraping on the slate floor.

"Please, Missus" said Mrs. Ames.

Kate walked in and spotted the half-eaten pie and tea. "I've interrupted your supper. I'll come back later." She turned to go.

"It's quite all right," said Mrs. Ames. "What can we do for you?"

Warmth crept into Kate's cheeks. "I'm thinking of having a tea party, in order to meet the ladies that live nearby."

Mrs. Ames and Lucy glanced at one another.

"You know everyone around here, don't you Mrs. Ames? You've lived here a long time."

Mrs. Ames pulled herself up to full height. "Of course, I know who lives in Chelsea."

"I thought as much," Kate said, clasping her hands together with excitement. "If you would make a list for me of names and addresses, perhaps a dozen who live nearby, I'll write the invitations. And Lucy, you and I will need to make a menu. It will be afternoon tea, and I want a good selection of pastries and biscuits. Anything else we should have, Lucy?"

Lucy beamed. "Petite sandwiches, Missus, for those who may not want sweets."

"Very well. Let's talk later. Will you come up with some ideas? Maybe a special recipe you want to try?"

"Yes, Ma'am."

"Very well, and Mrs. Ames, if I could get that list within two days, I can get busy on the invitations."

"Very well, Mrs. Casey."

Kate stood for a moment, smiling at the two women, then said. "I'll let you finish your supper." She pushed back through the door.

The two women sat down again and looked at one another. Lucy broke the silence. "Do you think they'll come? The ladies of Chelsea."

"Are you daft?" snapped the older woman. "They'll never set foot in this house. What is that woman thinking? They know that Lord St. John has rented his uncle's house out to a hired man and his wife, and they're not happy about it neither."

"She's going to be so disappointed if no one shows up," Lucy whispered.

"Serves her right." Mrs. Ames picked up her fork. "Does she think just by moving into a grand house you suddenly become one of them?"

She waved her fork at the neighborhood outside, then concentrated on finishing her kidney pie.

The next evening, James and Kate sat across the dining room table from one another as Lucy served leg of lamb with mashed potatoes and peas. "It looks delicious, Lucy," said James.

"Thank you, sir." Lucy blushed. "Anything else I can get you?"

"No, thank you, Lucy."

After Lucy left the dining room, James sliced off a serving from the leg and leaned across the table to place it on Kate's plate, then took one for himself.

"How was work today?" Kate asked, taking a sip of wine.

"Now that you ask, I have a surprise for you." James stood and left the dining room, and returned with a wooden box. "Close your eyes,"

Kate smiled and closed her eyes.

James took the lid off the box. "Now just breathe in."

"Oh," Kate said, "It smells heavenly."

"We got a ship in from India today carrying spices. You wouldn't have believed the aroma on the docks all day—pepper, cumin, nutmeg, and clove. I brought home samples."

Kate opened her eyes and looked at the cloth pouches in the box, each bearing the name of the spice inside. "Your timing couldn't be better. I just talked to Mrs. Ames and Lucy today about hosting afternoon tea so I can meet the ladies nearby. Mrs. Ames is getting me a list of names, and Lucy is going to prepare the food. With these spices, she should be able to make delicious cakes and biscuits."

James put the box on the table and sat back down. "That's a great idea, hosting afternoon tea. You're sure to make some friends."

Kate smiled. "It's not quite the same as welcoming a ship in from India, but I'm looking forward to it."

Mrs. Ames traveled from one servants' entrance to another warning butlers and housekeepers about the impending invitation. Then she served up the list of names and addresses to Mrs. Casey, as requested.

Kate set the date for tea a fortnight out, to allow plenty of time to prepare, then spent the next two days concentrating on writing the invitations, including a personal note about lovely Chelsea, and her eagerness to meet each and every invitee, in her best handwriting.

Two days later, as she worked with Lucy over possible recipes to include the fresh spices, Mrs. Ames entered the sitting room with two small envelopes on a platter. "For you, Mrs. Casey," she said, her expression neutral as she bent down and presented the letters to Kate.

"Thank you, Mrs. Ames." Kate picked up the envelope and opened the first letter. "Oh dear, Mrs. Corbyn is unable to attend."

Mrs. Ames cleared her throat. "That's Lady Corbyn."

"Yes, that's what I meant. Lady Corbyn." Kate opened the second envelope. "Isabelle Chapman also sends her regrets." Unsure of Isabelle's proper title, Kate opted to use the woman's first name to spare herself the brusque correction again. "Thank you, Mrs. Ames." She turned back to Lucy. "What do you think of biscuits made with clove?"

The next day, Mrs. Ames delivered three more envelopes to Kate, who opened each one.

> *Regretfully cannot attend.*
> *Conflict of schedule.*
> *Unable to attend.*

The day after, when Mrs. Ames delivered the mail, Kate tucked them into her pocket. "That will be all, Mrs. Ames. Thank you." She had grown weary of seeing the smug expression on the woman's face.

By the fourth day, a response had arrived for every single invitation she had mailed. Not a single person would attend her tea.

Kate pushed the door open to the kitchen on the afternoon that the last note had arrived. The aroma was intoxicating, but not even the bouquet of warm spices could lift her mood.

Lucy looked up, startled, then smiled. "The cinnamon and clove make some fine biscuits. Would you like to try one?" She turned to the counter nearest the oven and picked up a tray of freshly baked biscuits, and held them out to Kate.

"I'm sorry, Lucy, I'm just not hungry right now. For dessert tonight, perhaps? And there's no need to bother preparing any more for the tea party. It's cancelled. No one's coming."

Lucy set the tray down, smile fading. "Oh."

Kate tried to smile. "Mr. Casey will enjoy those very much. Thank you, Lucy."

At the conclusion of dinner that night, Lucy brought out the biscuits. "Mrs. Casey asked that I serve these tonight, for dessert." She turned to exit the dining room, glancing at Kate as she left.

"Thank you, Lucy," James called after her. He picked up a biscuit, took a bite, and groaned. "These are lovely. I can taste the spices. Is this the recipe Lucy created for your party?"

"Yes," Kate said, then added, "But there won't be a party. No one can attend. They're all busy—each and every one of them."

James stopped, set the biscuit down, waited a heartbeat, then stood and walked around the table to Kate. He leaned down and kissed her on the cheek. "Their loss, darling," he whispered.

She patted his hand that rested on her shoulder. She may be Mrs. James Casey, mistress of a beautiful home in a posh upper-class neighborhood, but now she knew: she would never be accepted in this society.

Kate put the disappointment out of her mind and concentrated on her fashion creations, and the next day, prepared a picnic for her husband—with Lucy's help. After picking up the picnic basket, she set out for the train station, drinking in afternoon sounds and sights. The only thing she missed about her old life was her daily treks in the Scottish hills.

She took the train a short ride east, and walked from the station toward the docks. By the time she arrived, a glance at her reflection in a window showed that her cheeks flushed rose on cream, and a few wisps of dark hair had worked loose. She stopped to watch the bustle of commerce. Warehouses sat a short distance back from the river. The brackish water of the Thames churned and swirled beneath the hulls of large vessels that crept in and out of the crowded shipping lanes. Men heaved cargo from ship to shore.

She thought about James, how he had become a part of this world that looked chaotic to the untrained eye, but in fact was a business honed to the finest detail. Most days, James had explained, he accompanied Mark on what they called their rounds—like doctors visiting patients in hospital. Together, they scrutinized the business from the ground up, evaluating each step of the operation as they went.

Both men enjoyed being a vital part of the industry, and while employees had at first viewed their presence with skepticism and unease, now they accepted and even welcomed them. One-word responses to inquiries had become full conversations about the weather and families, and ultimately business details that management might never have known in the past. Mark and James would discuss the details at the end of their rounds, turning them over and examining them, filing them away for future use. Their intimate knowledge of the business began to influence every decision they made.

Kate shifted the basket to her other arm, and started down the wooden stairs that led to the shipyard's main business office, where James worked. She knocked and waited, and when no one answered, she pushed open the door into a reception area with chairs against one wall, and a coat rack just inside the door. A large oak desk sat off to one side, and a doorway led into another office. She heard movement from behind the door and peeked inside. Mr. Bridger's eyes lit up at the sight of Kate and her sizable picnic basket. She walked into the office, set her burden down on Mr. Bridger's desk, and planted a kiss on his cheek.

"You're looking a little on the thin side, Mr. Bridger. Isn't the missus feeding you proper these days?"

He patted his belly. "Ever since you moved out, she's been feeding me gruel in the morning and soup at night. It's a pitiful existence for a hardworking man."

She glanced back at the basket. "Well, I'm sure I've brought more than James can eat by himself. Maybe you could help him out? I'd hate to think Lucy went to all that trouble only to have it go to waste."

"Why, that would be sinful, indeed," he said, eyeing the basket.

She smiled and glanced around the office—another desk, file cabinets, stacks of papers piled in labeled trays. "I've wanted to see where you and James work for a long time. He talks so much about it, I feel as though I've been here before. It looks just as I imagined it would. Where is James?"

"Down at the docks."

"You help yourself, Mr. Bridger. I'll go see if I can find him. Which dock?"

"Number two, but you shouldn't go down there by yourself." He looked toward the picnic basket and sighed. "I'll find him for you."

Kate grinned at the man's obvious struggle between duty and appetite. "Nonsense. No one will bother me. I'll find him and bring him back before you've had a chance to decide between the chicken sandwiches and pickled herring."

He never gave her a second glance as she left out the back door, lifting the hem of her dress with both hands as she started down another set of stairs onto a dirt road that led to the docks. The farther she walked, the more hectic the atmosphere became. A few men stopped their labors to stare at her as she passed by, and the odor of oiled wood filled the air as a fine layer of soot from the dark steam plumes of the ships settled on the ground.

As Kate searched for James, a somewhat disheveled older man hesitantly approached her, twisting his cap in his hands, encouraged by a grinning group of men behind him.

"'Ello miss," he spoke with a cockney accent. "Could I be of service to you?" At this remark, the men behind him burst into guffaws and laughter.

Kate glanced from the man to the group. "Thank you, sir. I believe you could be of great service to me." The men nearly fell over one another in laughter, but Kate ignored them. "I'm searching for my husband, Mr. James Casey. Have you seen him?"

The group fell quiet, and the man before her stood a little taller, no longer grinning. "Why, uh, Mr. Casey.... Well yes, ma'am, I think I saw him by that Dutch freighter over there." He pointed.

"Thank you. What did you say your name is?"

"Henry Brown, ma'am."

"Thank you, Mr. Brown. I shall be sure and mention to my husband that you were of great assistance to me."

"Ah, no need to mention it, ma'am, no need a'tall" He hurried back to his mates.

As she neared the dock, she stared in amazement at the ship towering above her, its iron hull gleaming in the noonday sun. How could the mountain of steel even float? At the end of the dock, she spotted James and Mark talking with a tall, fair-skinned man. As she approached, she could hear that the man spoke with a thick accent. She loved to imagine the exotic ports of call these ships visited, and envied these men who traveled the world.

"Kate!" James tucked a clipboard beneath one arm. "What a surprise. Kate, this is Captain Van Dam of the freighter Cojenrad. Captain, my wife, Mrs. Katherine Casey."

"How do you do?" Kate smiled as the man clicked his heels together and bowed.

"Kate...." Mark reached out and took her hand. "Good to see you."

"What brings you down here, darling?" James asked.

"It's such a beautiful day that I had Lucy pack a picnic for you. You had better hurry, though. I left it in the office with Mr. Bridger, and he looked famished. I hope you'll join us, Lord St. John."

"I hate to pass up Lucy's cooking, but I have a business luncheon," Mark said. "However, I will walk you both back to the office."

The captain excused himself with another bow.

Kate looked up at the captain's vessel. "She's a grand ship, is she not?"

"A grand ship, indeed," James agreed, offering his arm.

Kate placed her hand in the crook of his elbow and they started back toward the office. Mark fell into step on her other side, and they came upon the group of men she had encountered earlier. She said in a loud voice, "Oh, James, Mr. Henry Brown helped me find you."

Mark raised an eyebrow at her, then at the group of men. "Give you a hard time, did they?"

"Oh, nothing of the sort." She smiled, glancing over at Mark.

But Mark's attention had already turned elsewhere, as he watched a man sauntering toward them. "There's my business lunch," he said in a flat tone.

Kate followed his gaze. The air left her lungs in a rush and she turned pale as a sickening dizziness swept over her. A lesser woman would have fainted on the spot.

"Mark," the man boomed, hand outstretched.

Mark shook his hand, eyes veiled. "Hello, Des. I don't believe you've met James Casey. This is the business manager I told you about. James, this is the company's silent partner, Desmond McGregor."

James held his hand out. "It's a pleasure, sir."

Des McGregor gave James his full attention, shaking his hand and examining him.

Mark cleared his throat. "And this is Mrs. Casey, James's wife."

The business partner turned slowly toward Kate. He took a step closer, took her hand in his, and raised it to his lips, his gray eyes boring into hers.

Kate forced herself to meet his eyes.

"It's a pleasure, Mrs. Casey."

She tried to speak, but could only dip her head, then pulled her hand from his grasp.

Mark seemed to study his business partner, and turned back to James. "Why don't you two go on ahead, James?"

A flash of annoyance passed over Des's face, but his smile reappeared in an instant, and without taking his eyes from her, he said, "I hope we meet again, Mrs. Casey."

Kate remained speechless, walking blindly alongside James toward the office.

"Are you all right, Kate?" James looked concerned.

"The long walk to get here, even taking the train, made me feel a little faint. I think I had better go home."

"I'll take you," he insisted as they climbed the stairs to the office.

"No, no really. I'm fine, just a little tired."

When they reached the top of the stairs, she turned to him. His lips brushed her cheek, and she thought she would scream if she couldn't escape. She pulled away, calling behind her, "See you for dinner."

She hurried through the office, past Mr. Bridger, and out the door.

She didn't know how she made it home, but she ran upstairs to her bedroom and threw herself onto the bed.

Des McGregor, Mark's partner? Impossible.

She wanted to cry, but instead of tears, waves of anger washed over her. She was trying so hard to be a good wife. She stood and walked to the window, and stared down to the garden. She didn't focus on the roses blooming below; instead, she let her eyes close, and remembered the first time she met Desmond McGregor.

It had been spring in the Scottish Highlands.

Chapter 8 – Scotland, June 1910

Katie entered the servants' entrance to the McGregor house, and took the stairs two at a time down to the kitchen.

"It's about time you got here, lass," grumbled Mrs. Shaunessy. "I had to start the stove myself, and Lily needs help peeling potatoes."

Katie mumbled an apology as she plucked her apron from its hook on the wall, threw it over her head, and tied it about her waist. She joined Lily at the counter, picked up a knife, and began peeling potatoes.

Nature hadn't been kind to Lily Pickering, a tall and gangly young woman with sallow cheeks, bearing remnants of long-ago blemishes. Wispy hair peeked out from beneath her cap. She lived at the McGregor house, along with most of the servants.

Katie was a rarity, allowed to live at home with her mum, and arrive each morning for twelve hours of work or so, depending on the need. She thanked God each evening as she escaped the place, grateful to be free.

Mrs. Shaunessy studied Katie with watery eyes. "You've been acting mighty peculiar lately. Everything all right with your mum?"

"Aye." Katie nodded, concentrating on the potatoes. "She's fine and sends her respects." She struggled to act casually, but things had changed in the last several days. The arrival of a houseguest had made Katie look forward to coming to work every day, curious and excited.

The cook grunted and turned back to pull a rack of scones out of the oven.

The air filled with a buttery aroma that, most days, would have made Katie's stomach growl. Not today.

"They'll be down in five minutes and ready to be served."

Katie climbed the stairs from the kitchen to the dining room, and managed to set the tea and cups on the sideboard moments before Lord and Lady McGregor arrived along with their guest, a great-nephew by the name of Desmond McGregor. The elder McGregors were in their seventies, while Desmond—or Des, as they called him—looked to be around thirty, with ebony hair and eyes of gray.

Katie's cheeks burned as she rushed out of the room. She hesitated behind the door, leaving it open just a crack, listening.

"Uncle Geoffrey," Des said, "I haven't had a chance to get out and exercise since I've arrived. I would love to take one of your horses for a ride today, if you don't mind."

"What? Oh, yes. Certainly," Lord McGregor replied.

"The only problem," Des continued, "is that it's been so long since I've ridden in this part of the country. I'd prefer to have a guide come along."

Lady McGregor looked up in surprise. "Why, Des," she exclaimed in her quivering voice. "You've ridden every hill and glen around here."

"I was a youngster, Aunt Lucille." He leaned over and placed his hand on hers. "I would hate to ride away from here with the confidence of that young lad, only to find myself much older, a bit wiser, and very lost."

Katie could have sworn Des glanced her way, and she stepped away from the door, but not so far that she couldn't hear their conversation.

"Perhaps one of your servants could come along to guide me," Des said.

"Servants!" Lady McGregor's voice displayed her disdain. "Oh my, do they do that in London?"

"Perhaps Mr. Weatherby from down the way can go with you," Lord McGregor said.

"I wouldn't want to bother Mr. Weatherby just for a morning ride. I'm sure he's got better things to do than look after me."

Katie reluctantly started back down to the kitchen.

So, he lives in London. I'll take you riding, Des McGregor.

She rushed to wash the bowls Mrs. Shaunessy had dirtied making scones.

And you take me to London. Show me the city. I've never been out of Kirken.

After breakfast, she stood at the kitchen door and watched a stable boy accompany Des, riding several paces behind. As they passed by the kitchen, Des turned and looked at her. She thought she detected a faint shrug of his shoulders, and a vague smile tugging one corner of his mouth. She stepped back inside the door and ran smack into Lily.

Lily peered narrow-eyed from Katie to Des as he rode away, and back to Katie. "What is it you think you're doing?"

"Nothing at all," Katie said.

"You're making eyes at him. I saw you."

"Nonsense. Lily, how old are you?"

"Twenty-eight, and old enough to know a foolish girl when I see one."

"You've lived and worked here for how long?"

"Since I were fourteen."

"Is this all you want in life?"

"It's a good job, this. You're daft if you think you're ever going to find anything better."

"Maybe I'll find *someone* better," Katie said.

"Like the fine gentleman there?" Lily nodded toward the door. "You're crazy. Even if he looked at you twice, which he won't, what good do you think he would ever do you?"

"I never said I was thinking of him."

Lily stepped closer and leaned down to look Katie squarely in the eye. "You better never think of him in that way, because thinking like that brings nothing but trouble, girl."

"I won't be here when I'm twenty-eight." Katie stepped back, feeling at once sorry for and angry with Lily. "You wait and see. I won't."

Katie saw more and more of Des during the next few days. Her duties took her beyond the kitchen, wherever help was needed. As she dusted books in the library, Des would appear in the doorway, his gaze lingering on her for a moment too long. When she washed the windows overlooking the rose garden, he'd stroll past, arm in arm with his aunt, glancing in her direction as Lady McGregor chatted on unaware.

At seven Saturday evening, she untied her apron and hung it on the kitchen hook. Sunday — her one day off — had arrived too soon.

She stepped into the summer evening, still light and warm, and set off for home, walking past regal yellow irises and winking buttercups. She began the long, steady climb up the rolling hills through a purple carpet of heather.

A silhouette on the skyline up ahead stopped her, a man on a chestnut-colored horse, sitting perfectly still.

Her heart thudded in her chest.

The man nudged his horse and began descending the hill toward her.

Katie held her breath as he approached.

"It's Katie, isn't it?" Des McGregor asked as he reined in the nervous stallion.

"Yes sir," she replied, trembling. "Katherine MacLaren is my given name, sir."

He dismounted and stood facing her, stroking the horse's neck. "I've seen you many times around the house. You're a hardworking girl."

"Thank you, sir."

He looked around. "I'd almost forgotten the heather. When I think back to Scotland, all I remember is the cold and the mist." He turned to her again. "Or perhaps London has pervaded even my memories with its fog."

Katie tried to smile. He seemed so much taller than she had noticed, but she had never stood so close to him before. When he smiled, creases etched his cheeks. His skin had the rugged texture of a man instead of the smoothness of a boy. A shadow of a dark beard had grown since his morning shave.

"Do you have far to walk?" he asked.

"Oh no, sir, just a ways over the hill." She nodded toward the horizon.

"May I walk with you?"

"Oh yes. Yes sir," she stammered.

He led the stallion by the reins as they fell into step together.

"My name is Des. Desmond McGregor, actually." He smiled. "If you wouldn't mind, I'd like you to call me Des when we're away from the house."

Katie concentrated on the ground ahead of her. "Yes sir." Then, realizing her error, she stuttered, "I mean, no, sir, ah, Lord McGregor." She looked up at him blushing furiously. "Des, that is."

He burst out laughing.

She gave him a sheepish smile. No one had ever walked her home before, even as a girl of twelve when she started her work at the McGregor house.

"Tell me about your family," he said.

"I live with my mum."

"And your father...?"

"No, he died a long time ago. It's just Mum and me."

Des looked at her. "I'm sorry. My dad is gone, too. Aunt Lucille, Lady McGregor, is his mother's sister."

No resemblance linked this strong man to the frail Lady McGregor.

"You live in London, sir? Des."

"Yes, but I've been visiting my aunt and uncle here since I was a lad."

Katie didn't want to hear about his visits to Scotland; she wanted to hear about London. But too soon, they crested the hill overlooking her home, a stone cottage smaller than the gardener's shack at the McGregor house.

Instantly sorry she had brought him this far, she mumbled, "Here we are."

"That's it there?"

She nodded, embarrassed.

"It looks to be a charming cottage," he said. "I hope I haven't made you late." He held his hand out to her.

After a moment, she placed her own hand into his.

"I enjoyed our walk." He studied her face. "Perhaps I could join you again?"

Her cheeks burned red. She nodded, pulled her hand free, and dashed down the hill without a backward glance.

The next week passed like a dream. Des turned up throughout the day with increasing regularity, always with some excuse for being around.

"Did I leave my book in here?" he'd asked as she straightened the library. "That dessert was delicious, Mrs. Shaunessy. Could I have a bit more?" he'd inquired as she toiled in the kitchen. Best of all, every evening he appeared astride his horse at the top of the hill, well away from the McGregor house, to walk her home.

He told her of sailing on great ships and life in the city. Much of the time, they just walked in silence, keenly aware of one another. They never spoke of their respective stations in life.

One unforgettable evening, he invited her up on his horse to ride with him. She hesitated, but he persuaded her. When he pulled her up, placing her sidesaddle in front of him, she sat rigid, breathless, her senses stinging with the nearness of him.

Too quickly, another Saturday night came around, and when Katie arrived home late she found her mum sitting morose in the dim light of the cottage. Katie and Des had stayed for an hour on the hilltop overlooking her home, he reluctant to leave, and she unable to send him away. When she walked into the house, her mum stood with great effort, walked to the kitchen, and ladled mutton stew into a bowl.

"I already had something at the McGregor house, Mum," Katie said.

"You're a young girl, and you've had a long week, and a long walk." Her mum set the bowl on the kitchen table and sat in the opposite chair, cradling a cup of steaming tea in her frail hands.

Katie sat down without a word and began to eat. The stew tasted like dust.

"And how are Lord and Lady McGregor treating you these days?" her mum asked.

Katie hesitated, a spoonful of mutton stew halfway to her lips. Her mum — not one for small talk — sipped her tea, never looking Katie squarely in the eye.

"I never see them," Katie murmured. "I'm a shadow in that house, nearly invisible."

Except to one of them, she thought. *One of them sees me.* And she couldn't help but smile.

Her mum's eyes narrowed. "You need to do laundry early tomorrow. We're having company for dinner."

Katie held her spoon midair above the stew. "Company?" She could count on one hand the times they'd had company for dinner over the years. "Who's coming?"

"James Casey will be taking Sunday dinner with us," her mum said in a tone that made it clear no argument would be tolerated.

Katie sat stupefied. She barely remembered James Casey. He must be about six years older and had left Kirken years before. "Why on earth would you invite James Casey to dinner?" Even as the words came out of her mouth, a realization crept into her mind. He mustn't be married yet.

Her mum's look hardened. "You're no babe anymore. You're a grown woman. It's time to find a husband."

"If I do, I don't need your help, thank you very much."

"And who might you have found on your own?" her mum snapped. "That fancy gentleman who rides you home?"

Katie's mouth dropped open, but no words came out.

"Oh, you thought I didn't know? You're a silly girl if you think that will lead to anything. You have no business being with him a'tall. You're inviting trouble, lass. Bad trouble."

Katie struggled to keep her voice even. "I don't need a husband. I can take care of myself."

"If you don't find yourself a suitable husband, you'll end up just like me, living in a house just like this, until the landowner gets tired of you and sends you packing, or the rent goes too high to afford. And you'll work just as you do now, as I have all my life, until you drop dead."

They stared at each other, both surprised at the turn the conversation had taken. Katie stood and took her bowl to the kitchen. "I'll have the laundry done early," she said, and went to her room.

At two o'clock sharp, a wagon clattered up the road to the cottage. Katie's mum stepped out the front door and into the bright afternoon sunshine with Katie behind her.

Squinting, Katie shielded her eyes with one hand and watched the horse-drawn wagon make its way toward the house. A movement caught her eye on the top of the hill above the cottage, and she turned to look. There on horseback sat Des McGregor. Katie's mouth dropped open in surprise. She gave a nervous glance to her mum. Too late.

Her mum had seen the look on Katie's face and followed her gaze. Her mum's lips pressed together and she gripped Katie's forearm and propelled her toward the road to greet their guest.

James Casey jumped from the wagon and they said their greetings.

The next time Katie looked up to the horizon, Des had vanished.

Tall and lanky, James wore his honey-colored hair combed neatly to one side. Katie remembered him as a fair-haired, freckle-faced youth, and while the freckles had faded, his look remained boyish.

For dinner, they sat side by side at the table, bumping elbows occasionally since James was left-handed. He would apologize and scoot away a bit, only to bump her again. Katie tried to concentrate on her lamb, and what little conversation there was dwindled to silence. Soon, the only sounds were the clatter of forks against plates, punctuated by her mum's nagging cough and James's occasional apology.

Finally, her mum sat back in her chair, signaling the meal's end, and Katie jumped up to clear the table.

"Katie, I'm sure Mr. Casey would like to go for a walk. Dishes can wait."

Katie glared at her, then turned to James. "Come along."

She set a good pace along a dirt road that bordered a meadow behind the cottage, with James by her side. Behind low, endless rock walls, sheep paused in their grazing to watch them pass by.

James cleared his throat, glancing sideways at Katie as they walked. "I think we've been the victims of skullduggery, you and I."

"Skullduggery?"

"I was home visiting my mum when your mum came around last week and told me that you had been asking after me. Hadn't seen me all these years and just woke up one morning and said to your mum, 'Now what do you suppose has become of James Casey?'"

Katie felt like smiling at his imitation of her mum's voice, but didn't.

"Now, this doesn't sound like the Katie MacLaren that I remember, but it has been many years, so you never know. Your mum invited me to Sunday dinner—and a grand one at that—but I began to get the feeling that maybe this dinner wasn't your idea after all, that maybe a well-meaning mum decided to play matchmaker. Perhaps Miss Katie MacLaren was still that stubborn, independent twelve-year-old I remembered after all."

"Stubborn?" She stopped and plopped onto the rock wall.

James sat beside her, stretching his legs out in front of him.

"And what have you been doing all this time, James?" she asked.

"I've been in Glasgow attending university and working."

"University?" Katie glanced at him. "Now how did you manage that?"

James laughed. "I was a pretty good student, you know."

"I know that, but the money. How could you afford it?"

"You're right, I haven't any money. I worked loading ships while I went to school. A cousin of my dad helped out and I've been working for them since graduation."

"Well, I'll be. I would never have imagined it."

"I've just taken a new job, now that I've paid off my debt. I came back to Kirken for a visit before I start working for a large shipping company in London."

"London," she repeated. The whole world revolved around London while she remained stuck in the Highlands of Scotland. She glanced at James. "I'm sorry about the way I acted at dinner. You were right about my mum. She made me mad, trying to set me up with a beau." She stood. "We better get back."

"You're a grand lass, Katie MacLaren," he said, getting to his feet, "and it will be a lucky man who wins your heart."

Katie's face burned warm, and her thoughts turned to Des.

"I'm leaving for London next week," he went on. "I know I'll make new friends, just like I did in Glasgow, but would you mind very much if I write to you now and again?"

Katie looked at him in surprise.

"You wouldn't have to write back," he hurried on, "unless you wanted to."

"I'll write, if you promise to tell me all about life in London. Every detail."

James smiled. "I promise."

Her mum had seemed pleased when Katie and James returned from their walk, especially when she overheard the two promise again to write one another, but that was Sunday, and by Monday morning Des consumed all Katie's thoughts.

She arrived early at the McGregor house, excited at the prospect of seeing him. She caught a glimpse of him at breakfast, but Mrs. Shaunessy kept her too busy to see anyone at all.

When she finished with her kitchen duties, she was assigned to help the housemaids, who gave her a dirty job no one else wanted—cleaning out the fireplace in the library—a job after which she always wound up covered with ashes from head to toe, no matter how careful she tried to be.

On hands and knees, shoveling ashes into a dustbin, she heard the library door open and close behind her. Thinking someone was checking up on her, she turned around in exasperation, but it was neither Mrs. Shaunessy nor a housemaid.

Des McGregor himself stood there, smiling.

Katie's breath caught in her throat. She jumped to her feet, knocking over the ash can and sending a cloud of gray over the hearth and herself. She cried out in dismay.

Des laughed and walked to her, knelt down at the hearth, picked up a small broom, and began sweeping the ashes back into the fireplace.

"Oh no, you mustn't," she said, alarmed that he would end up as dirty as her, or worse yet, that someone would walk in and see him.

As if reading her thoughts, he reassured her. "Don't worry. My aunt and uncle have gone into town, Mrs. Shaunessy is busy preparing my favorite pastry in the kitchen, and...."He gave her a boyish grin. "I locked the library door."

His grin faded. "You're a young, beautiful girl, Katie."

A thrill ran through her at his words. *He loves me!*

She had known it. Now he had said as much.

Des set down the broom and took the ash shovel from her hand, and placed the tools carefully on the hearth. He took her hand and, as they stood face to face, touched her face, his fingers moving to trace her lips.

Katie trembled under his touch, and stepped with trust into his arms. He lowered his mouth to hers, pressing gently at first, then with more urgency. She returned his kiss, moving her body against his, drowning in the sensations of his touch, breathing in the exquisite, masculine scent of him.

A voice whispered in her head—*Stop*—but she pushed the thought away.

Des explored her slender neck with his lips and tongue, tracing a path downward to the hollow of her throat, then took her hand and led her to the couch. He kissed her again, and lowered her gently, expertly, to the couch.

Panic welled up inside her, and he sensed it. "Don't worry, my Katie," he murmured into her ear. "I'll take care of you. You're mine now."

Katie looked into his eyes. In those eyes, she saw her future, a woman loved and cared for—a life in London in a fine home, no longer a servant, but a woman of means. She wouldn't end up like her mum or poor, homely, single Lily Pickering.

Emboldened, she touched his cheek and ran her hand through his hair, trusting him. She gave up her innocence willingly. Only a moment of pain brought her out of the cloud of euphoria, and even so, their intimacy felt the most natural thing in the world. Happiness was hers for the taking, at last, here in the arms of Des McGregor.

In the weeks that followed, each day, somehow, somewhere, they managed to be together. One afternoon, she slipped out to the stables where Des waited. After a stolen hour with him, she remained weak-kneed for the rest of the day. Another day, they slipped into his bedroom while Lord McGregor read in the library, and Lady McGregor retired to her sitting room. Oh, how she loved being in his bedroom. She dreamed of spending the night there and waking in his arms. The room was so grand with its fine linens, fire crackling in the fireplace, and paintings above the hearth. Someday soon, she was certain, they would be together in a room even more luxurious than this in London, where they would live together as man and wife.

Mrs. Shaunessy had been quick to notice the change in Katie, and to realize her frequent disappearances. At first, she said nothing, and just glared at Katie with indignant eyes. Then, one day, she cornered her in the kitchen and unleashed such a tirade of scorn that Katie could scarcely breathe.

"We all know what you're up to," Mrs. Shaunessy hissed. "You're a fool, a disgrace to your mum. What do you think the gentleman is going to do? Marry you?" She coughed out a mean-spirited laugh. "You're behaving like you're feeble minded. Or worse, like a slut."

Katie covered her ears and ran from the room, refusing to let the jealous old woman's words diminish her happiness, and ran straight into Lily.

Lily was neither jealous nor old—at least not as old as Mrs. Shaunessy. She pulled Katie down the narrow hallway, into the tiny bedroom she shared with two other servants, and closed the door behind them.

"This house has eyes," Lily whispered. "The only people who are blind are Lord and Lady McGregor. Everyone else knows what you and the young Lord are doing."

"What you don't understand—" Katie enunciated each word as if talking to a child. "—is that Des promised to take care of me."

"Des, is it, now?"

Katie took Lily's limp hands into her own, and peered into the servant's eyes. "He's going to take me out of here, Lily. Don't you see? He loves me."

Lily shook her head slowly. "You're daft. You're dreaming."

"You just wait and see." Katie squeezed the girl's hands. "I'm going to travel and see the world, and Des McGregor is going to take me."

On an overcast Friday morning, when the summer warmth gave way to the first bitter day of autumn, Des's chair sat empty at the breakfast table. The first sense of doubt crept over Katie as she lifted her apron from its hook and tied it about her.

Out of character, Mrs. Shaunessy hummed a hymn as she prattled about the stove. "Better get busy setting the table, lass." Her eyes locked onto Katie's. The old cook looked happy for once.

The breakfast plates were stacked neatly on the counter—two plates, two cups, two saucers. Katie stared at the dishes, a sense of foreboding welling up inside. She walked toward Mrs. Shaunessy, reaching out to the counter for support.

Mrs. Shaunessy turned toward her. "What's the matter, deary? You don't look so good this morning. 'Tis probably the change in the air. There's a chill on this morning, that's for sure." She dried her hands on her apron, an uncharacteristic smile revealing several missing teeth. "Oh dear." She paused in melodramatic concern. "Is it Lord *Desmond* McGregor you're concerned about? It seems he received a telegram late last night. I just happened to overhear them talking, you know."

Katie nodded woodenly.

"Yes, well, it seems that Lord McGregor got called back to London because of an emergency." Mrs. Shaunessy's tongue snaked out to moisten her lips as she leaned closer to Katie's face. "It seems his wife has taken ill, and requires his presence at home."

Katie went numb. The strength drained from her knees.

"What's the matter now, Missy?" Mrs. Shaunessy crooned. "Don't be telling me the gentleman didn't mention his missus? Get on with you, I don't believe it."

Katie stepped backward, reached behind her, untied her apron and placed it back on its hook.

"You don't feel like such a grand lady now, do you, Missy?" hissed Mrs. Shaunessy.

Katie stood rooted to the ground in shock.

"Maybe now you feel like the fool that you are. You're just a servant girl who should have been grateful for a job. But no, you thought yourself better than the rest of us. You're no better. In fact, you're soiled goods now."

Katie moved to the door, opened it, and nearly fell outside, legs threatening to fold and drop her to the ground.

Des, married? How could that be?

His departure, without so much as a goodbye, had cut her to the bone. Like a thief in the night, he had crept away, taking her girlhood and innocence with him.

Chapter 9

After encountering Des at Lyman & Stonebeck, Kate spent weeks pacing about the house, worrying about James, agonizing about Des. With James, she had so many things she had never thought possible: a caring husband, a beautiful house in London, clothes, a cook, and a housekeeper. All these should make her happy.

Yet she couldn't get Des out of her mind.

The days crawled by in dull routine. She stopped shopping, instead retreating to her bedroom after James left for work, staring out the window, watching the roses bloom in riotous color. They brought her no pleasure.

One afternoon, the housekeeper, Mrs. Ames, a heavyset woman who always had a ready smile for James but not Kate, presented a letter to Kate that had arrived in the mail, addressed directly to Mrs. James Casey. Kate took the envelope and as her eyes widened at the return name on the letter, Mrs. Ames's eyes narrowed.

Kate mumbled a thank you and slipped into her bedroom. She examined the rich texture of the envelope, turning it over and over in her hands. At last, she broke the seal and slipped out a card with scribbled handwriting.

> Katie,
> Meet me at 1410 Hampshire Boulevard Tuesday at noon.
> Des

Kate stared at the message. He hadn't asked her if she wanted to see him again. He assumed that she did, and merely provided her with the time and the place.

Fury welled up inside her. *Preposterous — unthinkable — to consider meeting him.*

So many things had changed since those impetuous days at the McGregor house. She had been an innocent child, ripe for excitement and romance.

She bit her lip and walked over to the window. How many nights since their wedding night had she waited until James fell asleep before she slipped from the bed to this window, where she stared at the stars and tried to ignore her unsatisfied longing? James's lovemaking was sweet and kind and aroused desire in her—desire he was never able to quench.

Des knew how to satisfy her to the core.

She rested her forehead against the cool glass and closed her eyes, remembering the scent of Des's skin, the firmness of it beneath her open palms. It had been two years since he had left her, yet she could recall each moment they shared with precise detail.

Her eyes flew open.

Maybe she should see him. Perhaps if she could talk to him, if she could say goodbye, then she could finally forget him—get him out of her mind for good. She examined the note again, insulted once more at his brashness. It might just take him down a peg to see her again, a happily married woman doing quite well without him.

She made up her mind. She would go see him on Tuesday and finish it once and for all.

Kate sat at her dressing table examining her image in the mirror, and applied just a tiny bit of rouge to her already-flushed cheeks. She had gone shopping the day before, discreetly buying paint for her face, something she had seen but never used. She brushed a hint of kohl on her eyelids, accenting the blue of her eyes. Her lashes were the same charcoal color as her hair, but she added a touch of mascara and coconut oil. She had pulled her hair to one side and rolled it into a crescent, holding it in place with a silver barrette, and had sewn the dress herself, using midnight-blue velvet. Long sleeved with slight puffed shoulders and a scooped neckline, the dress fit snug at the waist, and draped in a full skirt to the ankle.

She stood and pulled a cape from the closet. The day had turned unseasonably cloudy and cold.

She let herself out of the house without a sound, walking for ten minutes before hiring a cab. After giving the driver the address, she tried to rehearse in her mind what she would say. She would be distant and polite but cool. She would listen with disinterest to his explanations of his abrupt departure, then she would make it clear: *I'm a happily married woman who has forgotten you. I've only come to be polite and to put an end to this foolishness once and for all.*

After too short a time, the cab pulled to a stop in front of a stone house two stories high. A matching stone wall continued along the street adjacent to the house, perhaps surrounding a garden or courtyard. The crimson leaves of maple trees growing inside the wall loomed overhead. As Kate stepped outside, the wind gusted and swirled leaves into the air. She shivered and pulled her wrap closer as she stared up at Des McGregor's house.

She paid the cabbie, and tried to put on a brave face as she walked up a short set of stairs and knocked.

The door opened faster than it should have, and a silver-haired butler appraised her. "Mrs. Casey," he stated matter-of-factly. "Lord McGregor is expecting you. This way, please."

Heart pounding, she followed him inside.

He led her into a sitting room, where a divan and matching Louis XVI chairs faced one another over an oriental rug.

"May I take your wrap?" he offered.

With some reluctance, she pulled the cape from her shoulders, handed it to him, and suddenly wished that she'd worn something less revealing.

She glanced around, tense as a cat, at once sorry she had come.

"Mrs. Casey." Des appeared in the doorway, and strode directly to her and took both her hands in his. "So wonderful to see you again."

He acts as if we're old friends.

"Duncan," he said to the butler. "Some tea."

The butler nodded and disappeared.

"Katie," Des said. "It's marvelous to see you again."

"Kate," she stammered. "I go by Kate, now."

"It suits you." He smiled. "What a coincidence that your husband works at my business."

Kate willed her heart to slow down its hammering in her chest. "Explain that to me. It's named Lyman & Stonebeck, yet it's owned by St. John and McGregor?"

"Quite right. Our fathers started it together. They named it after their wives' maiden names. My mother was a Lyman, and Mark's a Stonebeck."

The butler returned carrying a tray of tea and biscuits, and set it on a small table.

"That will be all, Duncan," Des said, never taking his eyes off Kate. "We won't need anything else."

The butler gave a nod and left, closing the door behind him.

With great effort, Kate lifted her chin and stared directly at Des. He still had her hands in his, studying her, standing so close she could smell the scent of his skin. She felt painfully aware of his touch, the warmth of his hands.

His eyes dropped from her face, traveling to the neckline of her dress and back again.

Kate pulled her hands from his and stepped away.

He walked to the table and poured them each a cup of tea. "Please, sit."

They sat across from one another, eyes locked over their teacups.

"You're looking beautiful, as usual," he said. "Marriage must agree with you."

Kate sipped, trying to keep her hands from trembling. "Marriage agrees with me very well." She set down her cup, afraid it might slip from her hands. "And you look the same, which must indicate that marriage has always agreed with you."

Des set down his cup. "Touché. I deserve that."

"Deserve that?" She made no attempt to mask her incredulity. "You deserve much worse than that."

"You're absolutely right. I couldn't agree more. Will you indulge me, Kate? Hear my side of the story?"

After a pause, she nodded.

"My wife's name is Margaret. We both come from very old families of a certain social standing, if you will. With privilege, comes responsibility, and duty."

"You left without a word," she said, voice hard. "I had to find out from the servants, who were only too pleased to inform me."

"I'm so sorry. You see, I—"

"I do see," she interrupted. "Only too well."

He leaned forward. "Love, Kate, is a luxury I couldn't afford. Marriage is about alliances, about producing heirs. I am married, to be sure, and we have children, and I live with them some of the time, but I live here—"He waved one hand, open-palmed, at the room. " —in my own house as much as I can. No one comes here unless invited. My family doesn't know about this house, or at least they pretend they don't know. Here, I'm free to do as I please."

"You left me with nothing," she said. "Not even a goodbye."

"The message arrived after I returned from walking you home. I had to leave right away. It killed me to leave you, but I had no choice.

And I couldn't very well leave a message for you, or write to you later, could I?"

Kate sat back, shaking her head. "You took advantage of me. It was wrong of you and foolish of me. I was too young to know any better. I thought we had a future together."

"But we do have a future together." He stood and stepped around the table, pulled her to her feet, and kissed her.

Kate, too stunned to think straight, stood stiffly in his arms. Without warning, her body began to respond. Des sensed it and pulled her tighter to him, pressing every inch of his body to hers, and she felt paralyzed.

His mouth left hers, traveling down her neck. Impatient now, he pulled at her bodice, freeing her breast and fastening his mouth over it.

She was at once astounded by his impertinence, by his boldness, and shocked at her own body's response. Desire gripped her, knocking the breath from her lungs, and all rational thought from her head. In an instant, nothing else mattered—nothing but this—and she gave herself over to ecstasy.

Chapter 10

A week later, James was late getting home from work, and Kate passed the time fussing at the dinner table, moving plates, straightening glasses, putting everything in order. Every day since seeing Des, she'd waited with a combination of fear and anticipation for a message from him, but so far, only silence.

Each night when Kate sat down to dinner with James, she could barely eat a bite. Food seemed to stick halfway down her throat.

But today she had worked with young Lucy to plan an elaborate menu, just to give herself something to think about besides Des. Dinner would begin with fish soup, followed by sorbet, poached turbot and salmon mayonnaise, quail and pigeon pie, with pears for dessert, all accompanied by wine. Extravagant.

This past week, her stomach had been tied in knots. It made her sick to think of what she had done and how it would hurt James if he knew.

When James arrived home, she met him in the foyer just as Mrs. Ames took his coat. "You're late," Kate said.

"Busy day." He smiled and tucked a newspaper beneath his arm.

"Lucy has outdone herself with tonight's meal." Kate turned to go, but James caught her by the elbow and pulled her back to him.

He looked at her long and hard. "You've changed."

She felt lightheaded. "Changed? What on earth are you talking about?"

"Who would have ever thought that little Katie MacLaren would grow up to be such a beautiful woman?" He leaned down and kissed her cheek, and drew back, smiling. "And who ever thought she would marry me?"

Kate breathed again. "Well, now I know why you're so late, Mr. Casey. You've had a long stop at the pub on the way home, that's certain."

He laughed. "Mark and I were going over the books." He followed her into the dining room and dropped into his chair, stretching his legs out before him as Kate rang the dinner bell. "Mark is thinking about expanding the business."

"Really?" She sat down. "That could be good for us, couldn't it?"

James smiled and leaned toward her across the table. "Yes, it might be very good for us."

"James, if things get busier at the office, is there a chance that I could help out?"

"Help out?"

"Yes. Help you with the paperwork or something. I learn quickly."

"There's no need for you to work."

"But isn't it different than *needing* to work, as I did in Scotland? I thought I might help out now and again."

"We've risen above all that, you and I. Just look where we are—living in a home like this, with our own cook and housekeeper. And you're the lady of the house who keeps it all running along."

True, James had risen above his station in life, bringing her along with him. And how had she repaid him? By behaving like the lowest whore in London.

Lucy pushed through the dining room door with the fish soup, served it, and exited again.

Kate felt sick at the prospect of food, but for appearance's sake, she picked up her spoon and tried to eat.

It had rained during the night, leaving the rose garden glistening in the morning sun. After James left for work, Kate took her tea outside into the garden, breathing in the clean scent of fresh air.

She hadn't been there long when Mrs. Ames came into the gardens with a scowl on her face. She clipped each word as she said, "There is a gentleman caller here to see you."

Kate raised her eyebrows. "A gentleman, for me? Who is it?"

"A Lord Desmond McGregor."

Kate froze. Mrs. Ames stared, and Kate hoped she didn't look as upset as she felt.

"Did you tell him Mr. Casey has already left for the office?"

"He asked for you," the housekeeper said, eyebrows raised.

"Show Lord McGregor into the sitting room, please, Mrs. Ames."

The woman nodded and turned back into the house.

Kate tossed the rest of her tea to the ground.

"Lord McGregor," she said too loudly as she swept into the room, grasping for an air of confidence. "What an unexpected surprise."

Des sprawled out on the divan, staring at the empty fireplace, wearing a two-day growth of beard beneath bloodshot eyes. He gathered himself and stood.

She glanced over her shoulder, fearful that Mrs. Ames might be about. "What are you doing here?" she asked evenly, in a low voice. "Have you lost your mind?"

A shadow passed over his face, then he sauntered toward her, closing the distance between them until he stood in front of her, almost touching. Kate took a step backward, but he reached out and began running his hands along her upper arms. Without warning his grip tightened.

"You need to understand something, my bonnie girl—where you are concerned, I'm always welcome."

This was a side of him she had never seen, and she willed her body to relax under his grip. She cocked her head slightly. "Indeed, you're welcome."

He let go and took a step backward. "Tomorrow... come over tomorrow."

Kate glanced toward the door, hoping Mrs. Ames couldn't hear their conversation. "No, Des."

He looked troubled. "I'll tell your husband what happened."

"No."

His voice hardened. "If you don't come, I'll tell your husband what you've been up to. He'll never look at you the same, if he keeps you at all."

She stared at him, stunned. "Why? Why would you do this to me?"

"We can still be together. We were meant to be together, you know that."

"Leave me be. You've wrecked me enough."

"I don't have a choice, Kate. Don't make me do something to hurt you, to hurt your husband." He released her and walked to the door. "Two o'clock," he said, and left.

The next day, Kate left the house determined to put an end to the foolish and dangerous business with Des. She walked off the edge of her nervousness before hailing a taxi. Near Leicester Square they hit a snarl of traffic, and Kate looked out the window at a crowd of well-dressed women chanting and waving signs. She picked out the words sisterhood and equality as the cabbie muttered under his breath.

"Suffragettes." She stared in awe.

"Women who think they should wear trousers," the driver said.

She had read about them, but never seen anything like this before — a row of bobbies lined the crowd on full alert. She sat back as the cabbie darted onto a side street. In a way, she envied those women and their courage. She had read in the newspapers stories of occasional outbreaks of violence at such marches, and wondered if she would have the nerve to risk danger for a cause she believed in. These women had already made that decision, and were lobbying for the vote, for equality with men. Kate knew what their opinion of her would be — a married woman on the way to rendezvous with her lover.

As the taxi pulled up to Des's house, she leaned forward and handed the driver extra fare. "I'll be back in ten minutes. Fifteen at the most. Wait for me."

No butler answered her knock. She tried the door and it opened.

"Des?" Her voice sounded small in the cavernous foyer.

No one came to take her coat or offer tea.

"Kate." Des's voice sounded from the top of the stairs. "Come up."

She hesitated. She wanted to tell him they were done, no matter what he threatened, but she wanted to do it in the safety of the sitting room with the butler hovering nearby. She pondered the situation as she climbed the stairs.

Des stood at the door to his bedroom, and moved quickly to greet her, taking both her hands in his. His eyes were bright and glassy, as if he'd been drinking. He leaned over and kissed her hands, his gaze never leaving her face as he pulled her into the bedroom.

Des unbuttoned his shirt and peeled it off. He took Kate's hand and pressed it to his chest.

She felt the familiar thick patch of dark hair and the firmness of his muscles and, caught off guard, froze.

Des pressed his mouth against hers, forcing her head back. Abruptly, he let her go and walked to the bed, then turned, his eyes locked on hers.

Kate started to back away, shaking her head, and stumbled out of the bedroom. She heard Des behind her and took the stairs as fast as she dared.

Partway down, he grabbed her from behind, whirled her around by the wrist, and pulled her to him. "You don't seem to understand. Don't you see? You're the only woman I want. You've ruined me. I have to have you."

She shook her head and tried to pull away from him. "I don't care what you do, who you tell. I will not see you anymore. Ever again. Do you understand?"

He gathered her in his arms and sat back on the stairs, pulling her down on top of him. He grabbed her by the hair and turned her head to face him, now just inches away.

She smelled a strange, sweet odor on his breath, and felt sickened by him and this whole ugly mess.

"Tell everyone what I've done," she said, spitting the words into his face. "Tell the whole world what a bloody whore I am! I don't care. But listen to me and listen hard... I won't ever see you again. Do you understand? We are done. I will never come back to you, no matter what you do."

She broke free of his grip and lurched down the stairs, and out the front door.

"You'll come back to me," Des shouted as the front door closed.

Chapter 11

Kate pushed Des McGregor out of her mind, vowing never to see him again, regardless of the consequences. Weeks had passed, and he'd made no attempt to contact her again. She dared to hope that he might have given her up.

The magnolia trees burst with blooms the day Kate felt queasy after breakfast. She managed to wait until James left for work before she ran to the toilet and was sick.

The queasiness returned the next day at the same time.

On the fifth morning of nausea, she wandered into her dressing room and stared at herself in the mirror. Her complexion seemed sallow in the morning light. Her breasts felt tender. It occurred to her that she couldn't remember the last time she had bled, and her eyes widened.

A baby?

She gazed down to her tummy, gently placing her hand on it, and counted the days back to that shameful afternoon with Des. She and James had continued their marital lovemaking, so surely he'd fathered this child. If not, if by some twist of cruel fate one mistaken afternoon tryst had created this baby, no one need ever know.

She thought of the suffragettes she'd seen on her way to Des's house that day. How strong and brave they'd looked, how sure of themselves. She envied them, their brashness and confidence and purpose. Most of them were probably mothers, as well as suffragettes. Now she was about to become a mother, too, but that didn't mean she couldn't dream of making something of herself someday.

And being a father would make James so happy.

Kate glanced down at her belly again and said, "I'll love you and take care of you in a way my mum never could for me. I promise."

She looked in the mirror again, surprised to see herself smiling.

She planned a dinner that would include hints of the news she would deliver after the meal. When evening arrived, she peeked over Lucy's shoulder, trying to make sure everything looked perfect. "This looks wonderful, Lucy. You're a fabulous cook, and we're lucky to have you."

"Why thank you, ma'am," Lucy said. "I'm happy to be here."

James arrived home at last, and as they sat down across the dinner table from one another, Kate made a point of mentioning each item as Lucy served. "Why Lucy, what perfect baby oysters. James, leg of lamb, one of your favorites. Oh, look. Baby carrots, peas, and onions."

James studied her as he ate, a puzzled look on his face as Kate dug into her meal. He abruptly put his fork down, staring at her.

It took her a few bites to realize that James had stopped eating. She put her fork down, dabbed her napkin to her mouth, stood, and turned sideways.

"Am I showing yet?"

James pushed back his chair, stood and circled the table, and gently took her in his arms and searched her face. "Is it true?"

She nodded.

He wrapped his arms around her and pulled her close. They held one another, swaying together, dinner forgotten.

Chapter 12

Mark loaded his suitcase into the Mercedes. His mother had written him a lengthy letter scolding him for his lack of attention to his family, and inviting him to her annual May Day party. He hated to leave the business, and disdained parties, but he respected his mother's wishes. He hadn't been to Stonebeck Hall for months.

The country roads twisted around obscure land boundaries drawn in the days before motorcars, but Mark found the drive relaxing as he followed the narrow lanes to Kent and beyond. Two kilometers out of Royal Tunbridge Wells, he turned into the long, sweeping driveway of Stonebeck Hall. Mark's mother, Lady Winifred St. John, spent a good deal of the year there, when not traveling, or in London for the season. The sprawling, three-story mansion rose out of the forest, an elegant gray stone monolith trimmed with white rock. Beneath a gray slate roof were intricately detailed cornices. Tall windows peered out to acres of formal gardens, filled with carefully groomed hedges, and beyond them hundreds of acres of forest, also owned by the St. John family.

As Mark pulled the Mercedes to a stop in front of the mansion, Lady Winifred herself appeared at the door to greet him, petite yet sturdy. Although fifty-five years of age, her regal—if mature—beauty seemed eternal. Her hair shone vibrant silver, always impeccably swept up in an elaborate knot, and her hazel eyes followed Mark as he trotted up the front steps.

"The prodigal son has returned at last," she announced.

Mark had inherited his eye color from his mother's—green flecked with brown. He kissed her smooth cheek. "Hello, Mother, you're looking beautiful, as ever."

"Don't try to flatter me, you errant child. You haven't visited me for ages, and don't think I haven't noticed." She put her arm through his as they turned to walk inside.

"My work keeps me very busy, Mother. You know that."

"*Too* busy, if you ask me. I don't suppose you've met an exquisite woman and settled down to start a family without telling me, have you?"

Mark smiled. "Not lately, Mother."

"I thought as much."

They walked into a sunny room filled with rattan and wicker furniture, imported from Africa, the air humid and musty. Greenery dangled from hanging baskets, and plants thrived in oversized ceramic pots on tile floors. A row of vertical windows peered out onto a garden. Mother and son sat in massive oval-backed chairs interwoven with bamboo and strands of green silk.

The butler, Stephens, who had been with the family for as long as Mark could remember, came in carrying a tray of tea.

"Stephens." Mark stood, and as soon as the tray settled on the table, shook the butler's hand. "Are you keeping everything shipshape around here?"

"I try, sir," Stephens said, giving a half bow and smiling. He poured their tea, set out a plate of biscuits, and retreated.

Lady Winifred sipped her tea, watching Mark as he sat back down. "You look too thin, Mark, and you haven't any color at all."

"I live in London, Mother, and it's just now spring. There hasn't been any sun to speak of since October."

"It's not just that." She set down her cup. "Really, Mark, you spend entirely too much time at the business. There are people who can do the work you're doing. Everyone always asks about you, and I'm constantly making excuses for your absence."

"I enjoy the work."

"You are getting older, in case you haven't noticed. You will be thirty-three in July, and still no wife, no children. As the last male St. John, you have a responsibility to the family name that you seem to have forgotten."

"Mother, I'm not going to marry someone just to perpetuate the family name."

"Why not? It's as good a reason as any."

He leaned forward and took her hands in his. "It's your fault. All women pale in comparison to you. They seem simpering and homely and not at all interesting. You've spoiled me."

"I'm serious. Your father, God rest his soul, is the one who should be having this talk with you. You're the future of this family. You're our legacy."

Mark patted her hands. They were cool and dry, slipping from his as he stood and walked to the window.

"I have always wanted a family, but it hasn't been a priority. The business is everything to me. It's all I have need of now."

"What about Lady Millicent, for example? You were a perfect match."

"She had black hair growing out of her chin at the age of twenty-two."

His mother made a most un-ladylike snorting sound. "She's from a family of exceptional heritage and social standing. She has a younger cousin, Lady Henrietta, who's very pretty. What about her?"

Mark sighed. It seemed that, for the last several years, each visit home dissolved into this same inevitable conversation. His mother had grown obsessed with his marrying, and constantly reminded him that the bride-to-be required impeccable pedigree, social standing, and hopefully a robust dowry.

"You're a romantic, you know," she accused. "Love at first sight is a myth. Take your father and me, for instance. I didn't love him when we married, and he didn't love me. He needed my money, and I wanted his title."

Mark turned to her. "Mother!"

"Oh, don't act so shocked. Those were perfectly good reasons for marrying. And as time went by a great fondness developed between us, and we produced two magnificent children. A good marriage and a happy life mustn't start out with anything more than friendship, or even a business merger."

"Are you trying to speak my language?"

"Don't be impolite to your mother. Now finish your tea and tell me what you've been doing, no matter how boring it may be."

The next morning after breakfast, Stephens leaned down to speak to Mark, who was sipping his coffee and reading the Times. "I believe your sister is arriving, if the rumbling sound of that motorcar she insists upon driving is any indication."

"Ah, yes. Muriel. Thank you, Stephens."

Mark folded up the paper and went outside to greet his younger sister.

Muriel sat behind the wheel of the family car, a sleek, bronze Bentley, while the chauffeur who should have been driving sat beside her, gripping the door handle, wide-eyed. As the car rounded the driveway and pulled up in front of the house, Muriel let go of the steering wheel and gave Mark a wave. She stepped hard on the brakes and the car slid on the loose pebbles of the driveway, sputtering to a stop.

She leapt out and took the steps two at a time. "Long-lost brother!" She threw herself into Mark's arms, then struggled to get away as he tried to tussle her hair. "I thought you would never come to visit."

He tweaked her gently on her nose. "It works both ways, young lady. You could always come visit me in London."

"Not true. You say I can come visit you, but Mother says no."

Over his sister's shoulder, Mark noticed the chauffeur helping a wisp of a young woman get out of the car. "Who's this?"

"God, I almost forgot." She smacked the heel of her hand dramatically onto her forehead, then ran to the bottom of the steps, grabbed the horrified-looking young woman by the hand, and dragged her toward Mark.

"Lady Anne Rutledge," she said, "allow me to introduce my brother, Mark St. John. Lord St. John, my chum—I mean distinguished guest—Lady Anne."

Mark took the girl's trembling hand and bowed over it. "Lady Anne." He looked up as he straightened, surprised to find a look of terror in her huge brown eyes.

"I'm sorry," he said. "Are you all right?"

"Oh, don't mind Anne," Muriel said. "She's as shy as a church mouse. She'll be better once she gets to know you." She grabbed the girl's hand away from Mark's and pulled her friend into the mansion. "We're going to get something to eat. Meet us for a game of croquet in an hour."

Mark smiled as they disappeared into the house. Some things never changed.

Lady Winifred St. John knew how to throw a party. Cars and horse-drawn carriages filled with families began to arrive shortly after Muriel's dramatic entrance. Mark stood with his mother and greeted guests until Muriel dragged him away for a quick game of croquet.

Lady St. John made sure the annual May Day celebration included an elegant luncheon for the adults, and fun for the children. Food was served beneath white canopies on tables set with linen and silver. As the adults sipped champagne and nibbled on hors d'oeuvres, the children milled around in anticipation. Dressed in traditional May Day style, the boys were outfitted in shirts with ties, and short pants. The girls wore white dresses with garlands of flowers in their hair.

The servants had spent several hours the day before erecting a tall pole with long ribbons hanging from the top.

Lady Winifred, in a long, slim-fitting lavender dress, walked to the pole. "Boys and girls," she said, holding her arms out. "It's time for the celebration. Come dance for us around the maypole."

The adults set down their food long enough to applaud as pairs of boys and girls gathered around the base of the pole, each taking the end of a ribbon. As a quartet of violinists pulled back their bows and began to play, the children weaved in and around each other, boys going one way and girls going the other, as their ribbons braided together around the pole. The ribbons pulled them tighter and tighter together with each revolution, until all the children met, laughing, at the base. The adults applauded again, and the children, relieved of their duty to perform, dropped their ribbons and scattered to play a game of hide-and-seek around the garden hedges and trees.

The luncheon marked only the beginning of a long day of festivities. Mark chatted with guests until the last one had retired for an afternoon rest.

To please his mother, he arrived first at the pre-dinner gathering that began at seven, wearing a black tuxedo, black vest, and gray-striped silk shirt and tie.

Muriel and Anne arrived arm in arm. Muriel's dress fell in straight lines, showing off her broad shoulders and narrow hips. The color was the shade of a blue bunting, one of her favorite birds. Anne wore pink taffeta, with a cream-colored sash wrapped tightly around her tiny waist.

"Ladies?" Mark held his arms out to the women, and they let go of one another and each took one of his arms. He escorted them in to dinner, and held out their chairs as they sat on either side of his own place.

Muriel chatted easily with those around her, but was uncharacteristically restrained when speaking with the gentleman by her side.

The man looked familiar, but Mark couldn't quite place him. He smiled at his sister, who'd never been at a loss for words or known a moment of insecurity in her life. What an odd pair they made, Muriel and Anne. He glanced at Anne, nearly swallowed up by the ruffles of her dress.

She examined her plate as intently as if she were a businessman reading the London Times.

He leaned toward her. "If there's anything I hate more than having to attend one of Mother's parties, it's having to wear a tie."

She started and stared at him, and said in a whisper, "I don't like parties either."

"Why did you come?"

"Because my mother made me."

Mark laughed out loud, causing Muriel to turn to him curiously. Mark ignored her, whispering to Anne again, "We're in the same boat, aren't we, since my mother made me come also. How do you suppose two grown adults let their mothers boss them around like this?"

Anne looked at him with unabashed curiosity, as if, at seventeen, no one had ever called her an adult.

"Here's a thought," he said. "Let's go have a dance after dinner, shall we? My mother will see us, and word is bound to get back to your mother. We'll make two women very happy. What do you say?"

She shook her head. "I couldn't."

Mark felt a wave of compassion for this girl who seemed so afraid of everyone and everything. "Just pretend no one is here except us. Close your eyes and believe that we're all alone. It won't be so bad, and I'll try not to step on your toes."

After hours of course after course, dessert arrived.

"Eton Mess, my favorite," Mark said to Anne of the mishmash of strawberries, meringue, and cream that looked like a smashed dish.

She tasted the concoction and smiled. "It's quite lovely."

When the last bit had been devoured, Mark stood and held his arm out to her.

She rose, put her hand on his arm, and allowed herself to be escorted out of the dining room.

In the ballroom, the fireplace crackled and cast a golden light as the strains of piano, violins, and cellos invited dancers to the marble dance floor.

Mark took Anne by the hand and led her to the center of the room—the first to take the floor. He pulled her gently into his arms and began to move.

Anne followed his lead stiffly.

"Remember," he said, pulling her close and whispering into her ear, "our mothers will be ecstatic."

Muriel and a tall, young man joined them on the dance floor. She mouthed the word "Thanks" to her brother.

Mark leaned near Muriel's young man. "Better keep an eye on my sister. If she thinks you dance better than she does, she'll challenge you to rugby."

"Rugby!" Her dance partner looked aghast. "A woman playing rugby?"

Muriel looked quite pleased.

Mark could feel Anne relax a little as they moved around the floor. The song ended, but he didn't release her. Soon, more couples crowded the floor, and no one gave them a second glance.

Muriel and her tall dance partner danced alongside Mark and Anne, until the man who had been seated next to Muriel at dinner tapped her partner on the shoulder. "May I?"

The young man looked displeased, then gracefully stepped aside.

"Hello again." The man took Muriel into his arms.

"Mark," said Muriel as she leaned toward her brother. "You remember Sir Leopold Whitlock."

"Ah yes. Good to see you again." The two men shook hands. "Lady Anne Rutledge," Mark said.

Sir Leopold bowed, then turned back to Muriel and swirled her away into the crowd, a slight limp marring his graceful dancing skills.

"Who is Sir Leopold?" Anne asked.

"A distant neighbor, but I can't remember any details. We'll have to ask Muriel."

"He seems quite smitten with her."

"He does, indeed." The music ended, and he said, "There, we did it. Made our mothers proud. May I get you something to drink?"

She nodded and, as they moved off the floor, Mark plucked two champagnes from a footman's tray.

"Here we go," he said, handing her the flute and holding up his. "I propose a toast. To mothers... may they appreciate the sacrifices their children make on their behalf."

Anne smiled and they clinked glasses.

When Mark noticed his mother watching with ill-concealed interest, he held his champagne flute up to her, and she beamed. He then turned his attention back to Anne. "How did you ever get mixed up with the likes of my sister?"

Anne studied her glass. "She chose me."

"Chose you?"

"At Missus Chapmans, where we attend young ladies' afternoons. It's often tiresome, learning all the proper ways to do everything from discussing politics to choosing hats, but they do have games to help make it fun. Muriel chose me to be on her team. She was captain. After that, she picked me as partner whenever we had to practice something with other girls."

Mark could imagine his little sister taking this shy creature under her wing. "I see. And how did you feel about being, as you say, chosen?"

She looked up at him as if he were crazy to ask. "Muriel is one of the most popular girls, and the best at any outdoor game we play. She's wonderful."

Mark smiled. "Yes, she is wonderful, isn't she? And she has excellent taste in choosing friends."

Anne looked confused, then turned crimson.

Muriel joined them, cheeks flushed and skin glowing.

"We were just talking about you," Mark said.

"I hope you were both nice in your gossip!"

Standing side by side, the resemblance between Mark and Muriel was striking. She stood nearly as tall as Mark, and they shared the same hazel eyes, straight nose and strong jaw, but where Mark was fair-haired, Muriel's hair was dark brown like a light molasses.

"No gossip," Anne said, sounding alarmed. "I told him you're the best in outdoor games. But he's your brother, so I'm sure he already knows." She looked alarmed, as if she had said too much. "If you two will excuse me, I'm quite exhausted, and must go up to bed."

"So soon?" Mark took her by the hand and kissed it. "Thank you, Anne, for a wonderful evening."

She blushed, and bustled from the room.

"You've quite bowled her over," said Muriel. "Good for you. She can use some attention."

"She has a certain beauty, like a fawn, with big eyes, and long, awkward legs."

"I'd say she's more like a porcelain doll," Muriel said. "Pale and pretty, but fragile. If she gets dropped, she'll shatter."

"Perhaps that's just her shyness."

"She is agonizingly shy," agreed Muriel. "That's why I've tried to make friends with her. She's afraid of her own shadow."

"Let's talk about you. What's all this attention from Sir Leopold Whitlock?"

"Mother's keen on me marrying him." She grimaced.

"I don't remember much about him, but isn't he married?"

"He was. His wife died last year. Pneumonia."

"That's sad."

"He's nearly forty," Muriel whispered, glancing about. "How can Mother think I would ever want to marry someone that old? But she's got her scheme going, and every time I come home, there he is. Just like tonight."

Mark nodded. "What's the allure for Mother?"

"Not to be crass, but title and money," she said under her breath. "He was knighted for bravery in the Second Boer War, which is commendable. I don't know if you noticed the limp. War injury. Maybe if I had known him twenty years ago, I would have been interested...."

"Only you weren't born twenty years ago."

"Precisely, dear brother. Precisely. Now I'm going to follow Anne's lead and go off to bed, before Leo asks me to dance again. How about going riding after an early breakfast tomorrow?"

"My pleasure."

Muriel stood on her toes and gave Mark a peck on the cheek. "Good to have you home, Brother, even if it is just for a short while. See you in the morning."

The dew still glistened on the apple blossoms when Mark and Muriel finished breakfast and headed outside the next morning.

The butler rushed after them. "Excuse me, sir, Lady Muriel!"

They stopped and turned.

"Good morning, Stephens," Mark said.

The butler caught up to them. "I'm sorry to bother you, but I have a favor to ask. My son, Christopher, is visiting, and I wondered if you would mind if he accompanied you on your ride? He can tend to your needs and the horses."

"I remember Christopher," said Muriel. "He visited here a long time ago when we were children."

"Yes, my Lady," said Stephens. "He lives with his mother in town, and I bring him out here every now and then. I hope he's not a nuisance."

"He's welcome to ride with us," said Mark.

"He'll be of service to you," said Stephens. "I took the liberty of having him prepare your horses."

"Oh dear," Muriel said, looking past Stephens back toward the house.

Sir Leopold strutted out the front door in full riding gear. "Good, I've caught you," he said, joining them, slightly out of breath. "If you don't mind, I'd like to come along this morning. My valet mentioned you two were up and off for a ride."

"It looks like we'll have a full entourage this morning." Muriel sighed.

Stephens rushed back inside, and Mark, Muriel and Leo walked to the stables, where a dark-haired young man stood holding three horses, two English-saddle and one side-saddle.

"You must be Stephens's son," Mark said.

"Christopher, sir," the young man answered, then spotting Sir Leopold, added, "Looks like I'll need to saddle up another horse."

"You've already saddled my horse," said Leo.

"That was my horse, sir," Christopher said. "I'll saddle another."

"The problem with an entourage," Muriel said under her breath, "means I have to ride side-saddle."

"Don't tell me you ride like a man when no one's around?" Mark feigned shock.

"Better than a man, I'd say," Muriel deadpanned.

Christopher laughed.

Muriel regarded him. "You find that funny?"

He looked at her with cool, blue eyes. "Amusing," he answered. "But not consummately funny."

"That's a bit impertinent," said Leo. "Let's get going, shall we?"

With great deliberation, Christopher handed the reins of the side-saddled horse to Mark, and the English-saddle reins to Muriel, then turned back to the stables.

"Somewhat amusing," Muriel called after him, smiling. "And perhaps a trifle clever."

The three of them took off at a gallop, with Mark and Muriel in the lead, followed by Sir Leopold. Before long Christopher caught up to them, hanging a suitable distance behind. They rode past the apple orchard and into the forest on a wide, dirt road. The cool, morning air was filled with the scent of fir and cedar, and they rode hard for a while, then slowed to a walk. They could have galloped for days and never breached the boundary of the Stonebeck estate.

At mid-morning, they came upon a stream and stopped. Christopher caught up and took the reins of all the horses and led them to the stream to drink.

"This is the only thing I miss living in London," said Mark. "Riding every day. It clears my head and stirs my blood."

"I ride nearly every day," said Muriel. "When I don't have to attend Missus Chapman's school of silly rules."

Sir Leopold laughed. "You're a breath of fresh air, my dear. But rules are rules, customs are customs, and they're good to know. My wife Isabel was a stickler about etiquette."

"Sir Leopold," said Mark. "I am sorry to hear about Lady Whitlock."

The smile evaporated from Leopold's face, and his gaze dropped to his hands. "Thank you. It's quite difficult, as I'm sure you can imagine, to lose one's wife. Quite difficult. They say time will heal all wounds." He glanced up at Muriel. "I hope that's true."

Muriel's eyes widened. "If you'll excuse me, I brought some treats for the horses."

She walked to her horse and pulled carrots from a leather pouch tied to the saddle. "Here you go, boy." She held the treat out to her stallion, stroking his velvety muzzle as he devoured the carrot. Christopher watched as she fed each horse, until she reached the horse he was riding. She held out the carrot to Christopher. "Shall I? Or would you rather?"

Christopher took it from her and fed it to his horse, scratching the animal's forehead as it crunched the carrot greedily.

Muriel turned away and studied Leo and Mark as they talked. Sir Leopold was a pleasant enough looking man, with hair growing a trifle thin and sporting a slight paunch, but overall, still quite pleasing to look at. She turned back to Christopher, who was watching her watch Leo. Christopher, with his wide shoulders and narrow waist, legs long and lean, was young and in his prime.

Now, as he watched her contemplate *him*, he grinned.

Muriel eyed him dispassionately, took her stallion by the reins, and the mare Leo was riding, and led them over to Leo.

"Shall we carry on?" She handed him the reins.

As they rode through the woods she rode abreast with Leo. "I love riding," she said. "There's no place I would rather be than here, with my horse in the forest. Polo comes in at a close second, although it's hard to find a team out here in the countryside. When Mark still lived at home, he and I used to play polo nearly every day, an abbreviated game between the two of us. What about you, Sir Leopold? Tell me what you enjoy. Polo? Cricket? Football?"

"Please, call me Leo," he said. "I rather enjoy going to the theater, reading a good book, and a rousing game of bridge. You might have noticed a slight limp when I walk. I'm afraid my old war injury makes those activities I used to enjoy as a younger man more difficult now."

"I am sorry," Muriel said. "So thoughtless of me."

"Not at all." Leo smiled. "Isabel, my wife, was a dilly of a bridge player. Quite clever. She threw grand garden parties, just like your mother. Loved to throw a party. And she gave me two wonderful children. She was such a good mother to my boys. Why, I remember a time when...."

Muriel smiled politely as Leo talked on about Isabel. She glanced once over her shoulder, to where Mark and Christopher rode side by side in silence, obviously eavesdropping on Leo's monologue.

"You will, too, I'm sure," Leo said loudly.

"I'm sorry," Muriel said, returning her attention to Leo.

"Make a wonderful mother someday, just like Isabel. You will, too." He repeated.

"What a compliment," Muriel said, an abrupt dull ache in the pit of her stomach. "Thank you."

Muriel tapped on the bedroom door where Anne was staying, then cracked it open. "Are you ready?"

"Nearly," Anne said.

Muriel walked in to find her lady's maid, Rose, putting the finishing touches on Anne's hair. Anne was swallowed up in another pink taffeta dress.

"Oh dear," Muriel said.

"What?" Anne gaped up at her friend.

"That dress looks so much like the one you wore last night, and frankly, dear, it's not terribly flattering. It doesn't show off your figure or your hair."

Anne looked down at her dress. "Most of my dresses look like this," she said as if apologizing.

"Stay right there. I've got a dress in mind that I think will look stunning on you."

"You're too tall," Anne said. "Nothing that fits you will fit me."

"I haven't always been tall, but I have always had to wear dinner gowns, once I reached a certain age. Don't move." She ran out to a seldom-used closet, grabbed what she was looking for, and returned moments later with an emerald green dress made of silk. "Try this on."

Rose helped Anne out of the pink taffeta and into the green silk, and buttoned up a row of buttons that cascaded all the way down the back of the dress, emphasizing Anne's narrow waist.

Anne stood and gazed at her image in the mirror. "It's rather low cut," she mumbled, placing a hand over the mounds of her breasts that squeezed over the top of the neckline, straining against the fabric. "Improperly so, I believe."

"You are more endowed than I," Muriel agreed, not mentioning that she had worn a camisole beneath—what had been, on her—the loose-fitting bodice. "But you look positively elegant, don't you agree, Rose?"

The lady's maid stared at Anne's bosom. "Oh, yes ma'am," she agreed weakly.

"I can't." Anne frowned.

"Come along, we'll be late." Muriel propelled her friend out the door.

Downstairs, they made an entrance into the dining room, Muriel gently pushing Anne to go in first.

Leo and Mark stood. "Ah, the ladies," Leo said, then froze.

Lady Winifred arrived a moment later, walking around to her seat at the table as the footman pulled back her chair. When she noticed that everyone else was standing, staring at Anne, she glanced over at Anne, her eyes darting to the daring neckline and away. She then looked at the men, who stood motionless.

"You look beautiful, Anne," Winifred said, breaking the silence. "That dress fits you like...." She searched for the right word. "...like a glove."

"I think the color looks stunning on her," Muriel said proudly. "The dress is one of mine."

"I don't remember it looking like that on you," Mark said, smiling.

Anne blushed furiously. One hand floated up to cover her chest as she drifted to her place at the table and sat.

Muriel sat beside her.

Mark gave Muriel a look, one eyebrow raised.

Muriel grinned at him. "I'd love champagne with dinner tonight, instead of wine. I don't know... it feels like a celebration, with Mark home and Leo visiting."

"Champagne it is," Mark said, and the footman rushed out the door.

Early the next morning, as Mark loaded his luggage into the Mercedes, Muriel came outside, sleepy-eyed. "You're off so soon? I was hoping you would stay another day, go for another ride, maybe practice polo with me."

He shrugged. "I would love to play outside with you every day, dear sister, but business awaits and I must get back to London. By the way..." He lowered his voice, although no one else was about. "...that dress you chose for your friend last night was a little risqué, *tu ne penses pas?*"

Muriel grinned. "Anne has attributes that most people don't see. I thought you might be intrigued."

"Devilish girl," he admonished. "Are you trying to lure me into marriage through temptation? Or did Mother put you up to it?"

"All my idea," she said, still smiling.

"And what attributes does Sir Leopold have that I should have dangled in front of you, to lure you into marriage?"

His sister's smile collapsed. "He's a nice man, and I'm trying to like him. I really am."

"Be a dear and say my goodbyes for me, will you? Then maybe I'll forgive you for dressing your friend like a tart."

"Don't be a fuddy-duddy," she said. "And come back soon. Or better yet, convince Mother to let me visit you in London."

Just then Winifred appeared on the top step, leading a sleepy-looking Anne by the hand.

"Don't run off without saying goodbye," Lady Winifred admonished, leading the poor girl down the steps to Mark's car.

"Mother," he said, and leaned down and kissed her on the cheek. "Another spectacular May Day party. You should be very proud of yourself."

"It was successful because you were here to host the occasion. Let your managers run the business, and spend more time here at Stonebeck, where you belong. You have duties here."

"Yes, Mother, I'll try to get home more often."

He turned to Anne and took her hand. "A delight to meet you. Thank you for a marvelous time. Don't let my sister get you into any trouble."

Anne stared at him, doe-eyed, and mumbled, "No, I won't."

"See you again, maybe in London one of these days, when Mother allows Muriel to visit. She can bring you along." He kissed her hand, and climbed into his Mercedes, rather pleased with himself for fulfilling his family obligations.

Chapter 13

"We're expecting," James announced as Mark walked in the door at the shipping company the next morning.

"What are we expecting?" Mark walked past James into his office.

"A baby."

Mark backtracked out of his office. "What did you say?"

James laughed. "A baby... we're expecting a baby. I'm going to be a father."

"Congratulations!" Mark pumped James's hand. "That's wonderful. Wonderful news."

"I'm going to be a father," James repeated with a cockeyed smile.

Mark laughed. "So you said. Let me buy you a drink later. We'll have a little celebration."

"I must be the luckiest man in the world," James said.

By late summer, there could be no doubt about Kate's condition. She'd been letting out the waist of her skirts for the past six weeks, but now, new, larger clothes were a necessity.

James doted on her, and they spent his days off strolling through the parks or along the Thames. Time stood still.

By a week before Christmas, Kate had grown large. "I'm as big as a house," she said while handing James sparkling ornaments and hand-carved animals to hang on their Christmas tree. He put his arm around her, and she leaned against him, admiring their work.

"It's a bit early to have a tree up," James said.

"I know, but it's so festive, and with Mark dropping by I thought it would be fun." Kate stretched, hand on her lower back. "I better go see how Lucy's coming with dinner."

"No, you just sit here and rest." James helped her to a chair. "Can I get you anything?"

She shook her head.

He leaned down and kissed her cheek, and as he stood to leave, she caught his hand.

"You're a good man, James Casey," she said softly, "and you're going to be a wonderful father."

He squeezed her hand. "I'm a lucky man, Missus Casey." A knock sounded at the front door. "The guests have arrived."

James returned with Mark St. John, a pale girl with large eyes clinging to his arm, a tall young woman who resembled Mark, and an older man.

"Kate," Mark said, smiling. "You're looking lovely."

"Liar." Kate offered him her cheek, and he leaned down and kissed her.

"I would like you to meet Lady Anne Rutledge. This is Kate and James Casey."

James took her hand, and Kate nodded her head.

"This is my sister, Muriel, and Sir Leopold Whitlock," Mark said.

Leo shook James's hand, then lightly took Kate's outstretched fingers.

The baby took this opportunity to kick Kate soundly in the ribs, and she sat back in the chair with a gasp, hand on her side.

"What's wrong?" James turned pale.

"I think I've got a bloody rugby player in here."

Mark laughed, while Anne and Leo looked shocked.

"Are you quite all right?" James kneeled by her side.

"Quite." Kate smiled.

"Good," Mark said. "Your tree is magnificent, Kate."

"Dinner's nearly ready." She pushed herself up and out of the chair. "Let me just check with Lucy."

In the kitchen, Kate peeked at the glazed duck and took a sip of the fish soup, looking sideways at Lucy, who struggled to open a jar of pickled beets.

"Lucy, you've lived in London for a long time, haven't you?"

"All my life, ma'am."

"Does the name Rutledge sound familiar to you?"

Lucy set the jar down "Oh yes, ma'am. Well-known name, Rutledge is."

Kate stepped closer. "Anne Rutledge?"

"Yes, that's right. She's an only child, I believe."

"A good family?"

"One of the best—very old, very distinguished." Lucy picked up the jar again, and glanced back at Kate. "Quite wealthy, if one can mention such things."

"Hmm... thank you, Lucy. We're ready for dinner."

"Yes, ma'am. It's all ready."

Lady Anne clung to Mark like a shadow, close but never touching, as Lucy served the soup and poured the wine.

Sir Leopold glanced around, puzzled. "You don't have much of a staff for dinner this evening."

"Mark speaks so well of you, James," Muriel said, changing the subject. "He says you're a real asset to the company."

"It's a privilege to be a part of Lyman and Stonebeck," James said.

"How did you two meet, Kate?" Muriel asked.

Kate and James glanced at one another. "As children in Kirken, a small village in Scotland. James was much older than me."

"I think that makes a good pairing," Sir Leopold said. "An older man is a stable influence on a young woman." He glanced at Muriel, color rising to his cheeks as he mumbled, "Not terribly older."

"You met as children," Muriel continued. "Then you married and came to London?"

"I came first," James said, "after graduating college and working at a shipping company in Glasgow. I got hired on here at Lyman and Stonebeck. Then I brought Kate to join me, and we married."

"You're a working man?" Leo asked.

"That's right."

Lucy brought the duck to the table, and hurried back to the kitchen for potatoes and vegetable as James cut the duck and served it.

"Now you're starting a family." Muriel smiled. "How lovely."

"Quite right," said Leo. "My children are fourteen and fifteen. I can't believe how quickly they've grown. I'm a widower, you see."

Mark tapped his glass and looked at Anne, who looked suddenly radiant to him, like a porcelain doll come to life. "A toast," said Mark, raising his glass. "To James and Kate and their new arrival, who will, I'm sure, make an already happy household even brighter."

"Here here," said Leo.

Lucy's red hair worked its way loose of its pins by the time she served dessert, and her cheeks flushed nearly as bright as her hair.

James poured glasses of port for the men, and servings of sweet wine for the ladies.

Mark leaned over to him and said, "I have something in the automobile. Would you mind lending me a hand?"

"Not at all."

"I have to tell you," Mark said as they stepped into the brisk night air. "You and Kate have changed my thinking."

"How so?" James asked.

"I'm a business man, and happy to spend long days engaged in Lyman and Stonebeck matters. Mother constantly encourages me to find a suitable wife, but I've had no interest. Yet seeing you two make a home here, and now having a baby, it looks positively alluring. And then my sister brought home Anne."

"A lovey woman," James said. "Quiet, but a beauty in her own right. Rather genteel."

"Yes, all of those attributes, I agree. I might not have seen Anne again, except if she visited again with Muriel. Now I'm seeing her regularly, much to my mother's delight, I might add."

"I highly recommend marriage," James said, smiling. "I'll let you know about fatherhood soon, but I predict it will be quite remarkable."

"Here we are." They reached Mark's car. "Help me with this package, if you would."

They jostled a large, brightly wrapped box out of the Mercedes, and maneuvered it in through the front door.

"What in the world is this?" Kate asked as he carried the package into the dining room.

"A Christmas gift."

"You shouldn't have," said James.

"May I open it now?" asked Kate, rising from the table.

Mark laughed. "Please."

Kate tore off the wrapping paper and bow, untied a string that held the box closed, and pulled open the top.

"Let us help," Mark said. James held the box as Mark lifted out a hand-carved cradle. "It's made of cherry wood," he said. "See the bears and lambs carved into it?"

Kate's eyes filled with tears. "It's beautiful."

"A work of art," James said.

"It's perfect, Mark." Muriel put a hand on her brother's arm. "Well done."

"Thank you from all of us," said Kate. "Me, James, and the baby."

Mark bowed. "You're all very welcome."

Anne approached the cradle and ran her hand along the surface, a slow smile coming to her face.

Leo held up his wine glass. "To a healthy, happy baby."

"Here, here," everyone chimed in.

"To James and Kate," Mark added. "A long and happy life with their new family."

Chapter 14 – London, January 1913

A week after the dinner, in the darkness of night, Kate nudged James. "Wake up."

"What is it?" he murmured.

"It's begun." She smiled, then cringed as an obvious wave of pain washed over her.

James shot out of bed, on his feet in an instant. "I'll get the doctor and Missus Ames."

Kate shook her head, eyes closed. "Please, just the doctor."

The doctor and his nurse arrived an hour later. After James showed them to Kate's bed, they didn't allow him back inside.

Mrs. Ames watched over him downstairs, bringing him cup after cup of tea as they both listened to the cries coming from upstairs. The night lasted forever, until finally, at six in the morning, January 2, 1913, Kate's cries were replaced with the lusty cries of a baby.

James froze at the sound, staring at Mrs. Ames.

The nurse came down the stairs, smiling. "Mister Casey, would you like to meet your new daughter?"

James grabbed Mrs. Ames by the shoulders. "A daughter, did she say?"

The housekeeper nodded, eyes shining.

He looked at the nurse. "Is Kate all right? And my daughter?"

"They're just fine. If you follow me, you can see them now."

Two lamps lit the bedroom. Outside, fog clung to the windows. James stood in the doorway trying to accustom his eyes. The air felt heavy with sweat.

The doctor stood near the bed packing his bag. "Ah, Mister Casey." He looked up without missing a beat. "Congratulations. You have a fine, healthy girl."

James stared at Kate lying in bed, her charcoal hair sticking to her wet, pale forehead and cheeks, dark shadows beneath her eyes.

He leaned down. "Are you well?"

She smiled wanly and nodded. "There's someone here who wants to meet you, Mister Casey." She pulled back the sheet to reveal a tiny face topped by dark hair.

James stared, awestruck.

"You can hold her," Kate said.

The doctor and nurse slipped out of the room as James reached out timidly to stroke the baby's cheek and pick her up. "Hello, Vanessa Katharine," James whispered, finally saying the name they'd deliberated over for months. "I'm your father."

The baby yawned, her mouth opening wide.

The month of May found Vanessa a cherub, with plump, rosy cheeks and roly-poly arms and legs. As spring flowers blossomed, Kate's daily routine was to take a blanket out into the garden and sit with the baby, watching as Vanessa gazed around, bursting out with laughter and smiles for no apparent reason. A baby's love for living, perhaps, before life leached away that built-in joy.

Kate and James, after much debate, asked Mark if he might consider being godfather to Vanessa. Though well aware the request stretched social propriety, he seemed so interested in them and the baby that they risked the invitation.

Mark agreed without a moment's hesitation.

The day of Vanessa's christening, sunlight fought its way through the fog. They decided to forego a godmother as they didn't want to burden Mrs. Bridger with any responsibility, and no one else stepped up to fill the role. So, a godfather it would be.

Kate invited Mark, Anne, and the Bridgers, to their home for brunch after the christening. She invited Muriel and Leo, as well, but they were back in the country and unable to attend.

Anne brought along an aunt—her Aunt Florence—a thin, quiet woman, much like her niece.

Mrs. Ames and Lucy had set up tables and chairs outside in the garden, piling them high with muffins, crumpets, hot and cold bread, eggs in napkins, bacon, little fishes, deviled kidneys, even hot turtle soup. There were hot cakes, cold cakes, sweet cakes, and Scotch shortcake. Lucy had truly outdone herself.

While everyone lingered over lunch, sipping champagne, Mark presented Vanessa with a delicate necklace of pearls.

"They're so lovely," Kate said, running her fingers over the necklace. "We'll put these away until she's much older, of course."

"There is one more thing, if you'll excuse me." Mark went outside to his car, and returned with a second box, rather large, wrapped in a pink ribbon.

"What's this?" Kate exclaimed. "Another present for Vanessa?"

Mark handed her the box, a sly smile on his face.

The expression on Kate's face changed as the box began to move on its own.

"What on earth...?" Kate untied the ribbon and out wriggled a puppy. "Oh, my goodness!"

"A West Highlander, in honor of Vanessa's parents' homeland," Mark said.

Kate set the puppy on the ground, and everyone couldn't help but laugh. Its legs were so short that it appeared to consist only of one large, whiskered head and a body of long hair.

"I hope you like him, and that he's not too much trouble, with the baby and all. If he is, say the word, and I'll take him myself."

Anne looked at Mark in surprise.

"Not at all," James said. "Every babe needs a dog for a friend."

The puppy discovered Vanessa and began licking her face. The baby responded with a whoop of delight, and grabbed a handful of the puppy's hair in her fists.

James rescued the puppy, setting it on the blanket with them. "Be nice to the puppy, Vanessa. We have to pet, not grab." He guided the baby's hand over the dog. "What shall we call this little scamp?"

"It must be a good Scottish name, in honor of his heritage," Kate said.

"How about Bruce," James suggested, as the puppy chewed on his finger, "after Robert the Bruce, King of Scotland's independence."

"Bruce it is," Kate agreed.

"And, if you don't mind, I have another surprise," Mark said. He put his arm around Anne, who blushed furiously. "We're engaged to be married."

"Wonderful," Anne's Aunt Florence said, voice high and trembling. "What a blessing."

James jumped up from the blanket. "Congratulations!" He shook Mark's hand and kissed Anne on the cheek.

"And he's waited a good long time for the right woman to come along," Kate said. "Do you have a date set?"

"These things take time," Aunt Florence interceded. "I should think at least a year to make all the necessary arrangements."

"A toast is in order." James grabbed the champagne bottle and topped off everyone's flute, then held his own in the air. "To Mark and Anne. May they be blessed with a long marriage full of love, laughter, and children."

As if on cue, Vanessa started to cry, and everyone burst out laughing together.

Kate set her champagne down, and gathered the baby in her arms. "She's jealous that we're all eating and drinking, and she's not. Please excuse us."

She carried the baby away and upstairs to the bedroom, where she pulled a chair up to the window that overlooked the garden where everyone was gathered below. She unbuttoned her blouse and offered her breast to the hungry baby, and thought about Mark marrying Anne.

Kate would never have imagined Anne as a wife for Mark. He was as handsome and smart as Anne seemed dull and timid. Kate pulled the curtain to the side and looked down on the gathering. As she watched, Mark glanced up to the bedroom window where she stood, and quickly looked away. Kate sat back in the chair, and let the curtain fall shut.

A few weeks later, on June 28, James arrived home from the office early, frowning as he took the afternoon paper from Mrs. Ames.

Kate hurried into the foyer. "James, you're early."

He barely looked up at her as he scanned the paper.

"Is something wrong?"

He glanced at her. "Archduke Ferdinand and Sophie were assassinated today."

"Oh, dear. Another war in the Balkans?"

James looked surprised. "Quite possibly, yes. I didn't realize you followed such matters."

Kate turned toward the kitchen. "I read the newspapers, like everyone else. I'll get us some tea."

Chapter 15

Kate pushed Vanessa in the pram down the sidewalk of Piccadilly Circus, with its jumble of motorcars, buses, and horse-drawn carriages, listening to snippets of conversations as she passed people on the streets, or groups gathered on a corner. The topic was always the same: the assassination and its implications.

Despite the gloomy topic of the day, Kate felt free, and alive, and happy to be out of the house. As much as she loved her home, and especially her gardens, she felt thrilled to be in the heart of London. She stopped at a corner where a woman sold cut flowers, to admire the colors, and moved down the street to peer into store windows. She kept a keen eye out for the women shoppers, to see what fashions they were wearing this year.

Vanessa slept. Kate had timed the trip by feeding Vanessa right before they left, and hoped for a few hours before having to return home to feed her again.

She began to cross St. James Street, and as she looked both ways to make sure a horse or motorcar wouldn't run them down, she caught sight of two men coming out the door of a men's club onto the sidewalk. They turned in her direction, and Kate recognized Des in an instant.

Shaken, she hurried ahead and stepped off the sidewalk into the street, causing a motorcar to screech to a stop, blasting its horn. She rushed on even as Des called her name.

He caught up. "Kate, slow down there." He came from behind, and stepped in front of the pram, forcing her to stop.

He looked disheveled, with at least two day's stubble and bloodshot eyes. Des's companion joined them, a compact man with round wire spectacles and thinning hair. The two of them had the air of feral dogs.

Des stepped to the side and peered into the pram. "Look at you," Des clucked at the baby, then to Kate. "So, this is why you've been so scarce. What a beauty. A girl, I presume, because of the pink blanket. What beautiful black hair she has, like her mum." He looked Kate square in the eyes and smiled broadly. "And me."

Kate felt sick.

"Where are my manners? Kate, this is Mister Langdon Hughes, a friend of mine. Mister Hughes, Missus James Casey. Kate, to her friends."

"A pleasure," the man said.

"We've been at the club. Good heavens, what time is it? What *day* is it?" Des laughed. "I did rather well last night, wouldn't you agree, Langdon?"

"Very well," the man said. "The cards were in your favor."

"And not yours." Des made an attempt at looking concerned. "Lady Luck will be on your side next time."

Kate began to push the pram. "I really must go."

Des caught her upper arm, stopping her. He stepped close. "It's been too long, Missus Casey. No time to chat with a dear old friend?"

She could smell tobacco and alcohol on his breath. "I'm afraid not. Nice to meet you, Mister...."

"Hughes."

"Yes. I must go."

She pulled her arm out of Des's grip and pushed the pram away as quickly as she could, breathing hard, as if running a race.

She heard Des remark to his friend, "Look at that woman. A beauty if ever there was one."

Kate's face burned as she hurried away.

Chapter 16

Muriel sat next to her mother in the back of the Bentley, watching the countryside glide past and trying to ignore the knot in her stomach.

Winifred had refused to allow Muriel to drive. "It's unseemly for a woman to drive," she had said when they left, "especially when visiting a suitor's home with her mother."

They were on their way to Sir Leopold's.

"Now remember," Winifred continued, "when you meet his children, be pleasant, but distant. You don't want them to think you're trying to take the place of their mother."

"I don't think I can go along with this anymore," Muriel said.

"Along with what? He's a very nice man, and lonely. He wants to be married again. And he's a good match for you, don't forget that."

"In what way is he a good match for me?" Muriel frowned at her mother. "He's twice as old as I am, he's as athletic as a hedgehog, and he idolizes his deceased wife. I don't see anything that makes him a good match."

"You're young." Winifred patted her daughter's hand. "It's hard for you to grasp the long-term benefits of marrying Sir Leopold. He's titled, he reportedly is quite financially solvent, and he fawns over you. He'll spoil you and give you anything you want."

"I have everything I want now."

"Yes, you do, but what about the future? Mark will inherit Stonebeck Hall along with everything we have."

"Mark will provide for me," Muriel argued.

"And what if something happens to Mark? Then what? Your cousin Albert inherits the whole thing. You hardly know the man. You think he'll provide for you? There's no guarantee. You have to look after yourself, and Sir Leopold is the perfect resolution to the situation."

"Really, Mother, I've tried to cooperate with you, but the whole thing makes me sick. The idea of moving into another woman's home, marrying her husband and trying to raise her children, is not what I imagined a marriage to be."

"It's not ideal, but listen to me. Love grows slowly. What begins as a practical arrangement often grows into a lifetime of contentment."

The Bentley slowed as they entered the driveway that culminated at Sir Leopold's home, an edifice even larger than Stonebeck Hall. The drive circled sculptured hedges and manicured rose gardens, leading up to the house. Two footmen stood waiting for the car to ease to a stop, then opened the passenger doors before the chauffer had time to disembark. They lent a hand to Winifred and Muriel, as Sir Leopold himself came out the front door, leaning on his cane as he limped down the steps.

"Welcome, welcome," he shouted, and taking Winifred's hand as he kissed her on one cheek and then the other. He turned to Muriel, pausing to admire her. "My dear," he said with satisfaction, and repeated the cheek kissing. "Come in, come in." He tucked Muriel's hand in his arm and started up the steps. "The weather affects my hip," he said, as if to apologize. "It's been unseasonably damp this year. Then out comes the cane."

A butler held open enormous doors and bowed as the three of them entered the mansion. A domed ceiling loomed above the massive foyer, at the end of which a grand staircase swept upwards in an elegant arc. Portraits lined the walls along the stairs, each subject's dress revealing the era in which they'd lived.

"This way, please." Leo held his arm out, indicating a short hallway with a closed door at the end.

As they approached, the door opened, and there, standing at attention as they entered the room, stood two boys, one a head taller than the other, both towheaded with fair skin and a spattering of freckles sprinkling nose and cheeks. Each boy wore a collared shirt beneath a vest and jacket, with a bow tie. Perhaps most importantly, both boys wore identical scowls.

Muriel felt ill upon seeing the expressions on their faces, but Winifred raised herself up to her full height and approached the boys. "Well, well," she said, her expression mildly pleasant with threats of stern not too far beneath the surface. "Two very well behaved young men, I see."

Leopold limped to Winifred's side. "This is Leopold the Third," he said of the taller boy.

"And how old are you, Leopold?" Winifred peered at him.

"Fifteen, ma'am." The boy looked Winifred in the eye, then reached out dutifully and shook her hand.

"And this is his little brother, Cecil. Say hello to Lady Winifred and Lady Muriel, Cecil," Leo instructed.

"Hello," the boy deadpanned, and said nothing more, and made no move to shake anyone's hand.

Muriel followed her mother, offering her hand to Leopold the Third, and peering cautiously at Cecil.

They entered a large sitting room filled with furniture that could only be described as well-sized yet feminine. Spirals and flowers, both carved and painted, decorated the wood. Needlework upholstery likewise sprouted colorful flowers.

An enormous fireplace covered nearly the entire wall at the far end of the room. Above a carved oak mantle hung a portrait of a woman, with generous, rosy cheeks, sparkling eyes, and a subdued smile, as if she found life infinitely amusing. Her neck was hidden behind a cascade of jewels—diamonds, jade, and rubies. Muriel didn't have to guess the identity of the woman.

"And here's the boys' mother, Isabel." Sir Leo stood beneath the portrait, one hand behind his back, the other on the cane, studying the portrait. "A saint of a woman."

Winifred and Muriel glanced at one another. "She was a lovely woman," Winifred said. "I enjoyed meeting her on a number of occasions."

Sir Leo seemed lost in thought for a moment, then turned back to his sons. "Very well, boys, you're free to go."

The boys disappeared in an instant—standing there at attention one moment, gone the next.

A footman brought in a large tray with tea service, cakes, and biscuits.

"Let's have some refreshments," Leo boomed. "And then what do you say to a rousing afternoon of bridge?"

Three hours later, after countless hands of cards, Muriel couldn't sit another minute. "If you'll excuse me," she said.

"A few more hands for Lady Winifred and I," Leo said, and grinned. "We're neck and neck, I believe."

Winifred studied the scores she had written. "I believe I'm ahead, and Muriel is pitifully far behind."

Muriel wandered to the far side of the room, where oversized windows looked out onto a lawn, bordered by sculptured shrubs and roses. A large pond sat along one side of the lawn, with cattails edging its shores, and ducks floated on the water. A statue stood at one end of the pond, hand outstretched, as if feeding the water fowl.

The boys had stripped out of their formal clothes and were playing croquet on the grass. As she watched, Leopold the Third swung his mallet and hit the ball as hard as he could away from the croquet wickets, sending the heavy ball soaring through the air and splashing into the pond, scattering ducks to the four winds. Cecil followed suit, only he sent his ball crashing into the statue, and Muriel couldn't be sure, but it looked like some fingers from the outstretched hand fell to the ground.

When the boys began aiming their shots at one another, Muriel turned away.

It had been the longest afternoon of her life, and she knew one thing by the time her mother and Lord Leo had played the final hand of bridge, and they headed outside for the drive back to Stonebeck. She would do everything in her power to never return to this house again.

Chapter 17 – London, August 1914

Kate pulled on a pair of canvas gardening gloves while looking over the glorious reds, pinks, and yellows of her rose garden. Her flowers thrived in the warmth of early August. As she worked, Vanessa slept in a bassinet beneath an ancient chestnut tree, with puppy Bruce napping nearby on the grass. Kate stepped among the bushes, breathing in the perfume as she plucked wilted flowers. She loved her roses, with their delicate yet colorful petals, and took their stinging thorns in stride.

Bruce woke and jumped to his feet, and barked.

Kate looked up in surprise as James walked toward her with Mrs. Ames on his heels.

"What are you doing home?" She smiled and pulled off her gloves.

James studied her, and glanced over to Vanessa. "We're at war, Kate."

Kate stared, uncomprehending.

"Britain declared war on Germany late last night. Mark is waiting out front. I stopped to let you know we're going to Buckingham. The king is expected to make an appearance."

"I want to come along."

"There will be too many people."

"Missus Ames will look after Vanessa. I'm coming with you."

Mark put the Mercedes into gear, and turned the car toward the city center. People lined the streets; the crowds grew thicker as they neared the palace. Finally, they were forced to park the car and walk. Thousands of men and a smattering of women filled the palace courtyard, cheering. People cursed the Kaiser — delirious with the prospect of war. The crowd roared to a deafening thunder, waving their hats in the air as, up on the palace balcony, King George V and the Prince of Wales, both wearing military uniforms, appeared with the Queen.

The crowd chanted, "Long live the king!" and, "Death to the Kaiser!" The moment that some had long anticipated, and that others had scoffed at, had come at last—an epic battle to show the world who wielded the most power in Europe. The time had come to go to war, and by God, they would answer the call.

Kate, wedged between James and Mark, clung to each man's arm as they stared, at once appalled and mesmerized.

People stayed in the courtyard long after the king, queen, and prince had left the balcony.

"Let's get out of here!" Mark had to shout to be heard.

They wound their way through the crowd and back to the car.

Mark hesitated, running his hand along the gleaming surface of the Mercedes. "I guess I'll have to get rid of this. Wouldn't do to be driving a German car around now, would it?"

James shook his head. "No."

When they arrived home, Kate's breasts ached with the fullness of milk. She hadn't had time to feed the baby before they left. When she walked inside, she heard Vanessa's lusty cries from upstairs.

"Lucy, we need some refreshments, please," she called toward the kitchen as she mounted the stairs.

In her bedroom, settled into the chair by the window as she nursed Vanessa, Kate tapped her foot impatiently. Bruce had followed them upstairs, and now tried to bite at her shoes. She usually enjoyed these quiet moments with Vanessa, but today she wanted to be downstairs to hear what Mark and James were discussing. With a gentle sideways swipe of her foot, she sent the puppy flying. He tumbled, sat up, shook his head, and scampered across the wood floor to attack her shoe again.

When Vanessa finally dozed off at her breast, Kate carried her into the nursery, placed her in the crib, covered her with a blanket, and hurried downstairs.

James and Mark were talking in low voices in front of the fireplace. When she entered the room, the conversation stopped, and the men glanced at her, then at one another.

James cleared his throat and walked over to take both of Kate's hands in his. "We'll be joining up."

"Joining up?" Kate's stomach knotted.

"For me, the Royal Navy would be the most logical choice," said Mark.

"And since I'm comfortable with ships and shipping as well," James said, "perhaps the Navy could find some use for me. Don't worry. We're on the side of right, and with the manpower of Great Britain, all of this will be over soon. We'll be home by Christmas."

Kate stared at them, and knew that after today, nothing would ever be the same again.

Talk of war permeated London, along with a strange euphoria, as if the potential of Great Britain's power had gone to everyone's head. An excitement buzzed through every conversation. "We'll show the dirty Hun who's in charge," one would say. Another would nod and say, "It's time to put the Kaiser and his henchmen in place."

Sunday morning, two weeks after the declaration of war, a knock — no, a pounding — shook the front door. Mrs. Ames, alarmed and a little frightened, peeked out, then opened the door.

Mark and Anne stood hand in hand. "Good morning, Missus Ames," Mark said. He brushed past the surprised housekeeper, pulling along a shyly smiling Anne.

"Is everything well, Lord St. John?" Mrs. Ames closed the door behind them.

"Very well, Missus Ames." He turned toward a sound from the stairs. "Ah, there you are."

James treaded down the stairs with Vanessa held in one arm.

"Where's Kate? We haven't a moment to waste. I've kidnapped Anne from Aunt Florence, and there may be hell to pay, but I'll deal with that later. Now the two of us are kidnapping the three of you for the day. We're taking a drive."

"Cook prepared a huge picnic," Anne said, breathless, just as Kate appeared on the stairs.

"I heard that," Kate said. "A picnic! Let me dash up and change." She ran back up the stairs.

She returned dressed in a knee-length cotton tunic with empire lines, cloud-blue with a darker blue skirt underneath falling below her knees.

Anne stared wide-eyed and stammered, "Kate, your skirt is scandalously short."

"Nonsense," Kate said. "It's practical for a hot summer day and a picnic. I saw a drawing of one very similar worn by Wallis Warfield at a party with Prince Edward, so it's quite fashionable." She turned to James and Mark. "I brought Vanessa's things, and we're ready to go."

Outside, Mark led them to a gleaming black convertible. He smoothed his hand over the hood, looking at once proud and sheepish.

"What a beauty!" James walked a circle around it.

"I admit it... I have a horrible weakness for motorcars. I couldn't very well keep driving the Mercedes, so I stashed it in the barn at Stonebeck and bought this."

"It's a Defiance, an Austin Defiance," James said. "Like the one that crashed in the Czar's Cup."

"Yes, and no," Mark said. "That Defiance was a race car, and this is a touring car, but I did manage to keep the 40-horsepower engine. They're putting 30's in now, you know."

"How fast will this one go?"

"Let's find out!"

"Don't go too fast," Anne pleaded, climbing into the backseat.

Kate followed, and James planted Vanessa safely in between the two women, then climbed up front with Mark. When the engine turned over, Vanessa squealed.

"You, little lady," James said, twisting back to look at his daughter, "shall have your very own automobile one day."

"What an outrageous idea," Anne gasped.

As Mrs. Ames stood in the door watching them go, the puppy skirted her legs and took off running to the car.

"I'm sorry," Mrs. Ames called, chasing after him. "Bruce! Bad dog! Come back."

"It's fine, Missus Ames." James opened his door and the puppy jumped into his lap. "Bruce can come with us. A run in the country will do him good."

Mark shifted into gear and eased the Defiance into the street, and they were off.

Once they left the city behind, Mark shifted up from one gear to the next until they sailed, wind rustling through their hair and clothes, trees blurring past with dizzying speed. After the initial euphoria faded, Kate, with Vanessa tucked tightly against her, concentrated on the feel of the smooth leather seat, the odd sensation when the road dipped or raised, the smell of trees and grass.

After nearly an hour, Mark pulled onto a dirt road and brought the Austin to a shuddering stop. "How's this for a picnic spot?" He climbed out of the car and rushed to open Anne's door. "This hill used to be sacred to the Druids, they say."

"I must have an automobile," James said, climbing out and taking Vanessa from Kate. "A sporty one like this Austin. You won't mind eating bread and butter every meal for a decade or so, would you Kate, so I could buy one?"

"I'll buy one for you, and one for Vanessa someday," Kate said, smiling.

"Ah, I've married a wealthy woman, have I?"

Anne listened to the conversation, looking puzzled.

Mark handed out picnic baskets, and they trooped up a gentle slope, Bruce running circles around their feet. At the top, the land fell away into a forest of elms and maples, and beyond that, the landscape flattened into fields that stretched away to the horizon.

"What a fine view," Kate said. She took out a blanket, snapped it into the air, and let it float to the ground. She then placed Vanessa in the center as Bruce ran toward the woods, circled back to sniff Vanessa, and took off again.

Mark unpacked their lunch. "Let's see now, we have smoked salmon and lobster. And here's some chicken and asparagus. Champagne is the beverage of choice, but there's also Pimm's for those who fancy a summer cocktail. And dessert shall be strawberries and cream."

James dug around and extracted champagne flutes, while Mark eased the cork from the champagne with two thumbs, and poured.

Mark held his glass high. "A toast to my lovely fiancée and wonderful friends. To a perfect future for us all."

Even amid murmurs of "a perfect future," they all eyed one another with unspoken somberness, knowing full well that war made for an unpredictable future.

"We're moving up the wedding date," Mark said as they sat on the blanket and passed around plates and food. "Our families are frantic and understanding all at once."

"It's bad luck to marry and then go off to war," James said.

Anne flinched.

James looked stricken. "Sorry. Silly old superstition, that."

"Given the present circumstances, an elaborate wedding well off in the future didn't seem practical," Mark said. "We're getting married straight away." He reached out and squeezed Anne's hand. "There. You'll be stuck with me forever."

They ate, drank, laughed, and pretended the day would never end. While the others settled into an after-lunch drowsiness, Kate decided not to lose a second of daylight. Vanessa slept on the blanket, thumb in mouth, Bruce by her side. "Would you look after her for a bit?" she asked Anne.

"Certainly."

"Let's go explore," she said to James.

They strolled along the hill and followed a trail down into the trees, engulfed by shade, birdsong, and the heady aroma of leaves and earth. After a bit, the trail widened into what appeared to be an old road, and soon they came upon a bridge over a dry canal.

"Would you look at this?" James stepped onto the bridge. It felt solid, so he crossed, with Kate close behind.

"Was it a bridge over a moat?" she asked.

"Could be."

Beyond the bridge, a scattering of large stones lay hidden in the tall grass. "An old stone house, or maybe even a castle," James said as they picked their way around the stones.

"I wonder who lived here," Kate mused. "A princess in a fairy tale, perhaps."

James stopped and turned, pulling her into his arms. "You're a princess." He kissed her. "Now a bit of unpleasant business, I'm afraid. If anything happens to me—"

"Stop it! Don't talk that way."

"If things get bad in London, and I'm not back yet, you must go back to Kirken, to my family. They'll take care of you."

"No matter what happens, Vanessa and I will never go back to Kirken," she said gently. "I'll take care of us in London. I'll always find a way to take care of us."

James kissed her again. "My Kate, always so independent."

"Come back," she insisted. "Then we won't have to find out how independent I can be."

Chapter 18

Mark and Anne's wedding was held in St. Paul's Cathedral. Given the unusually short time between the engagement and the ceremony, they'd limited the guest list to close family and friends, much to Anne's parents' dismay. The match, their only daughter with the most eligible bachelor, however, mollified any misgivings they may have had.

The wedding may have been small, but Anne's family spared no expense. Her wedding dress shimmered with pearls, and festoons of gauze, with a long trail that required three bridesmaids to carry to the altar. She looked beautiful and radiant, and hiding behind a veil seemed to comfort her and free her from her debilitating shyness, if only for a few hours.

Muriel served as maid of honor, tall and elegant in a robin's egg blue gown. Sir Leopold accompanied her to the occasion, watching proudly as she stood at the altar.

A cousin served as Mark's best man. Lady Winifred had suggested Des McGregor, but Mark had flatly refused. He'd suggested James Casey, but Lady Winifred put her foot down, so, he chose a distant cousin he'd known all of his life, but only saw on rare occasions.

Before family and friends, on the eve of the Great War, Mark and Anne pledged themselves to one another in holy matrimony.

Anne sat before the dressing table in her room at Stonebeck Hall, staring at her reflection. She wore a smart off-white cashmere dress with pearls across the bodice. A lady's maid—on loan from her mother-in-law-to-be—struggled to arrange Anne's fine, brown hair into an elegant French roll.

Muriel looked on, beaming.

The wedding had been the day before, but the large reception, tastefully removed to Stonebeck Hall, was about to begin.

Muriel stood watching her lady's maid struggle with Anne's hair. "You married my brother," she gushed. "You're my sister-in-law, Anne."

Anne tried to smile, but her lips trembled. Truth be told, she wished the reception were over. She hated being the center of attention, and memories of their wedding night kept pushing their way into her mind. Before the wedding, she'd had a vague idea of what to expect, but had been shocked at the complete lack of modesty her wedding night had required. Mark had been kind and gentle, but the consummation of the marriage, the act itself, had been surreal and disquieting. She had enjoyed the warmth and closeness of the touching, but it went too far, invading the very core of her.

"How about you?" Anne asked. "When are you going to marry Sir Leo?"

Muriel sighed. "You love Mark, don't you?"

"Yes," Anne said, trying to push away the disturbing thoughts of her wedding night.

"I don't feel that way about Leo," Muriel said almost in a whisper. "He's nice enough, and I feel badly for him, having lost his wife. And Mother would be ecstatic if I would, just like she's ecstatic that you and Mark married." She squeezed Anne's shoulder. "But I don't think I can do it."

"Don't do it," Anne insisted, covering Muriel's hand with her own. "What husbands want, what they do, is—"

There came a short rap at the door, and Lady Winifred swept in, her silver hair in an elaborate knot held into place by a sapphire-studded clip. Her blue silk dress gathered at the bodice and fell to a scalloped hem, shorter in front.

"Are you nearly ready, dear?" she inquired. "The guests have all arrived, and we should go down."

Anne dropped her hands to her lap, and stared at her mother-in-law with growing fear.

Lady Winifred dismissed the maid and turned to Muriel. "Why don't you run along, darling? We'll meet you in a couple of minutes."

"You'll do well." Muriel leaned down to Anne, a slight frown on her face. "Don't worry."

Muriel slipped out the door as Winifred sat next to Anne. "I am so happy to have you as a daughter-in-law, dear."

"Thank you," Anne whispered. "I'm honored to be a member of your family."

"You are exactly what my son needed, and after the war is over, he will have a reason not to spend so much time working." Lady Winifred reached out and took one of Anne's hands in her own. "He's been running around with the wrong people, dear. I know I can trust you to understand how important that is. He ignores invitations. He missed all the season's social events. But now you'll be in charge of all that, and it is very important that you start to entertain, darling, and invite the right people."

Anne stared at her mother-in-law. Her own mother had already held a slight variation of this same conversation with her.

"For example, the people who came with you from London."

"The Caseys?"

"Yes, dear, the Caseys. The man works for Mark. You can only imagine the shock I had when Mark wanted him to stand up as best man. It would have been appalling. Embarrassing. It's wrong." Lady Winifred stood up and began pacing. "James may be a college man, but he is not one of us. He's from a poor family in Scotland, for heaven's sake. And his wife is even worse." Winifred stopped in front of Anne. "Did you know she used to be a maid?"

Anne started to feel nauseous. "Kate? A maid?"

"Yes, a maid. And now my son forces me to have her as a guest in my house. It's shameful. I've had to hide that from your parents, dear. They would be horrified, as I am. But Mark has always been different, and so damnably stubborn when he gets his mind made up on something."

Anne's voice carried a slight tremor. "I assumed, because of the house and the neighborhood they live in, and because they were friends of Mark's...."

"Mark inherited the house from his uncle, and he's renting it to them." Winifred sounded disgusted.

"How did you find out about Kate being a maid?"

"I leave my son alone. I can't force him to do the things I would prefer him to do, but I can make sure that he doesn't go too far. I have friends in London who pass along news. Your Aunt Florence was suspicious when she met them, and did a little asking around. She knows, but swore to me that she wouldn't tell your parents, if you promise to stay away from them now that you're married."

Winifred's voice fell to a soothing whisper. "Let's talk about something more pleasant. You will live here with us at Stonebeck, while Mark is away. It will be such a comfort to me having you here."

"Oh, yes, thank you."
"Good. You look lovely. We must hurry along."

During the reception, Lady Winifred had another task to tackle—an urgent mission. After learning that her son had already joined the Royal Navy, she invited to dinner some old friends of her late husband's, who happened to have quite a bit of influence with the highest-ranking Naval officers. Mark had always been bullheaded, but damned if she would let him run off and get himself killed on some ship, although it would be an honorable way to serve king and country. No, she couldn't risk her only son, and resolved to secure Mark an honorable position... in a safe environment.

She would have to be careful to keep it all quiet. Mark would be horrified if he suspected what she was up to, but sometimes, a mother had to do what was best for her children, whether they would approve of it or not.

Chapter 19

James and Kate sat together on the divan, with Vanessa sleeping in her cradle nearby, as the fire crackled. James had his arm around Kate while she rested her head on his shoulder.

"I wish we could stay like this forever," she said with a sigh.

It was his last night home before reporting for duty, and they sat, intertwined, until the fire faded to ash. James gathered Vanessa out of the cradle and carried her upstairs with Kate close behind.

Neither of them slept as they held one another throughout the night, until at last the gray light of dawn filtered in through the window, and James left the warmth of their embrace and dressed.

Kate sat on the side of the bed, her hair cascading down her back, shadows beneath her eyes, waiting until he returned. He held out his hand to her, and she took it and stood. Together they walked to Vanessa's room. After James leaned over the crib to kiss Vanessa's chubby cheek, Kate followed him downstairs to where his suitcase waited in the foyer.

Too soon, a knock sounded at the door. "Taxi," a man's voice said.

Kate buried her head in James's shoulder.

He held her, kissed her hard and quick, picked up his suitcase, and opened the door.

The taxi driver glanced at Kate, and James, and his expression changed. He could likely see what was going on, having no doubt driven many an enlisting man to the train station.

James walked past the driver, suitcase in hand, toward the taxi.

"I hope to deliver him back here one day," the kind driver said to Kate.

She nodded and tried to smile, closed the door, and let her tears fall.

Chapter 20

Ever since the long, bleak afternoon at Sir Leopold Whitlock's country estate, Muriel avoided him as much as possible. Lady Winifred invited Leo to dinner often, and he begged Muriel to come visit again, but she always found an excuse not to go.

After one such visit, in the following morning, Muriel told her, "I'm not going to marry him. There's no sense making him think this courting will end in marriage, because it won't."

Winifred's expression turned to iron. "Don't be foolish. I didn't want it to come to this, but you leave me no choice. You will marry him. I insist upon it, and you can't defy me."

Muriel knew better than to argue with her mother, but her mind was made up. Damn the consequences, she would not live in that house, with that man, his dead wife's image hovering over them from above the fireplace, while his two mean-spirited children tried to kill one another, or perhaps her.

On a sublime October afternoon, when households all over England were in turmoil as the men joined up and prepared to go off to war, Sir Leopold sat with Lady Winifred in her drawing room, heads together, speaking in hushed tones.

After some time, while Muriel sat with Anne in her bedroom, a knock came on the door.

She opened it to Stephens, and as their eyes met, and a knowing passed between them.

"Sir Leopold requests your presence in the garden," the butler said as he peeked in the door.

"Thank you, Stephens. I'll be right down." Muriel stared hard at Anne.

"What are you going to do?" Anne asked.

"You know what I'm going to do."

"You can't! Your mother will be furious."

"Well, she has you, now, doesn't she? One good girl in the house, married to her son. That should help."

She was glad it would be done in the garden, where at least she could breathe. She had never forgotten Anne's entreaty to her the day after marrying Mark—the day after her wedding night. *"Don't do it. What husbands want, what they do...."* The words echoed in her head as she walked to the garden.

Leo sat at a wicker table, with lemonade, tea, and biscuits waiting for her. He stood when she approached, held his arms out with a big smile, took her by each shoulder, and kissed her on both cheeks. "Sit, sit. Lemonade or tea?"

"Tea." She tried hard to look pleasant, and vowed to be kind.

He poured a cup of tea and placed a biscuit on a small plate of fine china, and placed them both before her. He prepared the exact portions for himself, and sat.

"We're at war again." He sighed, sipped his tea, and nibbled on a biscuit. "I'm not too old to join up, but this old injury of mine... well, I wouldn't be much use, would I?"

"With your experience, I'm sure there's some contribution you could make, perhaps in an advisory capacity."

"Yes, perhaps I could." He seemed to ponder the idea for the moment. "But at this point in my life, I'm loath to leave home."

"Mark and James are both enlisting," Muriel said, frowning. "I wish I could, too."

"Don't be silly, darling," he said quickly. "War is a man's game, and it's a brutal one, believe me. But let's not talk about war. That's not why I've come today."

Muriel stiffened.

"I think you know why I'm here." He smiled. "I spoke with Mark at the wedding, and then again with your mother."

He stood up, then with great effort, leaned on the poor wicker table as he went down on one knee.

His good leg, I hope.

"Sir Leo, please...." She tried to stop him, but it was no use—he was determined.

"Lady Muriel St. John," he said formally, then earnestly, "Muriel, will you be my wife?"

He looked up at her, with a smile, and she realized that he believed she would agree.

She stood, stepped back, placed her napkin on the table, and tried not to tremble As she said, "I am so very sorry."

Leo looked puzzled.

"I am unable to accept your proposal. You're a fine man, Sir Leopold, and any woman will be lucky to have you, but that woman cannot be me. I cannot accept your proposal. Thank you. I'm sorry. Goodbye."

She stumbled away from him, unable to see through her tears as she found her way inside and upstairs to her room, never once looking back.

It wasn't that she was doubtful in her decision—not at all. She simply hated to hurt the man. He had been through enough pain in his life, losing a wife whom he loved eternally, and now saddled with two spoiled and mean-spirited boys. She had tried to tell her mother she would never marry Leo, in order to avoid this scene, but her mother hadn't listened to her, and so it had come to this.

Upstairs, she threw herself on her bed and cried, but only for a few minutes. When a motor started outside, she got up and walked to the window to see Sir Leopold Whitlock limping to his car, where his chauffer held the door open and helped him inside. As the automobile drove away, Muriel was overcome with a feeling of lightness, as if she were floating up into the air. It was over. Finished. No matter what her mother did to her now, she would never again have to set foot in Leo's home; would never have to pretend to be interested in Leo's conversation. She would never have to see him again.

She turned away from the window, and decided it would be a good afternoon to take her stallion for a long ride in the woods.

"May I have a word with you when it's convenient, my lady?" Muriel overheard Stephens ask her mother after dinner.

"Certainly." Lady Winifred put her napkin on the table and stood. "I'm finished here. Let's go to the library."

Muriel glanced over at Anne, who seemed absorbed in her dessert.

"Excuse me, Anne," Muriel said, standing.

Although she didn't quite know why, she felt compelled to hear what Stephens had to say. Or maybe she did know why, but wouldn't admit it to herself. She quietly left the dining room and wandered toward the library.

Stephens and her mother were inside, and they hadn't closed the door.

"I hate to bother you, but may I have a day off next week?" Stephens asked. "I would like to leave after dinner is concluded on Wednesday evening, and not return until Friday morning. I assure you there will be no lack of service in my absence. I'll see to that."

"Yes, you may, Stephens. I do hope everything is well?" Lady Winifred said, ending the statement as a question.

"My son, Christopher," Stephens said.

Muriel moved closer to the door, trying not to make a sound.

"What about him?"

"He's joined the Army, my lady. He's leaving Friday, and I would like to spend the time with my wife and son."

"How admirable of your son," Winifred said. "Give him our highest regards, will you?"

"I will, thank you."

Stephens's wife and son lived in a village nearby, but Muriel didn't know exactly where. If Christopher was going off to war, she wanted to say goodbye. They didn't know one another well at all, yet the idea of him going off to war without seeing him again was unthinkable.

The next morning, as Rose, her lady's maid, helped her dress, she asked, "Rose, would you ask Stephens to come see me?"

"Here?" Rose asked. "In your room?"

"No, you're right. Not here. Better yet, take me to see him, now, will you?"

"Downstairs, my lady? To his office?"

"Yes. Let's go now, quietly."

Rose looked unsure, but led Muriel down the stairs to the main floor, then to the back of the house and down another flight of stairs to the kitchen and servants' quarters, then to Stephens's office door.

"That will be all, Rose. Thank you. I can find my way back."

Rose curtsied and left, and Muriel rapped on the door.

"Come," the call came from within.

Muriel stepped through the door and Stephens stood. "My lady," he exclaimed, surprised.

"Sorry to bother you, Stephens." She closed the door behind her. "I don't want to intrude, but I have a favor to ask."

"Anything, my lady, you know that."

"This will need to be a secret favor," she whispered, "just between you and me. No one else must know, not even mother."

Stephens looked uncomfortable for a moment, then said, "Whatever you ask, I am pleased to assist if I can."

"I understand that Christopher is going off to war. Is that right?"

Stephens's eyebrows knitted together and he sighed. "Yes, he's joined the Army and will leave on Friday."

"It must be difficult for you."

"I'm proud of him," Stephens said. "But to see my son go off to war... well, it's something no father wants. And his mother is beside herself."

"I don't want to intrude on your time with your family, but, may I come by on Thursday to say goodbye to him?"

Stephens's eyebrows raised. "To our cottage in the village?"

"Yes, if that's all right. I don't even know which village you live in, I'm sorry to say, so you'll have to give me directions. And I won't stay long, just long enough to say goodbye and give him a going away gift from the family."

"But it's a secret," Stephens clarified.

"Yes." Muriel looked the older man in the eye. "*Our* secret."

He hesitated, then said, "Let me draw you a map."

Stephens left after dinner Wednesday night, and to Muriel, it seemed that Thursday would never arrive. She decided not to make up a story, a deceit, to tell her mother. Instead, she went about her regular routine. She waited until early afternoon then donned her riding clothes, and peeked into the sitting room where Anne sat embroidering, and said, "I'm going for my ride."

Anne looked up and smiled. "Have a good time." She then returned to her stitching.

Muriel held her breath on the way to the stables, fearful that on this day, of all days, her mother would stop her, demanding her company for some activity or other, but she made it all the way to the stables unobstructed. She had made arrangements ahead of time to have her stallion saddled and ready to go.

With a leg up from the stable boy, she mounted the horse and turned him out of the stables and onto the road. With the map in her pocket, she set off to Stephens's village.

It took over an hour, sometimes galloping, sometimes trotting, and walking to reach the village, and another twenty minutes to locate Stephens's house. She looked at the map Stephens had drawn for her, then the cottage, and knew when she spotted the place, a charming stone building with shake roof, paned windows, and wooden shutters.

She urged her horse to the fence that surrounded the cottage and reigned him to a stop. For the first time since she had hatched the plan, she grew nervous. Now that she was here, what was she to say to him? Yet it was too late to turn back.

The door to the cottage opened and there stood Christopher, filling the doorway. He shaded his eyes and looked up at her. "Wait there," he said, and closed the door.

It wasn't long before Christopher came around the house on a horse. "Shall we?" He said it as if they met every day for a ride.

Grateful, Muriel nudged her horse into step beside him, and they rode down the road to the outskirts of the village, and then followed a track through a large pasture. They rode in silence until they came to a river, modest in width, flowing lazily along.

Christopher stopped his horse, dismounted, and pulled a pack off the back of the saddle.

Muriel dismounted, watching as he took a blanket from the pack and spread it out on the ground, followed by plates, then cheese, bread, and fruit. Finally came a bottle of wine along with two wine glasses.

A dozen witty remarks crossed her mind as he laid out the picnic, but instead of making light of it all, she pulled off her riding gloves, finger by finger, and sank to the blanket.

Christopher uncorked the wine and poured a glass for her, then for himself. They held their glasses up to one another and stopped, eyes locked, glasses in the air. The moment held, then broke as Christopher took a sip and picked up some bread and cheese.

Muriel had no appetite at all. She toyed with a grape and sipped her wine, and finally worked up the courage to speak. "Your cottage is charming."

"You could fit three of my cottages into your ballroom," he said with a hint of cynicism, then lay back, propped up on one elbow.

She shrugged. "It's charming nonetheless."

"How is Sir Leopold?" Christopher tossed a small lump of cheese into his mouth, watching her.

"I wouldn't know." She looked him square in the eyes. "I broke it off."

"Why?"

"Why?" Muriel looked at him incredulously. "I don't love him."

"I didn't think love had to be a part of the equation." He popped a grape into his mouth.

"Now you sound like my mother." She grimaced. "And no, Mother wasn't happy. She's hardly spoken to me since, which in some ways is a bit of a relief."

Christopher laughed, a burst of pure amusement, no hint of cynicism.

It caught Muriel unaware, and she smiled. *If I could make him laugh like that twice a day,* she thought, *what a lovely life it would be.*

"I'm sure your mother wants what's best for you." He smiled and took a sip of wine.

"Her version of what's best for me doesn't match my version. Anyway, I've brought you a going away present, since you're leaving."

She stood and went to her saddle, pulled a wrapped gift from the bag, walked back to the blanket, sat back down and handed it to him.

He set his wine down, sat up, took the gift, peeled back the layers of paper, and pulled out several jars.

"It's cook's pickled beets, green beans, and asparagus," said Muriel. "They're delicious. Better, I thought, than the food they'll serve you in the army."

"I'm sure it will be. Thank you."

She didn't want to talk about the war, but couldn't stop herself. "Are you afraid?"

"Would you be afraid?"

She thought about it for a moment. "I think I would be, but I would go."

"And so, I'm going." His expression turned serious. "Why are you here?"

"To say goodbye," she said quickly, in a tone that asked, *what's unusual about that?*

When he didn't respond, she said in a quiet voice, "Are you glad I came?"

His gaze held hers, and he moved next to her, cupped the back of her head with his hand, and pulled her closer, face to face.

Her heart thudded in her chest so hard she feared it would burst, and her breath caught in her throat.

They stared into one another's eyes, motionless, each knowing that whatever happened next would change things, and couldn't be undone. Then, he leaned in and kissed her, softly at first, then harder.

She kissed him back, and ran her hand over his strong neck and pulled him into her even more.

After an eternity, he pulled back, both of them breathing hard, as if they had just run a race.

Anne's words came rushing back into Muriel's thoughts. *What husbands want, what they do....* And Muriel knew in that instant, that if Christopher were her husband, she would want what he wanted. She would gladly do whatever he wanted to do. And then her next thought....

How ridiculous even to pretend he could ever be my husband.

"Yes," he interrupted her thoughts. "I'm glad you came to say goodbye."

And he kissed her again.

As they rode side-by-side back to his cottage, Muriel wanted to blurt out, *I'll wait for you. I'll be here when you return.* But she couldn't, because how could she make promises that she would be unable to keep? So, she rode in silence. She felt guilty for having stolen these few hours from his parents, and knew she could linger no more. When they reached his cottage, they each sat on their horses, gazing at one another, but making no move to dismount.

She wanted to admonish him to take care, to come back safely, but even that seemed too clichéd. Instead, she said, "Goodbye, Christopher."

He gave a slight nod.

Then she turned her horse back toward Stonebeck Hall.

Chapter 21

James shrugged his rifle from one shoulder to the other, trying to get some feeling back into his arm. He had pulled night watch, and had been patrolling the deck of the battle cruiser *Invincible* for hours. It was nearly four in the morning, and fog obliterated the water, creating one shade of dark gray merging into another. James slapped his hands against his upper arms, trying to stay warm. When that failed, he pulled a cigarette from inside his overcoat and, with cupped hands, lit it—a new habit he'd adopted to pass the endless hours.

It was Christmas morning, and he closed his eyes, trying to remember Christmas of the year before. It seemed so long ago. Kate had still been pregnant with Vanessa. Now, here he was missing Vanessa's first Christmas. He sucked the smoke deep into his lungs, allowing the calming effect to relax his mind as he stared into the fog.

The ship sailed somewhere off the coast of Scotland in the North Sea. They were doing exactly what they'd been doing every day for the past two months: protecting the coastline against the enemy—an enemy James had only heard about, and never seen.

Footsteps approached, and soon a lieutenant appeared out of the fog. James flipped the fag overboard, stood aside, and saluted as the officer passed.

The lieutenant saluted in return, and kept going.

Without warning, two flashes of light appeared in the distance, followed by deep booms, and a thunderous explosion tore through the air. It felt to James as though the air had been sucked from his lungs. After a heartbeat of silence, the ship came to life. An alarm wailed, and after the briefest of hesitations, sailors scrambled to their battle stations. James ran toward his post near the bridge, battling his way through an onslaught of men running the other way, until reaching his assigned group. He'd been at his station for nearly a half hour when an officer arrived.

"Now listen up!" Warrant Officer Leslie Harris shouted over the din. "The bloody Huns have either torpedoed our sister ship *Newcastle* or the *Newcastle* hit some mines. In any case, she's going down fast.

We'll drop the lifeboats and search for survivors." He divided the men into groups of four, choosing James and two others to go along with him. "She's due west of here. Move!"

James's group scrambled for the lifeboats, and the four men clambered aboard just before two sailors manning the winches lowered the craft to the water.

The loaded lifeboat hitched at the last moment, dropping at a drunken tilt and crashing into the sea. It righted itself like a cork as the men held tight. They grabbed oars and began to row, fighting through the roiling waters toward the Newcastle. Waves broke over the bow again and again, soaking them to the skin.

A crackling noise sounded through the fog, followed by an eerie metallic groaning. Debris knocked against their boat.

James squinted through the fog. "There!" He dropped his oar, leaned over the edge of the boat to fish a man from the sea, and stared hauling him up and in.

Leslie Harris grabbed James by the arm and hollered into his ear. "Save that one for later, mate."

"What?"

"We need to pick up survivors. Get on your oar."

James stared uncomprehending as a curtain of water washed over them, then looked down at the man in his grip—half the man's face was missing. James dropped him back into the sea.

He grabbed the oar and rowed with all his strength. He spotted an arm waving rhythmically back and forth above the water like a metronome. As they slid alongside, James dropped his oar and leaned once again over the edge. The man's arm continued its slow wave, and James caught it mid-arc. He inched his grip up toward the shoulder, grasped the upper arm, and pulled the man toward him.

Leslie Harris grabbed the man by the seat of his trousers and the two of them hoisted him in.

The man stared straight ahead, eyes vacant. His entire right side looked charred. The sleeve of his coat where James had grabbed him had fallen away, revealing a bloody mess.

"Grab your oar, mate," Leslie shouted. "There's more where this one came from."

By the time they'd filled their dinghy with broken men, the fog and smoke had thinned. As they rowed back toward their ship, James pulled on his oar until he couldn't feel his hands, but he never stopped, never gave up.

He noticed Leslie Harris scowling, staring off in the distance. Without breaking rhythm, James turned to look. About a hundred meters away, the first rays of the morning sun glinted on the gray bow of the *Newcastle* as it nosed straight up toward the sky—all that remained of the battle cruiser, a ship identical to their own. The vessel shuddered and slipped downward. A gasp of water erupted, leaving behind debris bobbing silently in the morning light, as the bow slipped beneath the water forever.

Chapter 22

Lieutenant Mark St. John studied the message on the paper before him, smoothing the fingered edges as he struggled to see through the illusion of words. He sat at his desk at Naval Intelligence, in the Old Building of the Admiralty, in a place known only as Room 40. From this compact room, he and an eclectic group of men tried to decipher intercepted wireless messages from the Germans. The unit was a mixture of Naval personnel, civilians, scholars, and businessmen, chosen for abilities that ranged from mathematics to German linguistics. How lucky he had decided to study German in college, a useful skill that landed him in this group.

Only twenty-four by seventeen feet, Room 40 was packed with desks, file cabinets, ashtrays, books, and stacks of papers. Understated and obscure, it escaped the attention of inquisitive eyes, a deliberate goal set by its founder, Sir Winston Churchill, the First Sea Lord of the Admiralty, who wanted Room 40 shrouded in secrecy.

It was nearly midnight when Mark sat back and rubbed his tired eyes in the dim light cast by his desk lamp. The frustration of trying to make sense out of jibberish—trying to piece together a jigsaw puzzle for which there was no final picture to consult—wore on him.

He hadn't wanted to go into intelligence work three months before, when his assignment had come through. He wanted to go to sea, like James, but his desires had been frustrated. He didn't understand it, having assumed they'd want as many people as possible in fighting positions, but he'd accepted his orders and would do the best he could.

He liked his commanding officer in Room 40, a regular Naval officer named Commander Herbert Hope. A quiet, modest man, he possessed an uncanny ability to decipher German code with extreme accuracy, and to inspire others with his dedication.

Mark thought back to the slow, painful process of deciphering a page of code—code to German, German to English. He remembered the immense pleasure he felt the first time he'd cracked a code, until he found out he'd confused a German Army message for a German Naval message — an easy mistake to make, and one that didn't do any great harm. Commander Hope had assured him that despite the error, his skills were exemplary, but from that moment on, he kept his mouth shut until there was no doubt as to the accuracy of his work.

He blinked and leaned forward over the paper again. He tore the top sheet off a pad of paper, crumpled it, threw it into the trash, picked up a pencil, and began again. He opened their precious copy of the *Handelsverkehrsbuch*, a codebook used by the German Admiralty, its warships, and High Seas Fleet, captured from a German-Australian steamship in Australia. That book, along with two other purloined codebooks, the *Signalbuch der Kaiserlichen Marine* and the *Verkehrsbuch*, provided the entire basis of Room 40's code-breaking processes.

Mark stared at the words, suddenly startled by their clarity. Scribbling, he decoded the intercept and sat back, exhaling a whistle as he stared at the words — names, a list of eight names along with corresponding coordinates. It seemed he'd discovered the names and locations of eight German ships.

Even though it was late, he put a call in to Commander Hope, who listened to what Mark had to say.

"I'll call the commanding officer," Commander Hope said.

Mark knew the commanding officer, Sir Alfred Ewing, had been a professor of mechanism and applied mechanics at King's College, Cambridge before the war.

"He's an early-to-bed, early-to-rise man," Commander Hope continued. "I'll have to assure that nervous secretary who answers his calls that this is important."

Within thirty minutes, both Commander Hope and Sir Ewing stood in Room 40, examining Mark's interpretation. At length, both men agreed with Mark's conclusion.

"Get in touch with Operations right away," Sir Ewing said.

An hour later, back in his rented flat, just a five-minute walk from Room 40, Mark discarded his tired uniform and slipped into pajamas. The clock chimed three. Three in the morning, and Christmas — the first Christmas he hadn't been at Stonebeck Hall with his family. He had, in fact, volunteered to stay behind, since most of the officers had wives and children. He missed being home, missed Anne, and Muriel, and the rest of the family, but it had been correct for him to stay. It seemed he'd done some good, as well.

He turned off the light, eager for a few hours' sleep before an early morning, and more work.

Chapter 23

The week after Christmas, the holiday already seemed a distant memory to Kate. On Christmas Day, Vanessa had gurgled happily while playing with ribbon and wrapping paper, ignoring the gifts that had been enclosed in the packaging. Bruce the puppy had joined in, chewing whatever he could wrestle away from Vanessa. They made quite the pair.

Still, the Casey house had seemed hollow and empty, and Kate's heart ached with each present she unwrapped. James had sent her a pendant, a gold heart on a chain. For Vanessa, he had sent a stuffed bear. Other gifts arrived from Mark—specially wrapped chocolates for Kate, and for Vanessa a beautiful doll made of bisque porcelain with glass eyes and rosy cheeks, dressed in a lavender bonnet and a white ruffle-bottom dress. He also sent a stuffed dog that looked like Bruce. The doll would have to be placed out of reach for now, but Vanessa already kept the stuffed dog by her side.

At Lyman & Stonebeck, Mr. Bridger had taken over as director— Mark's duties—while Kate had volunteered to take on James's work at no pay. Mark had approved of Kate's position, but he wouldn't hear of her volunteering. The same paycheck arrived every month in the same amount that James had received, only with her name on the payee line instead of her husband's. Requisitions, invoices, and shipping schedules seemed like old friends after evenings of listening to James talk about his work.

Women all over London were stepping in to take the place of men marching off to war.

Mr. Bridger looked exhausted most of the time, and complained a great deal, but Kate could sense the pride he felt at being asked to take such an important role in Mark's absence. He seemed to feel entirely vindicated that he, with a modest education but years of experience, had taken up where the "college boys" had left off.

"Missus Casey."

The new, young clerk, Thomas Hart, stood at the office door.

"Yes, Tommy?"

"It's nearly six o'clock, Missus Casey."

"Please, call me Kate. I'll be ready in a minute."

He nodded, eyes blinking through the thick round lenses of wire-rimmed glasses. He wore his brown hair a bit floppy on the top, shaved in the back and around his oversized ears — Kate had to curtail the impulse to scratch him behind those ears. A nice young man of twenty, he insisted on accompanying her to the train station after work every night.

She had started calling him Tommy instead of Mr. Hart by the third day they worked together. He felt like the younger brother she never had.

His myopic eyesight had kept him out of the military and landed him behind a desk. Their loss, as his brilliance with numbers would have served them well.

Kate gathered the shipping schedules together and locked them in a file cabinet as damp, cold air rushed in. *Tommy must be in a hurry and gone outside already.* She turned to get her coat.

"Hello, Missus Casey."

She froze at the sound of the familiar voice.

"May I help you, sir?" Tommy asked.

Kate turned slowly.

"I'm Desmond McGregor." His eyes never left Kate. "Owner of Lyman & Stonebeck."

Kate thought she might be sick, but pulled herself together, and said to Tommy in a cool voice, "Lord McGregor is co-owner, along with Lord St. John. What is it we can do for you, Lord McGregor? We're about to leave."

Des strolled inside, glancing into office doors. "Mark, Lord St. John, always delivered a quarterly report to me. Now that he's otherwise engaged, I shall be coming around to check on things. I expect weekly reports, and a copy of expenditures, revenue, and schedules."

He stopped so close to Kate that she could smell the tobacco on his jacket.

He smiled down at her. "Missus Casey, a pleasure to see you again."

She stepped away, tugged her wool coat from the rack, and shrugged into it, struggling to maintain calm. "You'll have to discuss that with Mister Bridger. Now, if you don't mind, it's rather late and we were on our way out."

"I wouldn't want to keep you," Des said, smile in place. "May I give you a ride?"

"No," Kate said too quickly. "No, thank you."

His smile faltered. "I insist. No sense taking the train. My car is right outside."

Tommy watched the exchange, then stepped forward. "Thank you, sir, but no need. We have a car waiting for us. We best be off, Missus Casey, or my father will wonder where we are."

"Quite right, Tommy. If you'll excuse us, please."

Des didn't look convinced, but he gave a curt nod, eyes still fixed on Kate. "I'll see you soon." Then he turned and left.

After Des had gone, Kate sagged against her desk.

"Is everything well?" Tommy looked concerned.

She forced a smile and straightened up. "You're a genius, Tommy. Thank you for getting us out of that one. Let's just say that Des McGregor is the silent partner in the business, and we'll all be better off if he stays out of the day-to-day. Shall we go?"

Tommy offered his arm and Kate took it, grateful, and they locked the door carefully behind them when they left.

Chapter 24

Anne wiped away the beads of perspiration from her forehead with a wet cloth, but nausea gripped her again. She retched into the toilet, slumping against it when the queasiness passed. She had felt sick all during Christmas, and had hardly eaten a thing, much to her mother-in-law's concern.

Since moving to Stonebeck, she felt like a child, as Lady Winifred supervised her every activity, scheduled her days. Long gone were her dreams of running a home for her and Mark, of being a wife. She had changed locations and faces, but her life remained unchanged from living in her parents' house.

Until the war ends, and Mark comes home. Then it will be different.

She heard the bedroom door open and close and, without having to look up, she knew who had come in. A knock sounded on the water closet door.

"Anne, are you all right?"

Anne closed her eyes. *Every precious privacy gone.* "I'm not feeling well."

Instead of leaving, her mother-in-law opened the door a crack. "I've had some tea brought up to you, dear. It should make you feel better. Please, come and have some."

Anne took a deep breath as she stood, and walked into her bedroom.

Winifred sat with tea set up on a table between two chairs.

"Really, you shouldn't have gone to all this trouble. I would have been down shortly."

"Nonsense, dear. Come sit." She poured their tea, while watching Anne over the rim of her cup. "This is the ninth morning you have been sick, dear. Isn't that correct?"

A blush of red crept up Anne's neck onto her cheeks. "Yes, I believe it has been about nine days."

"The doctor will be here this afternoon to examine you. Is that agreeable with your schedule?"

As if you didn't know my schedule. "That would be fine."

"You know what this might mean?"

Anne nodded.

"I hope so. I would be delighted. Now, if you'll excuse me." Winifred stood.

Anne watched her leave before she put down the tea and returned to the water closet, in the grips of nausea once again.

Chapter 25

Mark hunched over his desk, muscles cramped. A long list of numbers coupled with German words and their English translation lay to one side of his desk, splotched with coffee stains and wrinkled from handling.

18276 = *erhalten* = receive

17694 = *nicht* = not

4473 = *gelingen* = success

19452 = *schlag–en* = blow or beat

The numbers, the German, and the English crowded together in his brain, until he couldn't think straight anymore. He'd been deciphering wireless signals from a vessel called the *Seeadler*, a ship suspected of destroying merchant ships. His assignment was to determine whether the raider was sailing homeward, or outward bound, and pass the information along so the Navy could warn the merchant ships.

The day before, they had intercepted a message from a Neumünster broadcast, confirming that the Germans were reading the Merchant Navy Code, the one used by the British Navy to communicate with merchant ships. The news had deflated everyone, but particularly Mark. Lyman & Stonebeck had lost two ships, which meant men's lives, and now that the Germans had the Merchant Code, they would be able to intercept naval instructions to merchant ships in the same way the Room 40 decoders located German ships.

Mark stretched. He needed a break to clear his thinking. He tapped on the open door of Commander Hope's office and peeked inside.

The commander, too, was hunched over a pile of messages and codes.

"I'm checking out for a bit," Mark said. "I need some fresh air, but I won't be gone long."

The commander looked up. "Go have a good lunch at a pub. Play a game of soccer. Enjoy the fresh air."

Mark smiled. "I'll do that, and still be back in under an hour."

"Good man." Hope returned to his paperwork.

After the stuffiness of Room 40, the cool March air took him by surprise. He took a brisk walk, taking in the trees filled with budding leaves, and the subtle splash of color from the first spring flowers. After so many hours and days in the smoke-filled confines of Room 40, it seemed that winter had passed him by. Next winter would be different, he promised himself. Next winter, he would be a father. Next winter, he would go home for Christmas *and* Boxing Day, if his commanding officer allowed.

The note from his mother telling him of Anne's pregnancy had been a shock, but a pleasant one. He would love to watch his wife grow with his child. He had so enjoyed watching Kate pregnant with Vanessa.

He walked down Whitehall Place and along the River Thames, relishing the exercise and the humid river air. Before long, the walk seemed a frivolous use of his time, and he turned and started back to Room 40. Every moment was too precious to waste—always another intercept coming in, another code to decipher, another German attack to thwart, another life to save. A war to end.

Chapter 26 – North Channel, May 1915

On the sunny afternoon of May 7, 1915, Leslie Harris leaned against the rail on the top deck of the *Invincible*, smoking and watching the graphite waters of the North Channel. He also watched James Casey make his way aft, skirting the 12-inch guns that lined the ship as if they were poison. Casey's combat duty station was feeding ammo to those giant guns. Pity he held such an aversion to them.

He saluted Leslie as he walked by.

"Where are you off to in such a hurry, Casey?"

James hesitated. "My bunk, sir, to write a letter."

"You're off duty. It's a beautiful May afternoon. Why don't you stop and catch a breath of fresh air?"

James hesitated, then drifted over to the railing. "May, is it? It doesn't feel like it."

"It's easy for a man at sea to forget what time of year it is."

A muffled sound and the ship shuddered.

"We're hit!" James cried.

Leslies squinted across the water. "More likely the sweepers found a mine and exploded it, and they didn't use the hull of the *Invincible* to do it, either."

James glanced at the officer, embarrassed. "I'm not very good at this, I'm afraid."

"Nonsense." Leslie leaned beside him, watching him carefully. "For someone who wasn't born with sea salt in your veins, like old Leslie here, you're doing fine."

The younger man pulled out a handkerchief and wiped his face. "I worked at a shipping firm before the war—Lyman & Stonebeck. Perhaps you've heard of it?"

Leslie shook his head.

"We have a fleet of merchant ships."

"I take it you never sailed with them?"

James smiled. "I'm afraid not."

"No matter. You don't get seasick, now, do you?"

"No, luckily, no. Thank God for that."

"You miss your family." A statement of fact.

"Yes, terribly. I have pictures, would you like to see?" James dug into his wallet and pulled out a creased photograph.

"She's a beauty, your wife. And a bouncing baby."

"Vanessa, my daughter. They are beautiful, aren't they?"

"That they are. Makes it tough to be at sea, with two beautiful women at home."

James took the photograph back, and stared at it for a long while before tucking it away.

Leslie patted him on the shoulder. "You'll be home with them before you know it."

James nodded. "I think I'll hit my bunk now, sir."

Leslie nodded, returned James's salute, and watched him until he disappeared.

On that same sunny afternoon, hundreds of miles away from the *Invincible*, a German U-boat fired a single torpedo into a passenger ship named the *Lusitania*. The torpedo hit the starboard side close to the bridge. It must have hit a boiler or coal burner, because a violent explosion tore away the entire superstructure above the point of impact. Fire broke out, a thick cloud of smoke enveloped the ship, and thousands of passengers, many of them women and children, began a mad scramble for life.

A mere two and a half hours after the torpedo struck, the ship disappeared completely into the sea, taking with it 1,195 civilians, 94 of them children, and 140 of them American citizens.

Its sinking incensed the world, and prompted many able-bodied men who'd not joined up before to leave their families and work behind, and enlist in the military, particularly the Navy.

Many men who worked at Lyman & Stonebeck joined up, prompting Mr. Bridger to call back former employees, bent-over men with a gleam in their eyes, happy to be of service once again. A handful of younger unfit-for-duty men joined the company as well.

At first, the men were surprised to see Kate working in the office and walking the shipyard with Mr. Bridger each day, as Mark and James had done. As time wore on, the workers grew used to her. After all, everywhere you went these days, women worked as bank clerks, streetcar conductors, railroad trackwalkers, locomotive wipers, and oilers. The world had turned upside down.

After an unusually difficult morning that included mistakes on a shipping order, and a merchant angry at the mix-up, Kate decided to get out of the office and take a stroll downtown during lunch. Regent Street boasted some fine shops. She left the industrial area behind and, as she stared into a store window, a reflection caught her eye. She turned to see Anne, walking between Lady Winifred and Muriel.

Muriel towered over them both, looking so much like Mark with her light molasses hair and handsome features.

And one couldn't miss Winifred St. John, who wore an enormous fur-trimmed hat, topped by a tall feather that trembled as she walked.

"Anne," Kate called out, smiling. "Lady St. John, Muriel. Hello."

Anne gaped in surprise and began to blink, as if the sunlight had grown too bright.

Muriel gave a warm smile. "Hello, Kate."

Winifred St. John promptly grasped each of the young women by the arm and propelled them down the sidewalk.

Kate took a step toward them, and called out. "Anne! Hello!"

At that, Winifred St. John dropped both girls' arms, did an about-face, and marched back to Kate.

Surprised, Kate took a step backward.

"Young woman," Lady Winifred said loudly. "You may have hoodwinked my son into socializing with you—a common maid—but you have not pulled the wool over my eyes."

"Mother, really," Muriel protested.

Winifred ignored her. "It is not appropriate. You are not a friend of my son's. You are an employee, nothing more."

It took a second for Kate to comprehend, but by the time Winifred had turned away, Kate's blood had turned red hot.

"My work at Lyman and Stonebeck," Kate snapped, "has brought income to your family, which helped to buy that ridiculous hat you're wearing."

Muriel snickered, while Anne looked horrified.

"And your son is, I believe," Kate continued, breathing hard, heart pounding, "old enough and perfectly capable of choosing his own friends, without his mother's approval."

The older woman stiffened, then turned and marched away down the sidewalk to Anne and Muriel.

Muriel broke ranks and returned to Kate, leaned down and kissed her on the cheek. "Kate, you're looking well, despite the circumstances in which we find ourselves. How's the baby?"

Kate smiled gratefully. "Vanessa is well, very well. Thank you for asking."

"Have you seen my brother? I wonder if he's stationed nearby."

"He writes, but I haven't seen him. You?"

"The occasional note, but no visits."

"Muriel!" Lady Winifred called.

Muriel smiled at Kate. "Don't mind her," she whispered. "You're a gem." Muriel rejoined her mother.

Lady Winifred grabbed Anne and Muriel by the arms again and, with talon-like fingers, propelled them down the street.

What bothered Kate most, as she stood on the sidewalk, staring after the retreating trio, was not the horrible Lady St. John—although she wondered how people as nice as Mark and Muriel could have been raised by such a woman—but the fact that Anne, who used to be a friend, hadn't uttered one word throughout the entire encounter. She hadn't even glanced back as they hurried away. She acted as if Kate had never existed.

Kate sat back against the sturdy trunk of the chestnut tree outside their house, legs stretched out. She wore a navy blue pleated skirt and a white blouse, unbuttoned at the collar due to the warmth of the afternoon, her hair pulled into a loose knot. The branches of the old tree filtered the light, as she reread the latest letter from James. As with all his letters, the Navy had blacked out all references to his location or mission. He wrote in vague generalities about life aboard the ship—the close quarters and dismal food. Regardless of how he tried to make light of his situation, the fact that he lived in constant danger screamed between the lines for both of them.

A soft breeze rustled the leaves overhead as she picked up a letter from Mark. He and Anne were expecting a baby in August, and he reported that Anne had been ill during the first several months, but felt better now.

Kate glanced up as Vanessa ran after Bruce, who scampered back and forth with excitement. The two were inseparable, except when Mrs. Ames chased the dog out of the house, a daily occurrence.

She watched their play, dreaming of having another baby. Vanessa, at sixteen months, would be the right age to befriend a little brother or sister.

She returned to her reading. Mark's letters weren't censored by someone else as James's were. He was scrupulous to avoid any comment about his location and duties, yet she felt that he wasn't too far away.

"A gentleman here to see you, ma'am," Mrs. Ames called from the veranda door in an unusually cheerful tone.

Kate looked up, seized by an unreasonable panic. Who would be coming to see her? *Dear God*, she prayed, *please don't let it be bad news about James*. Another thought paralyzed her. *Des*. She gathered up the letters and pushed them back into their envelopes with trembling hands.

"Please watch Vanessa." She brushed grass off her skirt as she rushed past Mrs. Ames.

Kate opened the doors to the sitting room, and there before the window, looking out into the garden, stood a friend.

"Mark!" Kate rushed to him and caught his hands in hers.

His sandy hair seemed to have darkened a few shades, and his complexion seemed pale, as if he hadn't seen the sun in a long while—not that the sun shone much in London, even in springtime.

"Good gracious, what are you doing here?" she gasped.

"I needed to see a familiar face." He grinned.

"I just read your letter. Congratulations. You're a father-to-be. It's wonderful, Mark. I'm so happy for you."

He beamed. "Thank you."

"I recently chatted with Muriel," she said.

"Really?"

"Yes, I ran into her, your mother, and Anne downtown."

"I'm in trouble there." He grinned again, a little more devilishly this time. "I haven't made it home to Stonebeck in a long while."

"Come on. Let's go see Vanessa." She led him out to the garden.

"Lord St. John. So good to see you," said Mrs. Ames.

"And you, Missus Ames."

Vanessa stopped toddling after the dog long enough to look up at the tall man with her mum, but when he knelt down before her, she frowned and started to cry.

"Vanessa, naughty girl! This is your Godfather," Kate admonished with a smile.

Mark laughed. "So that's the effect I have on my favorite girl these days? Look how you've grown."

Kate watched him. "It's so good to see you."

His smile faded as he stood. "You heard the news about the *Lusitania*."

"Yes. It's tragic."

"Over a thousand drowned. It went down fast, they think in twenty minutes. There's only one good thing that might come of it."

"And what could that possibly be?"

"Americans were on the *Lusitania*. This might be what it takes to make them get involved in this war."

"Let's not talk about the war. Please?"

"Forgive me. I came here to forget, if only for a short while."

"The garden is rather a mess, I'm afraid. I've neglected my roses. I love working, but my time is limited now, and the roses are suffering for it."

"I'm glad you're at the business, keeping an eye on the place. I feel better knowing you're there."

"Mister Bridger is doing a grand job." She hesitated. "We all took it hard when our ships were lost."

"Bloody Germans are sinking everything—merchant ships, passenger ships. They don't care. That's why merchant crews are being trained to follow Royal Navy practice, and zigzag when in dangerous waters."

"They warn us to change our shipping routes when they suspect enemy ships in certain areas. How do you suppose they know that information?"

Mark smiled. "Lots of blokes working damned hard, I suspect."

"Will you stay for dinner? Lucy has gone off to work in a munitions factory, so you'll have to put up with my cooking."

"I'd love to, but I can't." He took her arm, tucking it in his. "I have to go. I needed a break, and I wanted to see you."

"You must work close by?"

Mark shook his finger at her, smiling. "Confidential."

They turned back into the house, arm in arm. Kate tried to keep her voice steady as they walked to the front door. "I miss our old world." She thought of Lady Winifred. "Well, many things about our old world, that is."

"You'll never know how much I miss being with all of you. It's odd, everything appearing the same here, when my world has changed so much."

"Come back when you can."

He reached inside his jacket, pulled out a small notepad and pen, scribbled on it, tore off a sheet, and handed it to her. "If you need anything, call this number. Whoever answers will be able to reach me."

He squeezed her hand, opened the front door, and walked away, turning once to wave.

Kate waved back, and leaned against the door for a long time after he disappeared from sight.

Chapter 27

Anne clutched the bed sheet, white knuckled, as another contraction gripped her. She'd vowed not to cry out in front of her mother-in-law, but the pain had become unbearable, and before she knew it, another scream escaped.

When the wave of pain receded, she gasped for breath, sweat stinging her eyes as she tried to focus on the doctor. It was late evening. The five of them — Anne, Lady Winifred, Muriel, the doctor, and his nurse — had been together in the room since two in the morning. Lady Winifred and Muriel traded off taking short rests out of the room. Exhaustion had made itself at home, like an unwelcome dinner guest.

The doctor frowned at Anne as if she were a naughty child, and to Winifred, he said, "Nothing."

Winifred crooned into Anne's ear, "Sweetheart, you're going to have to push harder."

Anne bit her lip to keep from crying. *The baby is ripping me apart and they want me to push harder? How long have we been at it now?* She'd lost all track of time.

"I can't," she said, sniffling.

Winifred's voice hardened to steel. "You must. Do you hear me? You have no choice. Now, the next time the pain comes, push with every bit of strength you have."

Anne turned her head away, fearful her mother-in-law would see the hatred in her eyes. Nobody was helping her — instead, they accused her of not pushing hard enough.

"Push hard. Be strong," the doctor said.

Well, I don't feel strong. I'm terrified. I'm going to die! The baby is tearing me apart, and I'm going to die!

She cried into her pillow as another wave of pain gathered momentum, gripping her bruised and tired body. She pulled herself into a sitting position and strained with all her might.

"Push!" Lady Winifred shouted. "You're going to kill my grandchild if you don't push!"

"Come on, child," the doctor commanded. "You've got to try harder."

The nurse blotted her forehead with a cool, damp rag.

"Please, someone help me," Anne pleaded. "Get it out of me!"

"Mark," Muriel called as he climbed out of the Austin. She must have heard the car pull up. "The baby's coming, but it's been going on for eighteen hours, and something is wrong." Her words tumbled out. "Poor Anne."

Mark took his sister's hands in his, released them, and went inside. He took the stairs two at a time and, upon reaching the bedroom door, flung it open.

The odor hit him first—the air thick with sweat mingled with less pleasant odors. Something seemed off, terribly wrong.

His mother and a nurse were leaning over the bed, while a doctor huddled near the foot of it.

Lady Winifred's head jerked in his direction, and with one swift movement she moved away from the bed, grabbed Mark by the arm, and propelled him out of the room, closing the door behind them.

Mark pulled out of her grip. "Why didn't you call me sooner? What's the matter? Tell me."

Lady Winifred took a breath. "The baby's not coming."

For the first time Mark could remember, his mother looked old and tired.

She pushed her hair away from her face. "She started labor very early this morning and it's been this way—"She nodded toward the door. "—ever since."

Mark stared at her, then started back inside.

"Mark, stop. You can't go in there."

"The hell I can't, Mother."

He walked straight for the bedside, unprepared to see the pitiful figure who looked nothing like his wife. Thin hair stuck to her scalp and face in wet clumps. Blue veins spidered beneath translucent skin.

"Anne, darling, it's me. Mark."

"Mark?" her voice rasped.

"Yes."

She turned her head toward him, and seeing him, began to sob. "Oh, thank God. Help me, please. The baby's trying to kill me and they won't do anything to help me." Her voice came in ragged gasps, like a child who'd been crying for a long time.

He moved closer and cradled her head and shoulders in his arms. "There, there," Mark whispered. "I'm here now. I'll help you."

"I knew you would. I knew you would," she mumbled, her voice growing louder as another contraction began.

Mark looked at the doctor. "What can we do?"

Anne gripped his arms, choking with the pain.

"She's weak, already lost a lot of blood," the doctor said. "But I suppose we have no choice but to operate—a caesarean section. The hospital's too far away—she won't make it. I'll have to do it here, which is not ideal. I warn you, she's already weak, and I'll have to give her ether. I can't predict the outcome."

Mark stared at the doctor. "Do it."

He watched the entire procedure in tense silence, and thirty minutes later, Charles William St. John entered the world wet, pale, and flaccid. The nurse gently sponged the infant before handing him to Mark, who cradled him against his chest and stared at the tiny face. "My son." He let out the breath he'd been holding. "Thank you, God."

Winifred's arms encircled her son and grandson. "The family name lives on." She smiled at Mark. "An heir is born."

When Mark returned to Anne's side, he found her sleeping. The maids had taken away the bloody sheets and somehow made a fresh, clean bed beneath her. Mark picked up her hand and held it to his cheek. Her translucent eyelids fluttered but remained closed, her pale skin waxy.

"I know it's been hard for you," he whispered. "Be strong. I'll take care of you, and our son."

Chapter 28

Kate closed the file cabinet, and pinched the bridge of her nose between thumb and forefinger. It had taken most of the afternoon to finish the new shipping schedule. Routes changed so often now. She glanced at the clock; time to go before Des showed up.

Des had informed Mr. Bridger that he would drop by every Tuesday around five to pick up a weekly report. "Oh, one more thing," Des had said, flopping an envelope on Mr. Bridger's desk. "I'll be drawing a salary. The amount's in there. Weekly payment, included along with the report."

Mr. Bridger had not been a happy man. The amount of time it would take to write up the report and copy schedules would add to his hours, and those of Kate and Tommy Hart, every week. Not to mention the insult of paying the man for doing nothing. But what could a working man do against an owner?

When Kate heard about the new arrangement, she determined to vanish every Tuesday afternoon, long before his arrival.

She locked the file cabinet, eager to get home to see Vanessa. Now that Lucy had left to work in a munitions factory, she and Mrs. Ames had settled into a new arrangement. Mrs. Ames cooked Vanessa's meals, and Kate cooked her own. She couldn't complain, as Mrs. Ames took loving care of Vanessa, and was a most efficient housekeeper.

Kate slipped her hand into the pocket of her skirt and pulled out a folded telegram.

> Kate,
> Anne has given birth to a healthy baby boy. We've named
> him Charles William. The Christening will be Sunday next. Please
> try to come. My poor Anne. It went very hard on her.
> Mark

She refolded the telegram as the front office door opened and closed.

"Tommy?" She scooped together her coat and purse. "Tommy, is that you? I'm ready to go. I just—"

James stood in the doorway.

She stared, and when comprehension finally seeped in, she forced herself to breathe and cried, "James!"

When she ran into his arms, he buried his face in her hair.

After a long while, she pulled back to look at him. His uniform hung on him and blue crescents smudged beneath his eyes. "Why didn't you tell me you were coming home? How long can you stay?"

"I'm sorry I didn't let you know. Leave came up rather suddenly. Five days... I have five days."

He reluctantly let her go and glanced around the office. His fingers traced the surface of his old desk, and he turned around in a slow circle.

"I work at your desk, now," she said. "Isn't that something? I always envied you your work. It seemed like such a secret world with important things to do. And now I'm a part of all that. Mister Bridger is doing a capital job running the place, and we hired a young man, Tommy Hart. Did you see him when you came in? He's very smart. One with the numbers, he is."

James gave a slight, apologetic smile. "It's good to see the old place. I'm glad you're here, in my old job. I'd like to go home now, if you don't mind."

"Of course. You must be exhausted."

They slid their arms around one another's waists, and started to leave, almost running into Tommy at the door.

"Tommy, this is my husband, James Casey. James, this is Tommy Hart."

"Sir," Tommy said. "It's an honor."

"Tommy insists on walking me to the train every evening," Kate added.

James reached out and shook the young man's hand. "Thank you for that kindness."

"I'll see you tomorrow, but I'll be late," said Kate. "And I won't be working a full day. Good night, Tommy. You're a saint."

When they arrived home, Mrs. Ames looked as though she might faint. "Mister Casey! Welcome home."

James gave her a quick hug. "It's a joy to be here. Where's Vanessa?"

"Upstairs, having a late nap. She had a hard afternoon of play with her dog. Would you like me to get her?"

"No, we won't wake her. Thanks, Missus Ames."

Kate pulled Mark's telegram from her pocket. "By the way, I have some wonderful news. Mark and Anne had their baby. A boy." She handed him the telegram.

"How wonderful," he said, glancing at it before handing it distractedly back to her. He turned toward the stairs, stood staring upward, then began to climb.

Upstairs, he stood at the foot of Vanessa's bed, and Kate moved silently behind him. Together they smiled at the chubby cheeks, the dark, curly hair, and the bow-shaped lips.

"I have to memorize everything about her," he whispered. "It's important to remember the good and the beauty of a child, during...."

"During what?" Kate prodded after a few seconds.

"The war is hard," he whispered. "It's hard on me, Kate."

She put her hand on his shoulder. "You're tired, James. I'll go make some tea."

He covered her hand with his own, and nodded.

She left him to prepare the tea, and when she returned, he hadn't budged. She took his hand and led him downstairs to the kitchen, where she poured them each a cup.

"I'll step out to get a breath of air," he said, and fished in his pocket for a cigarette. He took his tea and smoke outside.

She threw a wrap over her shoulders and followed him out, breathing in the evening air while watching James over the rim of her cup, until long after his cigarette had turned to ash.

"Let me make you something to eat," she said. "You must be hungry."

He barely glanced over his shoulder. "In a bit."

She set out a plate with game hen and potatoes, but James told her he would eat later and to go on up to bed.

Try as she might to stay awake, she never heard James come to bed. When she woke in the morning she found herself alone. The cover on his side of the bed was thrown back. He must have come to bed late and left early.

Over the next several days, James seemed his old self when he played with Vanessa. Kate watched in fascination, as he involved himself for hours in Vanessa's games: throwing a ball back and forth endlessly, while Bruce barked and chased; arranging rocks in the dirt in the garden to make towns, roads, and rivers; reading storybook after storybook with Vanessa in rapt attention, while Bruce slept on her lap.

Mrs. Ames outdid herself preparing James's favorite dishes, and would often peek outside at father and daughter, and smile approvingly.

Kate, on the other hand, watched her husband and daughter with a sense of unease. It didn't seem quite right for James to be so absorbed in childish games.

In the end, on the day he had to go back, James sat staring vacantly in the garden for hours. Plum-colored shadows beneath his eyes betrayed the fact that he had slept very little during his stay. At last, he went into the house and gathered his belongings, set them by the door, and took Kate and Vanessa into his arms.

Kate felt exhausted as he pulled her tightly against him, weary of yet another goodbye.

Then he left.

Vanessa howled as the door closed behind him, and Mrs. Ames rushed forward to take the crying child upstairs.

Kate stood in the foyer for a long time, strangely relieved, and yet empty. Her head pounded dully as she turned and climbed the stairs, and she spent the rest of the afternoon lying awake and confused in the cool green shadows of her bedroom.

James trudged up the gangplank of the *Invincible* as the mingled smells of saltwater and oil assaulted him. The cool darkness below deck relieved his burning eyes as he made his way along the narrow corridors, duffel bag thrown over his shoulder.

He ducked into his sleeping quarters, which were blissfully empty, flung his bag onto his bunk, flopped stomach-down, and buried his head in his arms.

He had dreamt of those five days of leave for months, and now they were gone. Yet he felt no relief, no warm afterglow from being with his wife and daughter. Kate had looked at him oddly since the first evening he had surprised her at the office. Even when he'd played with Vanessa, he caught her looking at him, brow furrowed. No surprise, perhaps, as he hadn't been his old self.

Footsteps rang along the corridor and stopped at his door, and he buried his head deeper in his arms.

"You're back from leave, are you?" Leslie Harris said.

James answered without looking up, when he should have jumped to his feet and saluted. "Yes, I'm back."

"How are your wife and baby?"

"Well. They're both well."

James turned over and looked at the older man's weathered face, swung his legs around, and sat on the edge of his bunk. "It wasn't the same. It wasn't what I expected." He ran his fingers through his hair.

"Aye. I know what you mean, lad. I was married once myself. A fine young girl with red hair."

James glanced at him. "What happened with your wife?"

Leslie sighed. "I went home after being away for seven months. It had been a good trip—a run to India. She didn't live there anymore. We didn't have any little 'uns, so no harm done. I can't blame the girl." He looked at James. "But Lord, I did miss looking at that red hair."

James tried to smile, but instead covered his face with his hands.

He glanced up when Leslie reached out and squeezed his shoulder. "There, there," Leslie said, his voice low and gruff.

"I'm sorry."

"No need to be sorry, boy. That's what old Leslie is here for."

James looked up. "Have I changed so much in such a short time? That's what I can't understand."

"The sea has a way of changing a man. And war... well, war has a way of cutting open a man, and showing him what's inside. Sometimes, we see things we never knew were there—some good, some not. Perhaps your Missus saw something different about you. Maybe she wondered where the boy she married had gone. Or maybe she looked at you the same as always, but you saw things different."

Voices sounded outside and Leslie stepped back and stood in the doorway. "You know where I am if you need to talk."

Chapter 29

The christening of Charles William St. John, the third Earl of Tunbridge, had to wait until the first Sunday in September in the hopes that Anne's health would improve enough to make the trip to London. Instead, she remained tucked in bed at Stonebeck Hall.

Kate sat discreetly, several pews back, watching as Mark, with Lady Winifred by his side, held the baby while the priest performed the baptism. Charles William St. John didn't struggle or whimper when the holy water touched his skin.

Mid-ceremony, the door to the church opened. Yellow streaks of sunlight stabbed into the dimness before the door fell closed. Kate glanced over her shoulder, and her blood turned to ice as Des strode toward the front of the church, a package tucked beneath one arm.

He hesitated ever so slightly when he reached Kate's row, but continued on to the first pew.

Lady Winifred smiled, while Mark ignored the interruption.

There would be a reception after the ceremony, but Kate had already decided not to attend. Mark would welcome her, but his mother would not.

When the ritual concluded, Kate stood, walked down the aisle and through the door outside, and blinked at the brightness. She hadn't gone far when she heard Des call her name.

He hurried to catch up and stopped too close, looking devilishly attractive, like fire, mesmerizing to contemplate but dangerous to touch. "Motherhood agrees with you, my dear. You're looking splendid."

Kate glared at him.

"Now, now, not the silent treatment. I've been a good boy, haven't I? I've left you alone, as you asked. Isn't that so?"

Kate said nothing

He took her by the arm. "Good God, it's been a year and a half. Talk to me."

She pulled her arm from his grip and looked him full in the face. Des had obviously gone to great care for the occasion—face shaved, suit pressed, hair combed.

"I appreciate your absence," she said, words clipped, "and beg you to continue."

She turned and started down the street but he stayed by her side.

When he spoke, his voice was low and firm. "You haven't seen me, my dear, but that doesn't mean I haven't seen you. You and your darling daughter make such a handsome pair, my two dark-haired beauties. Such a waste, two fragile creatures living alone without a man to take care of them. Are you frightened at night, my dear, when the stairs creak after everyone's gone to bed? Wouldn't it be safer to lie within the safe, warm arms of a man who loves you, Kate?"

She stopped and faced him. "Leave me alone, Des. Surely, you have better things to do than bother about me. You've damaged my life enough already. Go find yourself someone who will make you happy. You might even contemplate Margaret, your wife."

Without waiting for a reply, she walked away.

This time, he didn't follow.

Kate straightened the papers on her desk Tuesday afternoon. Des would be in soon, so she hurried to leave early. Mr. Bridger had noticed her new pattern, but never said a word. She walked to the coatrack and reached for her new hat, a wide-brimmed style that scooped low over her forehead. This smart blue bonnet had caught her eye in a store window, and war or no war, she couldn't resist.

She walked to the door of Tommy Hart's office where he labored over a ledger. "I've had my fill today, Tommy. I think I'll walk home. Maybe catch a cab partway."

Tommy peered at her through thick spectacles. "I'm finished here. I'll come along, if you don't mind."

"Lovely."

They climbed the steps to the street, and Kate paused and turned. The buildings and docks of Lyman & Stonebeck sprawled before them as the River Thames drifted by. The scent of wood and creosote clung to the moist air as it rose off the river.

"Let's walk over to Pall Mall and have a spot of tea before going home," said Kate. "There's a café called Sebastian's that serves strong tea, and maybe they'll have a biscuit or two left over. What do you say?"

"Yes." He looked serious.

Kate smiled and slipped her arm again through his, and they set off. Chestnuts and beech trees lined the street, a few leaves spiraling to the ground in the first step of their journey toward decay.

Kate peeked at him from beneath the brim of her hat. "I know you came from Wales to London to join the army...."

He glanced at Kate. "And they wouldn't have me because of my bloody eyes."

"It's their loss, you know."

He gave a grateful smile. "Have you always lived in London?"

"No, but as a girl in Scotland, I used to have grand dreams of life in London."

"And they've come true," Tommy said.

"I suppose, but in a different way than I expected."

The traffic grew thicker as they neared the city center. Although most of the young men were off fighting in France, the sidewalks remained crowded. Nearly all of the faces were old, very young, or female, but occasionally, they spotted a young man, home on leave, or on crutches, or worse.

"I do love it here," Kate continued. "My life has been good. After all, I married James, and have my Vanessa. I live in a beautiful home, better than any place I would have lived in Scotland. Fate has been very kind, although I don't deserve it."

Tommy stopped. "How can you say that? Why, I can't think of anyone who deserves it more. You're pretty, and nice, and very smart...." He stopped, suddenly self-conscious.

Kate smiled. "Tommy, you're a dear. Now let's get that tea, shall we?"

They found Sebastian's and peered in through the café's large window. "Oh good," Kate said. "There are only a few customers. We won't have any trouble getting a table." She turned toward Tommy, but he wasn't listening.

Instead, he stared upwards, open-mouthed.

Kate looked up as a shadow passed over them. Strange cylindrical shapes blotted out the September sky, and then the world erupted into chaos. People screamed and ran in all directions, horses reared, backing carriages into motorcars, and traffic snarled to a standstill.

"Airships!" Tommy gasped. "My God, they're German zeppelins. They're dropping bombs!"

Then the Sebastian's Café window exploded outward to the street, knocking Kate and Tommy to the ground.

The air burned hot and Tommy threw his arms around Kate, too late to protect her. As her hat cartwheeled down the street, he pulled back and they stared at one another, faces bloodied.

"Are you hurt?" Tommy shouted.

Kate shook her head numbly. "I don't know."

"I've lost my glasses." Tommy let her go and bent down, feeling around blindly in the rubble, and the ground shook with another explosion.

Kate grabbed Tommy by the upper arm and pulled him to his feet, as a surge of people threatened to trample them into the broken glass. Among the cacophony, with bombs dropping, buildings exploding, and people screaming, a silence wrapped itself around Kate like a cocoon, and after what could have been an eternity, the silence whispered one name into her ear.

Vanessa.

She turned and ran.

"Kate, come back!" Tommy yelled.

She soon heard him calling again and running behind her, as she pushed through the crowd.

He caught up to her and grasped her by the arm. "It's not safe."

She ignored him.

"Kate, please, we need to find cover."

She shook him off. "I must go home."

He took her arm again, and pushed through the crowd and debris alongside her, through air thick with smoke and dust. A stream of people running from the airships came at them, but Kate and Tommy pushed their way through them as they ran toward Chelsea, chasing the airships along a path of destruction. Another explosion toppled a church steeple across the street, raining dust and debris.

As they rounded one street corner, the screams of a horse made Kate cover her ears. Still tethered to a carriage, the animal lay on its side, its hindquarters a bloody pulp. The driver of the carriage, reins still in hand, was dead in the driver's seat. Kate envied Tommy's myopic vision.

They ran faster, toward her baby, away from the horror. Ahead of them, the airships drifted farther and farther away.

They reached Chelsea and wound their way through the streets until they reached Kate's home, and they stopped, breathless. The house appeared the same, but not quite right. A shroud of smoke and dust hovered in the air, and Kate moved forward on legs gone heavy, taking one slow step after another toward the front door. With Tommy breathing hard right behind her, they climbed the steps and pushed on the front door. It groaned open, and a cloud of smoke and dust poured out.

"Vanessa!" Kate plunged headlong into the house. "Missus Ames! Vanessa!"

A wall of debris lay heaped where the hallway to the kitchen and dining room should be. Kate stared, frozen with shock.

"Let's try around back," Tommy said.

She turned to him with wide eyes. "Yes. That's where they are. Around back."

They retraced their steps and stumbled around the side of the house. The brick wall that had enclosed the garden had tumbled, and they climbed through a sea of fallen bricks. The entire back of the house had gone missing, exposing the rooms. She could see her bedroom on the second floor, obscenely bare to the outside world. Below, the rose garden lay crushed and buried beneath debris. The old chestnut tree had been split in half, its massive branches broken.

Kate tried to call for Mrs. Ames and the baby, but the words stuck in her throat.

They clamored over the rubble, searching, tossing bricks and debris behind them.

"They probably had gone to the park or for a walk," Kate said as she pulled away a large chunk of plaster and twisted pipe. "They couldn't have been here."

She moved a large brick, revealing a clump of dark, matted hair, and began to whimper. She reached out and pulled away more bricks, then sat back on her heels. Bruce, the Scottish terrier, lay crushed and lifeless before her. Tenderly, she brushed the plaster and dirt from his hair. Feeling suddenly weak, she picked at the rubble near the dog's body.

Not a foot away, peeking out from beneath a brick, a tiny hand appeared.

She clawed at the rubble furiously, crying and moaning. Tommy joined in, and together they uncovered the broken, lifeless body of a little girl.

My Vanessa.

Kate picked her up gingerly, held the child tightly against her chest, and rocked slowly back and forth.

Tommy looked on, helpless, tears coursing down his bloodied cheeks.

An hour passed, and it felt like an eternity. Then two hours, and twilight settled in, casting the broken remains of the house in shadow.

"Kate," Tommy whispered as the light faded. "Please, let me help you. We need to... to take her away from here."

She ignored him. When he tried to touch her, she shook him off.

Another hour passed. Tommy squinted skyward and swallowed, but the lumbering airships were gone, leaving only a dark sky full of stars, oblivious to the destruction below.

The hour had grown late when he heard voices around front. He stood, his legs nearly buckling beneath him, and made his way over the rubble toward the voices,.

A Royal Army truck sat parked in front of the house. "Do you live here?" a man in uniform called from the front step.

"No, but the lady who does is behind the house. We need help."

As they rushed toward the back garden, Tommy explained. "There's been a casualty--her little girl, and probably the housekeeper, although we haven't found her. I can't get the mother to leave."

The soldier peered at him. "You don't look so good yourself."

Tommy touched his eyes. They were swollen and sore.

The two men stopped at the sight of Kate rocking back and forth amid the debris, her face and neck darkened with dried blood, her hair matted.

"Damn murdering bastards," one of the soldiers muttered. "They did this all over the city, killed innocent women and children. It's indecent. Inhuman. War is bloody war, man, but you don't bomb women and children. It's uncivilized."

Together, Tommy and the soldiers approached Kate. "Ma'am, please let us help you and your child."

Kate's focus remained blind as she continued to rock, pressing Vanessa to her chest.

Tommy and the soldier looked at one another, and Tommy knelt beside her.

"Please, Kate, you're hurt. You need a doctor, and Vanessa does, too."

For the first time since she'd uncovered the tiny hand, Kate turned her head to look at Tommy. Her eyes flashed. "You're not taking my baby away from me."

The sound of footsteps in the rubble caused Tommy and the soldiers to turn and squint through the darkness. The silhouette of a man appeared on the edge of the garden, looking first at the men, then toward Kate.

He closed the distance in a few quick steps, stood over mother and daughter for an instant, then bent over and scooped them both up in his arms.

A strangled protest escaped Kate's throat at the sudden intrusion, and she clung tighter to Vanessa. When she focused on the face of the intruder, she stopped struggling. Tears spilled from her eyes, tracing a path down her once-alabaster skin, mingling with the dirt and blood.

Tommy and the soldier stared open mouthed, as Des McGregor carried Kate and her lifeless child out of the backyard and into the night.

Chapter 30

Tombstones sparkled as a fine drizzle fell on the cemetery where a knot of people huddled by the side of an open grave. Mark had arranged to have Vanessa buried at Highgate Cemetery, prestigious ground that occupied a south-facing hillside overlooking London. Ancient elms and maples solemnly watched over mausoleums and headstones, entwined in ferns, ivy, and rhododendrons. Concrete angels looked on while birds trilled in spite of the sad occasion. Mounds of dirt marked the newest graves in the cemetery, and there were plenty of them. As the minister murmured the Lord's Prayer, the rich smell of damp earth mingled with the vague scent of flowers. Vanessa's was the second funeral the reverend had performed already this Saturday morning, and he's said he had three more to go.

Kate wavered on her feet, face hidden behind a black veil as she stared unblinking at the tiny coffin. In uncharacteristic fashion, Mark had used his family clout to convince Naval authorities to grant James leave, and had delayed the funeral, until James got permission and transport home.

James stood on one side of Kate, Mark on the other, both in uniform, both pale and silent. Des stood behind them, a dark figure with hard eyes. Mr. and Mrs. Bridger stood behind Des, Mrs. Bridger weeping. Anne had stayed at Stonebeck, too weak to travel.

When the minister's voice fell silent, two roughly clad men stepped forward and seized a rope on either end of the tiny casket. With ease, they lowered it into the ground.

Kate stepped up to the grave, holding in her trembling hand a single red rose. She released it and it floated onto the coffin. She stood and stared until James wrapped his arm around her, turned her, and walked her toward the car.

They came upon Lucy, their former cook, and Kate paused in front of her without looking up.

"How kind of you to come, Lucy," James said.

"I'm so sorry, sir. It's a tragedy, a real tragedy. And Missus Ames, too." Her voice broke. "It don't seem possible."

"Yes, Missus Ames never let Vanessa out of her sight, did she?" He patted Lucy on the shoulder. "Thank you for coming. It means a lot to Missus Casey and me. We miss you."

They continued on to the chauffeured car, provided by Des.

Mr. Bridger, hat in hand, stopped James before he climbed inside. "James," he said, and paused. He cleared his throat, gaze darting toward Kate. "Can I speak to you a moment?"

James helped Kate into the car and turned back to him.

"The Missus and I are so very sorry...." His voice trailed off.

James nodded and put a hand on Mr. Bridger's shoulder. "And with you in the Navy and all, with your home gone...."

James looked away.

"What I'm trying to say is that we would like Kate to come live with us again."

"Thank you," James said. "I'm afraid I hadn't even thought that far ahead."

Mr. Bridger backed away as James climbed in beside Kate.

They rode in silence to Des McGregor's townhouse, where Kate had been staying since the bombing, and Mark followed in his Austin.

As soon as they arrived, Kate climbed the stairs to the guest bedroom on the second floor—her bedroom now—and closed the door.

The men gathered in the sitting room, an awkward group—Mark paced, James perched uneasily in one of the Louis XVI chairs and stared at the floor, and Des gazed out the window while sipping a brandy.

"I want her to move into my house," Mark said at last. "I'm never there. I'll hire someone to look after her."

Des waved his brandy in the air. "She's settled in here. Why move her again?"

Mark shook his head. "I don't want her living here."

"I don't see where you have any say in it, old man," said Des. "I keep this house for business purposes. It's the least we can do for a valuable employee's wife."

James interrupted them. "Myron Bridger asked if Kate would come live with them again." He turned and stared out the window. "I never really gave her a home."

"Nonsense," Mark said. "You've given her a wonderful home."

"I could never have afforded to buy a house. You let us pay such a decent rent, but now your house is gone. Destroyed," James said, as if just realizing the turn of events. "You have no responsibility for us."

Mark walked over to him. "Indeed, I do. We're colleagues and friends. I think Kate should go to my house, or to Stonebeck Hall."

James shook his head. "You're both so generous. Thank you."

Mark flushed, took a step closer to James, and lowered his voice. "Damn it, man. Stop being so bloody grateful. You've worked for everything you have. You're not a charity case."

James blinked at him.

"Don't leave Kate here," Mark said with more firmness in his voice.

"Leave him alone," Des said from across the room. "Kate's safe here."

Mark walked to the bottom of the staircase, looked up, and took the stairs two at a time. He tapped on the door.

"Kate, it's Mark." He waited... nothing... and knocked again. "I'm coming in." He pushed open the door and stood in the doorway.

Kate sat in a chair before a dressing table, perfectly erect, hands in her lap. The veil absent, the high collar of her black dress enfolded her neck, a stark contrast to the paleness of her skin and the angry red cuts that crisscrossed her face.

Mark had learned that Des had called in a doctor as soon as he'd gotten Kate and Vanessa to the house, and the doctor had given Kate an injection of something to make her sleep. It didn't take long before her grip on her child had relaxed, and Des had lifted Vanessa from her arms, and called an undertaker.

The doctor had probed and extracted glass fragments from Kate's face and arms for two hours as she came in and out of consciousness. The wounds would heal, the doctor had said, and only a faint web of scars would remain, with the exception of one long, deep gash. It started beneath her left cheekbone, arcing back toward her ear and dropping down beneath her jaw to the top of her neck. A few centimeters lower, and it would have severed her artery. The doctor had stitched it up the best he could, but said it might leave a permanent scar.

A chill washed over Mark, seeing Kate this way—not just her physical wounds, but her devastating grief. He walked over and knelt beside her. "Kate." He struggled to find the words to begin. "I'm so sorry. This is the blackest hour."

She stared at nothing.

"I want to get you to a safe place, and I want to take you there now. Stay at my house here in Chelsea. I'll have someone stay with you. Or I can take you to Stonebeck Hall to be with Anne and Mother."

Kate winced.

He covered her hands with his own. They felt cold, lifeless. "I know things seem impossible right now. I understand how you feel, but—"

"No." Kate blinked, shifted her gaze to Mark, and said in a coarse voice, "You don't understand anything. You don't even know me."

"Know you? Of course, I know you."

"I'll stay here," she said. "I belong here."

"Here? With Des? You're not thinking clearly."

Kate's mouth twisted. "Des McGregor was my lover. Did you know that?"

Mark recoiled as if she'd slapped him across the face. "You've been through a terrible shock," he managed finally. "You don't know what you're saying."

"I gave him my virtue when I was only a girl in Scotland," she continued in a monotone. "But it didn't stop there. After I came to London, even after I married James, Des and I were lovers again. Des might have been Vanessa's father. I never knew for sure. It didn't matter."

The expression on his face was terrible to see—astonishment, disbelief, and a trace of disgust.

She looked away, closed her eyes, and shook her head. "Go away."

Chapter 31

Mark leaned forward over the mare's long neck and urged her into a full gallop. The horse snorted, sweat dampening her chestnut coat despite the early morning chill, as they raced along a path through the trees. He ducked a low limb, but it scraped along his back and soaked his shirt with morning dew.

After leaving Kate, he'd driven James to the train station. He'd intended to go back to work himself, but after arriving at Room 40, he found himself arranging a day's leave and driving straight through to Stonebeck, desperate to see Anne and Charles. He'd arrived before dawn, went directly to the stables, and at first light, had thundered off.

Now he pounded through Stonebeck's forest, trying to make sense of the whole mess.

The death of that beautiful child. Kate's unbelievable confession.

Blood pounded in his ears as he tried to sort out the truth. At first, he hadn't believed Kate—thought her to be rambling, despondent with grief—but the more her words echoed in his head, the more they began to make sense. The day at Lyman & Stonebeck when he, James, and Kate had run into Des, she'd acted strangely, and so had Des. He'd wondered about it at the time.

He pulled on the reins, slowed the mare to a walk, and turned back toward Stonebeck. Sweat stung his eyes as he thought back to the conversation with Kate. The revelation about her and Des echoed in his thoughts, unfathomable.

The mare perked up as they neared the stable, trotting the last hundred yards without any prodding. Mark dismounted and led the horse inside. A stable boy, who looked relieved that the mare had returned, reached out for her halter, but Mark waved him off and put the horse in a stall himself. He pulled off the saddle and blankets, hung them on the wall, and brushed the mare down, a routine that calmed him. After he finished, he started out across the yard toward the house.

Despite the early hour, Winifred waited at the top of the steps, impeccably dressed in a smart wool coat and a scarf over her hair, fastened at the neck by a sparkling brooch.

"Mother! How did you know I had come home?" He climbed the stairs and kissed her on the cheek.

"You think I don't know the minute my son comes home for the first time in months?" she said, as if offended, then smiled. "The stable boy told Stephens, and Stephens told me when you arrived."

"I needed to see the baby, Anne, you, Muriel... I needed my family."

Winifred hesitated. "I heard about the Casey child." She paused. "I also heard that Des McGregor has a new houseguest, one that his wife Margaret will ignore, I'm sure."

Mark said nothing.

"I can tell you're upset," she went on. "That's what happens when you allow work relationships to get confused with real family and friends."

"Enough." He didn't want to argue with his mother. He draped an arm around her shoulder. "I have twenty-four hours, and I won't be back for who knows how long. I want to have breakfast. I want to play with Charles. I want to forget the war. What do you say, Mother?"

"Your favorite breakfast is being prepared right now, and we'll start off with a good strong cup of tea."

The day passed by all too fast, but the night wore on endlessly. The peace Mark had desperately sought at Stonebeck Hall eluded him.

Muriel watched him silently, brows knitted together as he told her about the bombing of Kate's home, which killed Vanessa. "Where is Kate? Who's taking care of her?"

Mark shrugged off her questions. "I tried to help, but she's staying with a friend."

He went to his room, where Anne protested his presence in her bed. She was still too weak, too fragile to share the bedroom with her husband, she said. So he strolled into his old room, lay in his boyhood bed, and stared sleeplessly at the ceiling.

Hours later, he threw off the covers, swung his feet to the floor, and sat on the edge of the bed thinking of his son. At four months, Charles seemed undersized and docile. When Mark held him, the baby could barely hold up his head—didn't smile, didn't cry, simply watched Mark's face with a solemn expression. Although troubled by the lack of spark in his son, Mark loved being a father, and considered the baby heaven-sent.

He threw on a robe, walked to and opened his bedroom door, and stood in the dark hallway, flooded with childhood memories of creeping around the house at night after bedtime. He thought of his own father.

His father had spent many days and nights in London, away from the family. At age fourteen, Des had told him that both their fathers had mistresses. Mark hadn't believed him, and never questioned his father. He only knew that he never wanted that type of marriage. He always hoped to find a woman with whom to share ideas—a friend, a companion, and an equal.

He went downstairs to the kitchen to fix himself a cup of tea. He planned to return to his room and wait for the gray light of morning, but Muriel joined him long before anyone else was up.

She made herself a cup of tea and sat beside her brother. "Something more is wrong than you're telling me," she said.

He shook his head. "How is Leo?"

"A sad widower who wants me to make his life gay again, but I can't. I broke it off."

"How did mother take it?"

"Not well."

"You did the right thing." Mark stared into his tea.

"Where are you stationed? What kind of work do you do?" Muriel prodded.

"For once, curious cat, I cannot answer your questions, hound me though you may."

"I miss you. I want to come to London."

"It's a very bad time in London. Bad, indeed." Mark stood and kissed her on the top of the head. "Soon this will be over, and you can stay with Anne and me in London all you want. I better get back."

He went upstairs, dressed, and packed the few things he had brought. At least in Room 40, his mind could stay occupied piecing together odd bits of intelligence.

When the household finally started to awaken, he said goodbye to his mother, and left word for Anne, who still slept. He shrugged on his coat to leave, and paused at the nursery to kiss his sleeping son.

Muriel stood at the front door, watching as he climbed behind the wheel of the Austin.

As he slipped the car into gear, he wondered if his father had been happy. Maybe Des had been right about their fathers. Maybe they'd been unfaithful husbands.

God knows I don't trust my own ability to judge character after the bombshell Kate landed on me.

He gave Muriel a wave and sped away, back to the city.

Chapter 32

James stood on the deck of the *Invincible* as it cruised into the port of Gibraltar, a British Crown Colony near the tip of southern Spain. The cloudless December sky nudged the afternoon into a gentle warmth, a welcome change from the penetrating fog of the Irish Sea. Although filled with weary anticipation for a couple of days' leave ashore, James's head pounded.

For the last several weeks, the crew of the *Invincible* had been living on a few hours of sleep as they sailed south searching for subs, cruisers—any enemy presence. On edge as the ship crept south, the sailors knew that at any moment they could hit a mine, or become the target of a submarine. The sweepers accompanying them had found and detonated several mines along the way, mines that would have blown a hole the size of a train engine in the *Invincible's* hull.

James joined Leslie Harris as they made their way down the gangplank. He blinked in the brightness of the afternoon sun, shielded his aching head with a hand, and glanced sideways at the older man. "You've been here before?"

Leslie looked at James. "Many times, my boy. It's a most accommodating port of call." He donned a concerned expression. "You don't look well. You're pale."

"Headache," James answered. "It's killing me."

"Old Leslie has just the place where they know how to take away the pain." He smiled.

Gibraltar pulsed with life, streets brimming with merchants whose businesses thrived on the money of British sailors. James followed Leslie as he wound his way through throngs of people in a marketplace, lined with stalls displaying breads, meat, fine silks, and jewelry. The smell of human sweat mingled with spices and fruits in the humid air. When the merchants saw sailors coming, they hawked their wares twice as loudly, pushing melons under the men's noses, caressing their own faces with fabric.

James pushed them away, uncomfortable with it all.

Leslie, on the other hand, laughed, and stopped frequently to haggle as they made their way through narrow streets jammed with humanity.

Soon they left the crowds behind and walked through lanes lined with small houses made of cool gray rock. Leslie found his destination, climbed a short set of stairs, and smiled at James as he tapped on the door. The door cracked open and Leslie mumbled a word or two.

The door swung open, and once inside, Leslie pushed James along as they followed a thickset man down a hallway.

"What is this place?" James asked.

"It's a public bath, mate. You can take a bath, get a massage, and relax."

The man led them into a dressing room, gave a half bow, backed out, and closed the door. The air, filled with an acrid sulfur odor, felt humid and warm. Through a door, a large room held a number of sturdy beds, each divided from the other by curtains. A doorway out the opposite side led to a tile-lined pool, where a couple of heavyset men sat shoulder-deep in steaming water.

Leslie began to undress. "Take off your clothes, boy. You'll soon be forgetting about that blasted aching head of yours. First, we'll sit in the pool awhile, then you'll get to experience the ancient art of massage."

James was hesitant even to unbutton his shirt, while Leslie dropped the last of his clothes onto the floor, grabbed a towel from a pile, wrapped it around his waist, and headed toward the pool.

James undressed, took a towel, and followed. He paused at the edge of the pool as Leslie sank into the water, nodding at the men already there.

They nodded back.

"Come on, boy. It's a mineral bath, that's why it smells of sulfur. This water bubbles up from a natural spring, hot and steaming to soothe the tired bones of sailors."

James finally dropped his towel and sank into the pool. Despite the aroma, the water felt wonderful. In fact, it was the first time since standing in front of the fireplace at home that James could remember being truly warm. His knotted muscles began to relax.

Two olive-skinned boys arrived without a sound at the pool's edge, each carrying a bottle wrapped in steaming towels.

The two heavyset men climbed out of the pool, wrapped themselves in their towels, and followed the boys, bare feet slapping on the wet stone floor.

Thirty minutes ticked by before two more boys arrived.

"We're next," Leslie said.

Leslie climbed from the warmth of the pool, wrapped his towel around his waist, and followed the boys into the other room with James trailing behind. The two men each climbed onto a table, belly down. One of the boys drew the curtain between the beds.

James flinched as the boy poured warm oil onto his neck and back, but relaxed when the boy began kneading his tired muscles. The warm oil, the expert hands, and the humid air all worked together to create a tranquilizing effect. The boy's hands worked their way down his back, squeezing and rubbing the tension out of his body. By the time the boy reached his buttocks, James felt completely relaxed, headache forgotten. It felt so good, he simply allowed himself to drift away in a cloud of sensation. He lost track of time. All that mattered were the smooth, firm hands and the wonderful sensations they coaxed from his tired body.

After a while, the hands pushed him over onto his back, and poured a stream of warm oil onto his chest.

James became vaguely aware of Leslie on the other side of the curtain; his breathing had grown raspy and quick.

As the boy's smooth hands worked their way down James' chest, it seemed the most natural thing in the world that they should continue down over his belly and beyond. James felt himself grow hard beneath the expert hands.

Then the hands stopped.

James lay still, eyes closed, loins aching. After a few minutes, more warm oil dripped onto his skin, and a different pair of hands resumed where the others had left off. These hands were larger, rougher to the touch. Somewhere in James' mind a warning rang out. He almost resisted, sprang from the bed and ran, but he kept his eyes closed and ignored the impulse, subdued it until it faded away. Nothing else in the world mattered—war, fear, rolling ships, drowning men, babies killed by bombs.

All the ugliness vanished, leaving behind only his hard, urgent body, and the persistent, loving hands of Leslie Harris.

Chapter 33

The incessant drumming of rain filled the upstairs of the townhouse. Kate peeled back a corner of the thick curtain covering the window—blackout conditions imposed since the zeppelin bombing—and stared blankly out into the darkness. She had spent the better part of the last three months sitting by this window, looking out into the winter dullness of fog and rain and soot.

With great effort, she uncurled her legs from beneath her and stood, pulled her robe about her, and walked on unsteady legs across the room. She tried to look away when she passed the dressing table with its oversized mirror, but tonight she remembered too late, so she faced her reflection full on. A smattering of thin, red lines marred her pale skin, but the large, angry-looking cut along the side of her face caused her to turn away.

Des had gone out, leaving Kate and the servants alone. She didn't care, except that she had run out of powder. That, she cared about.

When she first arrived, the doctor had extracted each fragment of glass from her tender flesh, and had given her a cream-colored powder, a medicine used for to ease the pain—morphine.

Each night thereafter, Des mixed the powder into a glass of wine, and when she drank it, her aching soul didn't merely ease, it morphed into a warm cocoon of comfort, a subtle hum of well-being.

Then Des began to prepare a second glass for himself. He sipped it as he watched her—sometimes for hours—long after her mind went numb. He never touched her except for an occasional caress of her cheek or neck, but some part of her always remained aware of him there beside her, watching, and whenever he left, she always let out her breath and gave herself over to the medicinal comfort.

She heard the front door open downstairs, letting in the thunderous sound of rain, before closing. Men's voices drifted up the stairs—Des and someone else.

She hadn't wanted anything since the day Vanessa died—hadn't been curious, hadn't cared who came or who went—but tonight, for some reason, she wanted to see the visitor.

Perhaps it's Mark.

She crept out her bedroom door, partway down the stairs, and leaned over the banister, but her head swam and she sat down hard on the steps. She could hear them talking.

"What in the devil is that?" Des's voice boomed.

"A gift," said a man's unfamiliar voice.

Kate leaned forward and peered through the banister as the stranger set a heavy-looking package on the floor. "Open it," he said.

After a minute of paper rustling, Des said, "A radio?"

"A Marconi wireless." The man's voice sounded pleased. "It's the latest. They've been talking about them at the club. You can listen in on all the war chatter, and after the war, you'll be able to talk with other radio operators. It's the future."

"Sounds amusing," Des said without much enthusiasm, "but no need for you to buy a gift like this for me."

"Nonsense. You've introduced me around, made me feel at home. What do you say we set it up in the library and see how it works?"

Kate waited until they were gone, then pulled herself to her feet. She turned to climb the stairs back to her room, but her robe twisted around her legs, and she tumbled, sprawling onto the stairs with a loud thud.

A few heartbeats of dead silence were followed by the staccato of hurried footsteps.

Des arrived first, and frowned when he spotted her. Behind him came the visitor—a short man, quite lean, wearing round wire spectacles, his sparse hair combed back from his forehead.

Kate took a quick glance at the man and then looked away, but not fast enough to miss the disgust on his face.

His lips pressed together into a thin, disapproving line as he peered up at her.

She recognized him as the man she'd met downtown the day she'd been pushing Vanessa in the pram. He'd been gambling with Des.

She reached up first with one hand, then the other, and grabbed the banister to pull herself to her feet. She stared straight at Des and ignored the disturbing little man. "I don't have any more medicine," she said. "Did you bring my powders?"

Embarrassment flashed across Des's face. He turned to the man. "You'll have to excuse my houseguest. She's been through a terrible tragedy and is not quite herself."

Des turned back to her. "Kate, this is Mister Langdon Hughes. Mister Hughes, Missus James Casey."

"We've met," said the man. "A pleasure to see you again, Missus Casey."

"Go up to bed, Kate," Des said. "I'll bring your medicine up soon enough."

She started to go, but stopped. "What day is it?"

Des glanced at his guest and sighed. "It's Tuesday."

"Did you go into the office today? Did you pick up the reports?"

Langdon Hughes's eyes never left her face.

"Yes," Des answered with exaggerated patience. "Like every Tuesday."

"And Tommy. Tommy Hart." She hadn't given a thought of poor Tommy all this time, and felt ashamed that she hadn't considered him even for a second since the bombing. She remembered he had lost his glasses, and that he had been nearly blind without them. "Was he at work? Is he well?"

"The kid who does the numbers? Didn't see him. Now run upstairs."

She turned and climbed slowly, and as she went, she heard the men talk.

"A tragedy?" the guest asked.

"The dirigible bombing," Des said in a low voice. "She lost her daughter."

Kate's eyes flooded and overflowed without warning. She continued up the stairs to her bedroom and closed the door firmly behind her.

Chapter 34

James shuffled along the galley queue, a slender, pale figure. He held out his tray as one server after another smacked food onto his plate. It didn't matter what they served; it all tasted the same. He shuffled between long rows of tables, and found a spot away from the others.

Soon Leslie Harris sat down opposite him.

James glanced at the man, then dropped his gaze.

"They know," James mumbled.

Leslie tucked his napkin into his collar and took a heaping forkful of food, replying with a full mouth. "Who's they, and what do they know?"

James indicated the men who wolfed down their food elbow to elbow with a nod of his head. He leaned across the table, and mouthed the words in the barest of whispers. "They are everyone on this ship. They all know."

Leslie never skipped a beat, but kept eating. After several minutes, he glanced at James. "First of all, no one knows anything. There's no man here who's going to make accusations. No one cares, boy. Did you ever wonder if there would come a day when you would have to make a choice? Perhaps a choice between satisfying other people, like these blokes here, or yourself?"

James stared at his plate. "I never thought there would be any difference between the two."

"It's a tough world," Leslie said. "A tough war." Leslie studied him, sighed, pushed his plate away and leaned back. "Look around you, lad. Who do you see?"

James's eyes darted around the galley. "Sailors."

"That's right. And where are the officers?"

"You're an officer."

"Ah," Leslie said, leaning forward. "A warrant officer, mind you. An old sailor who hung around so long they had to do something with me. Even so, I have another place I could be eating. Where are the other officers?"

"In the officers' mess. What's your point?"

Leslie ignored the question. "And your boss, your... friend. Lord...."

"St. John. Lieutenant Mark St. John."

"Ah, yes. Lieutenant St. John. Now, where is he?"

James shrugged. "Right now? I'm not sure. He's in Intelligence."

"Now let me get this straight. You're a college boy. So is this Lieutenant St. John. Yet you're out in this bucket fighting the war while your friend sits behind a desk. Is that correct?"

"He wanted to be on a ship," James said. "He wants to fight."

"And further," Leslie continued, "you're sitting down in the galley while the officers smoke cigars and sip brandy in their dining room. Is that right?"

"Again, what is your point?"

"My point is, nobody cares about us. Nobody is going to take care of you, my boy, not the officers, not your lieutenant. Maybe not even your wife, I don't know. Mine didn't."

He leaned forward again. "No one is going to make you happy except you. There's no use living your life trying to satisfy these other blokes. They'll never be satisfied. You've got to do what makes you feel good in here." He tapped his chest. "If it don't feel right in here, it ain't worth doing, because that's where happiness comes from."

James snorted. "Happiness? I don't know what happiness is anymore."

Leslie spoke in low tones. "I think you've found some happiness, despite this bloody war. At least, I hope you have."

James looked up at the weathered face across the table. The world had gone crazy. He tried to speak—his mouth opened and closed—but nothing came out.

Leslie looked on in alarm. "Are you all right?"

A sudden look of panic passed over James's face. He began shaking his head back and forth. "Oh, God! What have I done?"

Other sailors looked over and stared as tears streamed down James's face.

Leslie came around the table in an instant, gently helping James up and out of the galley. "Get a grip, boy." He led James outside.

Out on deck, the air had cooled considerably since Gibraltar. James gripped the railing and breathed in ragged breaths, occasionally brushing his face with an impatient gesture. Leslie lit a cigarette, gave it to James, and then lit one for himself. The color had faded from the cloudless blue of day to gray. Already the sea and the sky were mingling at the edges, and soon they would be inseparable.

"Say goodbye to the blue Mediterranean," Leslie said, eyes never leaving James. "We're sailing north at a good clip, and I'd wager we'll be back in the cold, wet fog of our homeland before you can blink an eye."

James glanced at Leslie. "I love my wife, you know. We've had our problems, but I love her. I'm not cut out to be a...."

Leslie looked away and stared at the sky. "No one said you have to be anything. Sometimes, when you're in a strange port, things happen that would never happen at home. Let's leave it at that. We're mates, you and I. Friends."

James nodded, smoked until dropping the last burning embers into the sea, and with a quick glance at Leslie turned to go below deck.

Chapter 35

Lady Winifred, Muriel, Anne, and the baby came to London to visit Mark for Christmas, but the war had stifled all the festivities, and their visit turned into a disappointment. The fear of bombings and the blackout laws made dinner parties impossible, and the air raids made the three of them long for the peace of their country home. They were able to spend all of Christmas and Boxing Day with Mark, who took great joy in their company. Anne spent most of the time sitting quietly, wrapped in a shawl, watching Mark or Muriel play with the baby.

Muriel could make Anne smile, and even laugh now and again, and while Anne seemed happy at Stonebeck Hall, Mark felt troubled. Anne had barred him from her bed. He had his own room, his own bed, and on each occasion when he had visited her bedchamber, she had quietly yet firmly turned him away, fear stamped on her face. His meek little Anne had become a stubborn woman. He knew why she rejected him—the memories of childbirth—but that didn't stop the pain as he lay in his lonely bed. The day after Boxing Day, he took breakfast with them, kissed them each, and returned with relief to Room 40, where he felt he belonged.

Mark leaned back in his chair, leafing one by one through mail that had piled up during his days off—notices of meetings to attend, and new directives handed down. He sorted and scanned each memo and correspondence, but he couldn't concentrate as thoughts of Anne crowded his mind. She had never been a demonstrative woman, physically, but she had loved his attention. Now she barely looked at him, and seemed repelled by his touch. She fit in well with his mother and sister, and for that, at least, he was grateful. They formed a fine trio, a good mix with ample care and love for the baby.

His thoughts turned to Kate. He felt a mixture of sorrow for the loss of Vanessa and, for the hundredth time, disbelief at her confession, hoping it had been a lie or the confusion born of a mother's grief. If her words were true, how could she have done it? And with Des McGregor, of all people? She and James had appeared so happy together. Had that been merely an illusion?

"Did you have a good holiday?" Commander Hope broke the stream of Mark's thoughts.

Mark stood and saluted. "Yes, thank you, sir."

"Come along, I'd like to introduce you to Sir William Reginal Hall," Hope said. "Captain Hall, that is. He co-founded Room 40 with Sir Alfred Ewing."

They approached an office at the end of the hall, away from the hubbub of desks jammed together, and the general over-crowded feel of Room 40. Hope rapped on the door.

"Come," boomed a voice.

"Someone I want you to meet," Hope said as they entered. "This is Lieutenant Mark St. John."

Hall was balding on top with a fringe of white hair, an aquiline nose, and a dimpled chin. He stood, held his hand out and shook Mark's hand. "Commander Hope tells me you're sharp, fluent in German, and have taken to code like a duck to water."

"Thank you, sir. It can be frustrating, but I've always enjoyed a good challenge."

"Were you a mathematician before the war?"

"Only basic accounting. I own a shipping company, Lyman & Stonebeck. Perhaps you've heard of it."

"Of course, I have. An admirable business. And your mother must be Lady Winifred."

Abruptly, the captain's cheek twitched, then his mouth and eye joined in a series of spasms, before falling still.

"Yes, that's Mother," Mark answered, wondering if the mention of his mother had caused this odd reaction in the captain. Her presence often affected people in unexpected ways.

"Charming woman. I knew your father. My sympathies that he left us so soon."

"Thank you."

"Now, is there anything you need that you don't have?" The captain seemed oblivious to his convulsing face. "Any tools, any information, anything at all that will help you do your job?"

"I'm well equipped for now."

"Good. Let's do our jobs to put a stop to the Germans, and get you back to your business and family, shall we? Nice to meet you." The captain sat back at his desk, signaling the end of the meeting.

They stepped outside, Hope closing the door behind them, and started down the hall.

"You may have noticed," Hope began.

"I did," said Mark.

"It's chronic, that twitching face of his. Comes and goes with stress, I suppose. We call him Blinker."

Mark raised his eyebrows. "To his face?"

"In informal situations, yes. He takes it in stride. He's got bigger things on his mind than his overactive face." They reached Mark's desk. "Glad you had a good break. Now back to it, hey? The bloody Hun never take a holiday."

Mark forced his attention back to business, gathering the mail together and starting over. One paper caught his eye—a routine military ship maintenance schedule. It listed the name *Invincible*—James's ship—due in to the Devonport Naval Base at Plymouth soon. He needed to talk to James, to convince him to get Kate out of Des's house. No matter what had happened in the past, he had to get Kate away from Des. It might already be too late, but at least he could try.

Mark pulled his collar tighter about his neck, as he watched the *Invincible* ease into port. Sailors crowded the deck and, once their officers gave them the go-ahead, they poured down the plank and off the ship, dissolving into the maelstrom of the naval base. Mark searched the faces until at last he found James, who stood near the bottom of the gangplank, cupping his hands together with an older man as they both lit their cigarettes from a single flame.

They hoisted their duffel bags and walked along, puffing smoke into the moist air.

"James!" Mark walked toward them.

The two men stopped as he neared, and turned to look.

"James," Mark said as he caught up to them. "I saw the *Invincible* was scheduled in, and I hoped to see you."

James sat his duffel on the ground, stuck the cigarette in his mouth, and shook Mark's hand. "What a surprise."

The older man stuck his hand out. "Harris is the name. Warrant Officer Leslie Harris." He shook Mark's hand firmly. "You must be Lieutenant St. John. James has told me all about you."

"Warrant Officer Harris, nice to meet you. Let's find a pub, shall we? Drinks are on me." He led them up to the street where he had parked the Austin.

Leslie Harris whistled, and glanced at James. "She's a beauty, Lieutenant. A real beauty."

Mark ran his hand over the hood and wiped off an imaginary smudge. "Kind of you to say so."

The three climbed in, and Mark drove to a little pub far enough away from the base to avoid being filled with sailors.

When they each had a pint before them, Mark turned to James. "How's it going out there?"

James shrugged. "As well as can be expected."

Mark sat forward, leaning on the table. "How's Kate?"

James shifted restlessly and lit a cigarette. "I should be asking you that question. You're the one here in London. I haven't heard from her since... since the funeral."

"Six months? That's a long time. I'm worried about both of you."

Leslie held up an empty pint. "Think I'll head to the bar for my next, and let you gents talk."

Mark waited until Leslie was out of earshot. "I don't think Kate should stay at Des's house any longer."

"Why not?"

"I don't trust him."

James looked puzzled. "He's your business partner, and you don't trust him?"

"Look, James, Des's family and mine go a long way back. That's why he's my business partner, and it works because he stays out of the business, or at least he did before the war. So, yes, he's my business partner, and no, I don't trust him. Talk to Kate, will you? We'll find another place for her to live."

James stuck a cigarette in his mouth, inhaled deeply, and squinted at Mark through the smoke. "Frankly, I can't see any difference between the generosity that Des has extended to Kate after our tragedy, and the generosity you showed us by renting us your house. Without you, we'd have been stuck in a tiny flat. Now Des is allowing Kate to stay at one of his houses—a property that he owns. He's being extremely generous, and I'm in his debt, as I am in yours."

Mark felt like shaking James. If Kate's confession was true, James was expressing gratitude to the very man who had made a cuckold of him. But James looked exhausted, thin... like a twig that would snap if the wind blew too hard. He couldn't bring himself to tell another man that kind of news.

He shrugged. "I would feel better if I could help out, that's all. Talk her into staying at my house. The servants will look after her. I'm never there. I have a flat a few blocks away from my office now. When you see her, will you please convince her to go to my house?"

The conversation stopped when Leslie returned and sat down, ale in hand. "Let's drink a toast, shall we, mates?" He looked from one glum face to the other. "Come on, you two, no time to be down, not when you've found a nice pub and have a few days' leave. Let's have a toast to... let me see... how about Naval Intelligence?"

Mark raised his eyebrows.

"We want you chaps to do your jobs and do them well to keep our arses from getting blown out of the water. Don't we now, James?"

Mark slowly raised his glass. "We do our best."

James stayed the night at Mark's new flat, and the next morning took a cab to 1410 Hampshire Boulevard—Des's townhouse. He stood across the street and stared for a long time before finally working up the courage to knock on the door.

"Madam, please wake up. You must come downstairs. Please, madam, wake up," the butler, Duncan, pleaded with her from the other side of the bedroom door.

Kate struggled to gather herself together, struggled to coax her legs out from under the covers and onto the floor. She grabbed her robe from the foot of the bed, shrugged into it, stood, shuffled to the door, and opened it a crack, suspicious. The servants usually avoided her.

"What is it, Duncan?"

"There's a gentleman here to see you. Your husband, Mister Casey."

"James?"

"Shall I tell him you're on your way down?"

"Yes, please. I'll be down in a few minutes."

She closed the door and walked over to the dressing table, and picked up a brush. As she raised it to her hair, she looked at her dismal reflection in the mirror. She didn't want to see James, didn't want him to see her like this, but she couldn't hurt him any more than she already had. With deliberate resolve, she ran the brush through her tangled hair.

When Kate finally got downstairs, James sat in the same Louis XVI chair in which he'd sat after Vanessa's funeral. She stood in the doorway and watched him. When he looked up, he couldn't conceal his obvious astonishment, no doubt because the cuts on her face weren't healing well.

He stood. "Kate."

"Hello, James." She walked past him over to the window, and stared out into the garden.

"Are you seeing a doctor, Kate? Your injuries...."

She raised her hand to her face. "I saw a doctor at first, I think. I really don't remember."

A maid, whose name Kate couldn't think of, shuffled in with a tray of tea and scones, carefully avoiding looking directly at either Kate or James.

"May we have tea in the garden?" James asked. "It's not too cold out."

The maid nodded, picked up the tray, and walked toward the French doors that opened to the outside. James rushed to open it for her, but the door stuck and it took some force to pop it open.

"If you don't mind, sir," said the maid, nodding toward a far corner of the courtyard. "There's a table and chairs stacked over there. They're heavy, made of iron, and haven't been used for some time."

James retrieved the pedestal table and four chairs one by one, setting them up in the center of a stone patio surrounded by a tall, ivy-clad stone wall, the perimeter lined with rosebushes and maple trees.

The maid set the tray on the table, produced a white towel from her apron pocket, and dusted the table and chairs. "Anything else, sir?"

"No. You've been very kind...." He hesitated. "I'm sorry, I don't know your name."

"Hillary, sir," she said, and blushed. "They call me Hilly."

"You've been more than kind, Hillary. Did you make the scones yourself?"

"No, sir. Cook did. Missus Cooper. We don't have company often, so mostly she cooks just for us, and now for the Missus," she said, nodding at Kate. "Although she eats like a bird."

"Thank Missus Cooper for us, will you?"

"Yes, sir." She dropped an awkward curtsy, and hurried back inside the house, closing the reluctant door behind her.

James pulled out a chair for Kate, scraping it across the slate patio floor. Kate sat and allowed him to scoot her forward. He poured the tea and joined her.

They sipped their tea in silence. Finally, when the shadows stretched over the garden, James stood. He bent down and kissed the top of Kate's head, like a father to a child. He helped her out of her chair, and placed her hand on his bent arm. He opened the troublesome door and led her inside.

She stood at the bottom of the stairs as James let himself out.

He returned the next day, and the next, and they repeated the long, silent garden ritual, until his leave was up.

"I'll be back again when I can," he said on the final day, holding her gently. "Please heal, my love."

Chapter 36

In May, the *Invincible* sailed through the English Channel and the Strait of Dover, heading for a place called Skagerrak Strait in the arm of the North Sea, and off the coast of Norway. There, they joined a convergence of Naval power that included four other battle cruisers and twenty-two battleships. Something big was brewing.

Mark and his colleagues in Room 40 spent the days monitoring the wireless traffic, as usual. They never knew which tidbit of information would be important, and add to the growing body of knowledge about the German fleet. Recent chatter had indicated a strong buildup of Germany's High Seas Fleet in the North Sea, and that information had been communicated up the chain of Naval authority. At 9:06 that night, the Room 40 staff deciphered a German message: *C.-in-C. to Airship Detachment: "Early morning reconnaissance at Horns Riff is urgently requested."* The message, sent to the fleet's commander-in-chief, gave away their intended route.

Mark handed the message to Commander Hope, who in turn fired it off to Admiral Oliver, his usual contact. As the night passed, they intercepted and deciphered six other messages, all indicating the position of the German fleet, and ultimately pinpointing the juncture of assembly of all German flotillas: 2:00 a.m. at Horns Reef.

The men of Room 40 took pride in knowing their hard-earned and accurate information would make it to Fleet commanders in time to save the men at sea.

Admiral Oliver, evaluating intelligence he had received over the previous several weeks, drew an entirely different conclusion. He sent a message to his superior that said, "No definite news of enemy...

Apparently, they have been unable to carry out air reconnaissance, which has delayed them."

Persuaded that no urgent situation was eminent, the destroyers, which had been powering at high speed toward Horns Reef, slowed.

The *Invincible* cruised at a steady 25 knots toward Skagerrak Strait. Its original design as an armored cruiser, with a heavy main armament and steam turbines to produce high speed, enabled the *Invincible* to slice through the water like an iron shark. Speed, however, had its price, as they'd engineered it with a thinner armor to create a lighter, faster ship.

The *Invincible* firepower included eight 12-inch guns, sixteen 4-inch guns, and four torpedo tubes. James's duties included feeding ammunition to one of the 12-inch guns. The crew had been told to expect engagement with the enemy sometime within the next twenty-four hours.

James stood on the starboard foredeck as the ship thrust through the sea, spray stinging his eyes as he peered ahead, probing the steel-gray wall of fog for any indication of the enemy. Late in the afternoon, he spotted them, and the sight that met his eyes made every muscle in his body contract in astonishment—only 7,000 yards away sailed an entire German battle squadron. He nearly fell down in shock, and almost immediately, the salvo began.

The air erupted with the deafening shriek of shells. The water next to the *Invincible* boiled under the German assault. The gunner screamed at James to man his post, and he jumped into position, concentrating on feeding the ammo as the gun came to life. All the guns on the ship now fired in a deafening roar.

James worked mechanically, forcing himself to focus on his task, and to ignore his racing pulse and ragged breath. A shell exploded behind him, tearing a hole in the deck, followed by another, then another. The deck heaved with every hit, but James remained locked in position, feeding ammo.

Below the surface of the water, a volley of torpedoes streamed toward the *Invincible* with deadly accuracy.

The first torpedo pierced the armor of the bow. On deck, the explosion felt muted, a dull quivering in the bowels of the ship. Yet explosion after explosion shook the ship as more torpedoes found their mark. Water burst through the fissures created by the blasts, and soon the ship began to list to the starboard side.

The sailor next to James fell against him, and a split second later, a shell exploded, knocking James flat on his back. Stunned, he couldn't move. The ship lurched to starboard, and he felt a weight upon his right side, and a wet warmth; the sailor who had fallen lay half on top of him. James grabbed the man by both shoulders and gently pushed him aside, but the man felt oddly light. Then James saw that the man's legs were gone, and he turned his head to the side and wretched. He then surrendered to a welcome blackness.

Leslie Harris had seen James go down when the shell hit. He lurched along the deck, ducked flying debris, and pushed his way to James. He hooked his unconscious mate beneath the arms and dragged him toward the lifeboats.

Leslie fought his way onto a skiff already packed with sailors, lowered James into outstretched hands, and climbed in himself. They lowered the lifeboat, which pitched and reeled against the hull, and finally dropped the last ten feet into the sea.

Once in the water, as chaos exploded around them, the able-bodied grabbed oars and rowed away from the sinking ship.

The Battle of Jutland, as it would come to be called, cost the British Navy three battle cruisers, three armored cruisers, eight destroyers, and 6,097 men.

Chapter 37

A knock came at Kate's bedroom door, followed by Duncan's voice, sounding odd and urgent. He said that Mr. Casey and a guest were downstairs.

James home... again?

She uncurled herself from the chair in front of the window, moving as if underwater, then slipped off the robe and pulled a dress from a wardrobe stocked with clothes she never wore. She stepped into shoes, ran a brush through her hair, and went downstairs.

James sat in a wheelchair, and an older man looked up from tucking a blanket around him when Kate walked in the room.

A fleeting expression of surprise crossed his face. "Missus Casey, I'm Warrant Officer Harris. I'm a mate of your husband's."

Kate barely nodded at the man, unable to take her eyes off James. His complexion had gone gray, and he didn't acknowledge her presence. He sat slump-shouldered, gaze unfocused, eyes glassy, with his mouth hung open.

"I'm afraid he's had rather a bad time," Leslie said. "Our ship is sunk and... perhaps you might want to sit down?"

"No." Kate's voice trembled. "Go on."

"I'm sorry to have to tell you that your husband has lost a leg."

Her thoughts jumbled. "A leg?"

He reached down and pulled the blanket from James's lap. His left leg stopped above the knee, encased in a bulk of surgical dressing.

Kate felt dizzy.

"He's a lucky man," Leslie continued. "A shell exploded not three meters away from him. Another man took the brunt of it."

Kate found a chair and sank into it. "What cruel fate would kill my baby and do this to James?" she murmured, dazed.

Leslie froze, looked at James, and back to Kate. "Forgive me for being so thoughtless," he said slowly. "I'm truly sorry for your troubles. Your husband is hurt and needs tending. I don't want to bother you, but the nurses at the hospital trained me to clean and change his dressing and take care of his needs. Your husband is a good friend, Missus Casey. I would be grateful if you would let me visit each day and attend to him."

"Visit?"

"Yes. He's home now, for good, and I have been granted leave for a month."

"Home?"

"Yes, home." Leslie frowned. "This is where you live, isn't it? And you'll be keeping him here with you, won't you?"

It took a few moments for the words to sink in—James... injured... had been dismissed from the war permanently... needed to be taken care of. He needed to come home, and they were in the only home they had—Des's house. Kate wondered how Des would react to this turn of events, and decided in the same instant that she didn't care. If he kicked James out on the street, she would go with him.

"In that case," she said, "I would be grateful, Mister..."

"Harris. Leslie Harris. For now, is there a room that could be made up for him?" The man had kind eyes.

Kate struggled to collect her thoughts, to think hard about what she needed to do. "I'll have the sitting room made up on this floor so we won't have to worry about the stairs to the bedrooms."

Duncan, Hilly, and Leslie Harris carried a bed downstairs to the sitting room, and the men went back for the mattress while Hilly gathered sheets and blankets.

Des didn't appear that night, and after James had been tucked into bed, Kate mixed her own powders and drank the mixture down. She couldn't sleep without them anymore.

The next morning, she woke late, her body a dead weight, her mind groggy. Then she remembered James, and climbed out of bed. She moved to the chair by the window, pulled back the blackout curtain, and squinted down at the garden below as the sun streamed into her room.

As she watched, the older man....

What was his name? Leslie.

Leslie wheeled James outside, stopped the wheelchair in a shady spot beneath a maple tree, and tucked a blanket about James. He smoothed James's hair back away from his face, leaned down, and gave her husband a gentle kiss on the forehead.

Kate leaned forward, now wide awake.

Leslie pulled up a chair close to James and opened a book. She couldn't hear the man's voice, but could see that he began to read aloud to James. He paused every now and again to fuss with the blanket, and to turn the wheelchair to keep the sun out of James's blank, staring eyes.

Kate watched Leslie's every move. After a while, she sat back in her chair, considered what she had witnessed, and pondered this new turn of events.

James home, grievously wounded. Leslie Harris, caring for James so tenderly. And Des. What will Des have to say when he arrives home to find James and another man under his roof?

The inevitable arrival of Des took place the next day at noon. He took the stairs two at a time to Kate's room, only to find it empty. Duncan stood at the bottom of the stairs as Des came pounding back down.

"Mister and Missus Casey, along with their Royal Naval officer friend, are in the garden, I believe," Duncan said. "May I bring you some tea?"

Des stared at the butler. "Mister Casey? A friend? What the hell are you talking about?"

Without waiting for an answer, Des stormed out the French doors to the garden.

James, with an afghan draped around his shoulders and a blanket covering his lap, sat staring, while a tough-looking older fellow sat on one side reading from a book.

Kate sat on James's other side, face turned up to the sun, eyes closed.

"What the hell is all this?"

Kate's eyes flew open and she stood, as did Leslie. "Hello, Des," Kate said evenly. "I'd like you to meet Warrant Officer Leslie Harris. He brought James home."

Leslie gave a quick nod toward Des, but didn't take a step away from James's side. "Sir," he said.

Des stared at James. "What's wrong with him?"

"He's sustained injuries in a battle at sea," Leslie answered.

"James has lost a leg," Kate said quietly.

"And his senses, by the looks of him." Des stood a moment longer, then turned and walked back into the house.

He poured himself a brandy and drank it down in one swallow, then refilled his glass and returned to the door outside, where he simply leaned against the frame.

"My apologies," Kate said, chin rising slightly. "It seems we find ourselves in an awkward situation. If you'll bear with us for a short while, we'll return your home to you."

Des looked at her through narrowed eyes. "What does that mean?"

"We are moving out, James and I. We'll leave you in peace."

Des actually smiled. "Where will you go? You have no money, no means to live, to say nothing of the expensive little habit you've developed."

Kate's whole body wavered. She glanced briefly at Leslie, who, instead of looking shocked or disapproving, gave her a subtle nod of encouragement.

"Don't trouble yourself with any thoughts about me," she said.

"Don't trouble myself," Des repeated. "Sage advice, Missus Casey. Sage advice."

He pushed himself off the doorframe, set his empty glass on a table as he passed through the sitting room — which apparently had become a bedroom — and slammed out the front door.

Kate and Leslie looked at one another, then sat back down next to James. Leslie resumed reading until Duncan interrupted them, announcing dinner.

Dinner for James consisted of soup broth, which Leslie tried, without much success, to spoon into James's slack mouth.

Kate watched in dismay, with no stomach at all for her own soup, not to mention the chicken and dumplings that cook had prepared.

Leslie had no compunction about spooning a mouthful to James, then enjoying several bites of his own meal. "One of my favorites, chicken and dumplings," he said as Kate watched.

After dinner, Duncan assisted Leslie in whisking James away to be cleaned, toileted, put in pajamas, and tucked into bed.

Kate hovered nearby but out of sight, grateful for these two men for taking care of her poor, broken husband.

In Room 40, Mark stood and stretched. He had been at his desk since seven in the morning, and although it was nearly nine at night, the room still hummed with activity. Waste baskets overflowed with crumpled paper, and ashtrays heaped with ash sat beneath air thick with smoke and sweat.

The French had lost thousands upon thousands on the western front, and the British waters were crawling with U-boats. The British were losing more military vessels than the enemy, and to make matters worse, the Germans were sinking civilian vessels with abandon. Along with the pressure to perform, morale had been dismal since the Jutland fiasco, when the information they'd intercepted could have saved lives, but hadn't.

Mark picked up the next intercepted message. As he skimmed it, his heart began to pound. The page held a list of names, dates, and times. He had seen these names hundreds of times. It was a shipping schedule, and the list—the ships and the timetables—were quite familiar. The shipping schedule came from Lyman & Stonebeck.

The signature below the message read: *der Spazierstock.* The Walking Stick.

Chapter 38

Kate stood across the street from Lyman & Stonebeck, pale, and nearly swallowed up in a black wool coat. Her brain felt as thick as the rain that poured down on the city, and her hands shook. She hadn't ventured outside the townhouse since Vanessa's funeral. She waited for a couple of cars to pass by, then stepped off the curb to cross the street. Her black leather shoes, the same shoes she had worn on the afternoon of the airship attack, splashed through the puddles as she walked toward the office.

"Kate!" Mr. Bridger took off his reading glasses and stood when she appeared in his office.

"Mister Bridger." She hugged him.

When she stepped back, she could see him examining her face. The cuts were healing, but still red.

"Kate, girl," he said, afraid to say anything else.

"How is everything here?"

He pulled a handkerchief from his pocket and wiped the lenses of his glasses. "Not good right now. We've lost another ship, Kate. Lost men. Those bloody Huns must have known it were a merchant ship, not a military vessel they were shooting at, but they didn't care. Security is tight." He shook his head and sighed a long, lasting breath. "Things have changed."

"How is Tommy Hart?"

"When you two were caught in the bombing, he got glass fragments in his eyes. Both eyes hemorrhaged—nearly blinded him—but we cannot get the boy to stay away from work. He helps out wherever he can. The doctors think his eyes may heal, so we're waiting until he can see well enough to read the numbers again."

Kate stared. *Poor Tommy.* She'd been so wrapped-up in her own grief she hadn't thought of anyone else.

"Come to dinner," Mr. Bridger said. "Missus Bridger misses you something terrible."

"Thank you. Please tell her hello for me." She took a deep breath. "Mister Bridger, James is home."

"On leave, is he?"

"I'm afraid not. He's been wounded in battle. He's lost a leg, and he's... well, shell-shocked. We're hoping he comes out of it. The doctors say he may, in time."

"My poor dear, I'm so sorry."

"I don't know if you're aware of it, but since we lost Vanessa, and with James being away most of the time, Lord McGregor has let me stay at his house."

Mr. Bridger pulled at his ear. "Aye... uh... I did hear something about that."

"Mister Bridger, if I could get work, I've already got a little money saved, and James will be getting a modest pension, we would be able to rent our own flat." She searched his face.

"My dear, if you want your job back, it's yours. I would have to get approval from Lord St. John or Lord McGregor, but that won't be a problem."

Kate shook her head. "I need a fresh start. I don't want to be anywhere near...." She stopped. "May I give your name as a reference when I apply for jobs? You know I've handled all the paperwork in the office. What I don't know, I can learn."

"You're welcome to use me as a reference. I'll have a letter written up. Not only that, but I'll check around to see if someone needs a good office hand. I'm sure something will turn up. With so many men away, there's a need."

She held a hand out to him. "Thank you."

He took her hand. "No thanks necessary. You know that."

A few days after Leslie Harris's arrival, Kate decided she needed to stop taking the powders, at least for now. She wanted to be clear-headed, and needed to awaken earlier in the day to look after James. A full brown bottle of powders sat on the dresser. She picked it up, took it to the wardrobe and placed it carefully into a red purse, then snapped the clasp closed and placed it high on the shelf. She felt safe knowing it was there.

The first night she abstained, she didn't sleep at all. Her head pounded without relief.

Somehow, she made it downstairs the next morning, and found James and Leslie in the courtyard, in their usual spots--James in his wheelchair, Leslie sitting at the table next to him.

Kate collapsed into a chair, queasy.

"Top of the morning," Leslie said, then noticed her pale countenance. "Are you ill, Missus?"

"I'm afraid I must be coming down with the influenza," she said weakly. "I didn't sleep last night, and I have a dreadful headache."

"Let me fix you a piece of milk toast." Leslie stood.

"No thank you, Mister Harris. I can't eat a thing."

She tried her best to linger with the men but, at Leslie's insistence, she climbed the stairs and returned to bed.

Sleep came in short spurts and her body moved restlessly, twisting the sheets into a jumble. She awoke in the dark sweating and aching, frustrated that illness should arrive just when James needed her.

It was nearly noon the next day by the time she dragged herself down to the courtyard. She dropped into the chair and attempted a weak smile. "How is he doing today?"

Leslie looked at her and frowned. "Maybe better than you."

She met his gaze, startled at the knowing she saw in his eyes. It dawned on her that perhaps she didn't have influenza after all. Could this illness be what the powders had wrought? Could their absence create pain and sickness, in place of numb comfort?

"Don't worry, Missus," Leslie whispered as Kate shivered in the garden chair. "This will pass. It will take time, but this, too, shall pass. And old Leslie's here to look after you."

He stood and disappeared, and returned shortly with a cup of tea and a glass of water for her.

"Thank you." She sipped the water but ignored the tea. "Where are you staying at night?"

"A little flat I found that rents by the night."

"Stay here," she said. "We'll make the divan into a bed for you, so you can be near James."

"Thank you, but I don't think Lord McGregor would be pleased."

"We need you, both James and I. Don't worry about Des," she said softly, but the palms of her hands began to sweat as she spoke.

The old sailor looked at her, and then to James, and smiled. "By all means, I'll stay."

The first two weeks were torment as each night Kate fought a battle within herself. She wanted one drink of the powders, a sip to ease the pain, but each night she promised herself that she wouldn't give in. She had to be there for James. She had to be there for Vanessa, although that was crazy—Vanessa had been taken from her. It didn't make sense, but it got her through the nights.

During the worst times, she wondered if James felt pain and suffering, as she felt, or if his mind had totally vacated the premises. If so, she envied him that.

When she began to feel a little better, Leslie taught her how to care for James—changing the bandage on James's stump, feeding him. It gave her something to concentrate on besides how wretched she felt.

Leslie watched as she attempted to spoon soup into James's slack mouth, her own hand trembling so badly that much of the broth ended up on his chest.

Whereas Duncan and Hilly had avoided Kate before, now they began to help, unbidden. Hilly brought sandwiches and tea outside. She collected soiled clothing and returned it the next day, crisp and clean. Duncan helped lift James into and out of the wheelchair, and hovered in the house, watching out the window at the odd trio in the garden.

All too soon, Leslie's month of leave elapsed. He was being assigned to a new ship. The last thing he showed Kate was where he had left off in the latest Charles Dickens novel.

Touched by this tough yet tender man, when the time came for his departure, she left him alone to say his goodbyes to James.

Leslie's departure left a void. His constant, cheerful presence had brought optimism to the house, and his absence was sorely felt.

Kate took over nursing James, and in a strange way, it almost felt like caring for Vanessa. She fed him one spoonful of soup at a time, dabbing his chin when the broth dribbled. She wheeled him into the courtyard every morning, and would read to him for hours each day, picking up where Leslie had left off. She no longer spent long, dark hours in bed, trying to block out life.

Duncan helped without being asked, attending to the delicate matters of hygiene for James, earning Kate's gratitude for his quiet kindness.

"Fresh air is an important ingredient for health," Duncan announced one afternoon, when the sun warmed the slate tiles of the courtyard and Kate had grown weary of reading aloud. "And exercise is the other. It's a lovely day for a stroll."

He gently lifted James from his chair, wrapped James's left arm around his own shoulders, hung on to James's left hand while wrapping his right arm behind James's back, and began to walk. He pulled James forward as if pulling a weed from the garden.

At first, James stayed put, but with continued pressure, he yielded. Duncan stepped forward with James leaning on him, right leg left behind where it had started, and Kate feared they would both topple to the ground. James leaned harder onto Duncan, bent his knee, and took a step.

And they were off.

From that moment on, every day, twice a day, they tottered around the perimeter of the courtyard like a couple of happy drunks careening down the street, arms about one other.

Then, only two weeks after they had begun their walking routine, Duncan procured a crutch and brought it to the garden.

"No, Duncan," Kate cried. She put down some mending she'd been doing and stepped out of earshot of James. "He won't be able to use it."

The butler put one finger to his lips, and walked over to James. "Mister Casey, time for our walk."

James, expressionless, stood.

Kate gasped, and Duncan smiled. "We're trying something a bit different this morning, sir," Duncan said, and slipped the crutch under James's left arm. He wrapped James's fingers around the handgrip and patted them into place. He then wrapped his right arm around James's shoulders, cemented the crutch between them, and began walking.

James leaned on the crutch and took a step.

"That's right, sir. Very good."

Duncan took a step, and James leaned on the crutch and stepped. Over and over, they repeated the process, and soon they'd plodded a quarter of the way around the courtyard.

Kate watched, hands covering her mouth in worry and hope.

They made it full circle, and Duncan took the crutch from James and lowered him back into his wheelchair.

Kate clapped her hands together. "Bravo, James! You did it!"

"You certainly did, sir," added Duncan. "Admirably done."

James stared straight ahead, but Kate could have sworn that something about his countenance changed.

They repeated the routine in the afternoon, and again the next morning. Only this time, after they'd been walking about twenty minutes, Duncan quietly stepped away. James wobbled a bit, and Duncan's hands were close by to prevent a fall.

Kate gasped, watching with hands clasped over her mouth once again, forgetting, for an instant, the dull ache of mourning Vanessa, and the constant longing for the solace of the powders.

Without Duncan's guidance, James continued to walk—lean, step, lean, step—but he weaved a circle instead of walking a straight line. Round and round he thumped, as if the crutch were a fulcrum. Duncan rejoined him, resting his hand on James's shoulder to straighten the path, and they resumed their walk.

As the days passed in the same routine, the daily exercise seemed to be repairing the broken connections in James's nervous system. While his gaze remained unfocused, he stood or sat when asked, and chewed when fed. His mouth no longer hung open as it had upon his arrival home.

One afternoon, right in the middle of The Pickwick Papers, Kate stopped reading, distracted by a striking orange-colored butterfly flitting past, and when she looked back to James, he was leaning forward in his chair, seeming to urge the story to continue. Surprised and encouraged, she resumed reading.

The next day, she concentrated on mending a pair of his trousers so the leg wouldn't hang down past his stump. She glanced up and found him gazing right at her, face relaxed, like the old James. She dropped her sewing.

"James!" She sat forward and put a hand on his arm, but his eyes didn't follow her when she moved. She searched for the spark she knew she'd seen, but he stared past her. She sighed and picked up her sewing.

"Sorry," James croaked, voice rusty for lack of use.

Kate abandoned her sewing and dropped to her knees in front of him, grasping his hands in hers. "James, oh, James, are you back?"

"Sorry," he mumbled again, still staring sightlessly. "Sorry."

"It's all right." She answered every "sorry," tears falling on their joined hands. "I'm here, and there's no need to be sorry."

That night, long after she had tucked James in, the house dark and quiet, she lay in bed unable to sleep. She needed to make a plan, to find a way to make enough money so that she and James could afford a place of their own. He wouldn't be returning to work soon, that much was certain.

A sound interrupted her thoughts. Uneven footsteps pounded up the stairs and stopped outside her door.

"Duncan?" She sat up, holding the covers to her chest.

The bedroom door opened.

Des leaned against the doorframe, jacket buttoned one button off, hair a mess, as if he had run his hand around in circles on his head. "Were you asleep?" His words slurred.

Kate's skin crawled, and she held her breath.

He closed the door behind him, leaned heavily against it, then pushed off, reeling toward her bed. "Brought your medicine, my beautiful Kate."

She could smell the drink on his breath, and the cigar smoke that clung to him. She shrank back as he sat on the side of the bed, picked up her hand, raised it to his lips and kissed it.

She pulled her hand out of his grasp and turned it over, palm up. "Give me the medicine." She had quit the powders, but he didn't know that.

He grinned and dropped a brown bottle full of powdery comfort into her hand. "It's been too long since we've made love," he slurred.

Kate tensed and closed her hand over the bottle. "No, Des. What time is it?"

His easy manner vanished. "No? I don't believe you have a choice, madam. You are, after all, under my roof, to say nothing of indebted to me."

Fully awake and wary, she said, "I owe you nothing. You've taken more from me than you could ever repay. You used me all along for your selfish reasons."

"I used *you*?" he said, voice incredulous. "My dear, you were an open book to me from the first day we met. I never forced you."

"I was a child! I made a terrible mistake."

"You loved me between your legs." He made a sloppy attempt to reach beneath the covers and thrust his hand into intimate places, but Kate scooted away from him. His expression darkened, and he reached out and grabbed her upper arm, fingers sinking into her flesh, and pulled her back across the bed to him. He kissed her hard, teeth bruising her lips, and rolled over on top of her, pushing her onto her back.

Panic filled Kate as she struggled to get away, but he pinned her hard to the bed. She had to do something now.

"Yes," she said breathlessly.

Des stopped.

Kate placed her hands on his hips and drew him to her.

His expression changed to triumphant, and he pulled back and began to unbutton his trousers.

With his weight eased off her, Kate slid away, jumped out of bed, and lunged toward the fireplace. She grabbed the poker and pointed it toward Des like a sword. "Get out."

He seemed confused by the sudden turn of events, and his eyes darkened. "*You* get out! Take your bloody war hero husband and get the hell out of my house! Do you hear me?" He stumbled off the bed, attempting to button his trousers as he lurched toward the bedroom door. "All my luck has gone sour. At the club, at cards...." He stopped trying to button his trousers long enough to wave one hand in her direction. "With you! I saved you, and this is the thanks I get. You'll be sorry, you... ungrateful whore. You'll curse the day you crossed me." He staggered out of the room and slammed the door behind him.

Kate stood shaking. She dropped the fireplace poker and walked to her dressing table, picked up the chair, and propped it against the door, wedging it beneath the knob.

She backed away, staring, afraid he might return, but heard a door close down the hall. Maybe he had gone to bed and passed out. She could only hope. Frozen in fear, the minutes ticked past, and the house remained silent.

At last, she let out a breath, walked back to the fireplace, and reached down to pick up the poker. There on the floor lay the little brown bottle of powders. Hand trembling, she picked it up, unscrewed the cap, held it close to her nose, and inhaled the medicinal perfume of bliss. An overwhelming sense of longing gripped her, and she imagined pouring powder into a glass, filling it with wine, stirring with a spoon, and drinking it down. Euphoria followed by sleep. Blissful sleep.

Hands trembling, she replaced the lid, walked to the wardrobe, opened the door, reached up and plucked the red purse from its hiding place. She opened the clasp and dropped the bottle inside, where it clanked against the other bottles. She snapped the purse closed and replaced it on the shelf.

Sleep be damned.

Chapter 39

After Des's dangerous visit, Kate knew she had to find a way to get herself and James out of there. The next morning, after telling Duncan she had to go out, she took the list of businesses that Mr. Bridger had given her and set out to apply for jobs.

One thing she could say about Mr. Bridger: he had a diverse number of business acquaintances. She applied at a haberdashery, a bakery, even a toy shop. One by one, the proprietors shook their heads. Business was lousy, no work to be had.

After the sixth rejection, she stood on the sidewalk, discouraged. She had to find a means to independence. She had saved all the money James had sent home — all his pay from the Navy. She could use that to rent a flat initially, but they needed a steady income, and she had to provide that income until James got better. She didn't want to go to work in a munitions factory, like Lucy, and she couldn't return to Lyman & Stonebeck because Des would find her.

She started toward home, stopping at the window of a women's dress shop out of old habit. As she studied the fashions behind the display windows, she got an idea. On impulse, she went into the shop. With the help of Mr. Bridger's letter of recommendation, and the deposit of a modest sum of money to secure the return of a few dresses waiting for alterations, she convinced the woman to give her a chance to do the work. Along with the deposit, she offered to do the alterations for free, to prove both her trustworthiness and seamstress skills.

Kate hurried home, settled in the courtyard next to James with her sewing basket, and began mending. Her idea took form as she worked. She would begin by mending for as many shops as she could find, and after she gained their trust, she would bring out her own designs. She had experience in memorizing the dresses at Harrods, and could craft duplicates for herself. More importantly, she knew she could create original designs. She would convince the dress shops to buy the beautiful dresses that she made for a higher price than mending would bring.

It could work. It has to work.

The next morning, hours before she took the dresses back to the shop, Kate decided to make breakfast for James. Hilly had taken to bringing him a bowl of porridge each morning, but Kate decided he needed something more to help him get well. Thanks to Mrs. Shaunessy—a surprising thought, indeed—she knew her way around a kitchen. Food had become even more difficult to get, and crazily expensive during the war, but Des's kitchen somehow remained stocked with remarkable items, like eggs.

She positioned James in his wheelchair at the dining table on the main floor.

"Don't go away." She leaned down and kissed his forehead. "I'm coming back with breakfast."

She skipped down the stairs to the kitchen, where an immense stove stood at the ready, plucked an apron from its hook and tied it around her waist. She opened cupboards and searched until she found a heavy iron skillet, then found some lard.

"What are you doing at my stove, Missus?"

Kate whirled around. A heavyset woman with gray hair peeking out from beneath a cap stood in the doorway, frowning.

Kate remembered Mrs. Shaunessy with a twinge of unease. "You must be the cook, Missus..." She couldn't recall the woman's name.

"Cooper," the woman said. "And you must be Lord McGregor's houseguest. I never set eyes on you before." The tone of her voice conveyed her opinion of the Lord having a live-in female guest.

"Yes." Kate wasn't going to let this woman's sour attitude diminish her enthusiasm for preparing James a good breakfast. "You'll have to excuse my intrusion. I'm preparing breakfast for my husband. Might I have some eggs? And I recall a breakfast of lovely brown bread and marmalade. May I have some?"

The cook seemed to consider the request, then disappeared, returning a few moments later with the requested items. "Ain't easy to come by, eggs, during these hard times."

"Thank you so much," Kate said. "We'll savor them. I'll be out of your kitchen in no time."

Kate cracked four eggs into the skillet and, while they sizzled, placed the bread and marmalade onto a tray. She flipped the eggs, scooped them from the skillet, and slid them onto two plates—three eggs for James, one for her. She wiped her hands on her apron before untying it, and returned it to its hook while the cook watched.

Kate put plates, silverware, napkins, and tea on a tray. "Thank you, Missus Cooper."

She backed out of the kitchen, pushing the kitchen door open with her derriere, as the cook made no move to help. She climbed the stairs to the dining room, where she had left James sitting.

"Breakfast, dear," she said.

"Sorry," he said, sitting erect and staring ahead.

"I brought marmalade this morning. Your favorite." She set a plate in front of him and spooned marmalade onto his bread.

"Sorry," he repeated.

She tucked a napkin about his neck, picked up a fork, placed it in his left hand, wrapped his fingers around it, and guided his fork to the plate.

He took over from there, lifting the fork to his mouth. Like a good soldier, he chewed.

She pulled her own chair next to him, and took bites of her own breakfast while watching him, sometimes taking the edge of his napkin and dabbing bits of food from his chin.

"You have a good appetite this morning."

"Sorry," he said.

"I have to go out again today. When I get back, I'll have lots of sewing to do, so Duncan may have to read to us both. I bought a new book for us by an American author named Willa Cather. It's called O Pioneers! Doesn't that sound interesting?"

"Ah," James said.

Kate stared at him, surprised at this new sound.

"Ah mare can," James said slowly.

She shook her head, and then realized what he was saying. "Yes! American! She's an American author."

Encouraged by his expanding vocabulary, she hoped to see some other sign of consciousness. She stared into his eyes, but his gaze focused off to an unseen landscape while he chewed his breakfast slowly.

She sat back, fighting disappointment. After all, he had said a new word. "We'll have our own place soon, James. I'm going to be making enough money to take care of us. You'll see." She smoothed a strand of hair from his forehead. "Back into a flat we'll go."

"Sorry," he said.

"Well, I'm not." She smiled at him. "I'm not sorry at all."

"The light fell upon the two sad young faces that were turned mutely toward it," Kate read aloud to James from the American novel. "Upon the eyes of the girl, who seemed to be looking with such anguished perplexity into the future; upon the sombre eyes of the boy, who seemed already to be looking into the past."

It occurred to Kate that the characters created by Willa Cather weren't too unlike herself and James—the girl perplexed about the future, and the boy looking into the past.

She stopped reading for a moment to enjoy the beautiful September morning. James had been home for a little over three months, and the time had flown.

The French doors opened. "Lord St. James is here, Missus Casey," Duncan announced. "Lieutenant St. James."

Kate slipped a ribbon into the book to keep her place. "Please show him out."

Mark, following closely on the heels of the butler, stepped outside.

Kate stood and turned to him.

He avoided her eyes.

Why won't he look at me?

Then she recalled their last conversation, when she had told him about her and Des. The trauma of that night, followed by endless nights of the powders, had all but erased their talk from her mind. She had told him the truth, and now he was sickened by her. She couldn't blame him.

Mark looked past her to where James sat in his wheelchair. He walked toward his former employee, around the wheelchair, and stopped in front to look at James head on.

James's head was cocked slightly, and he leaned toward where Kate had just been sitting, gazing vacantly toward the ground.

"Hello, James," Mark said.

James didn't move, didn't utter a sound.

"Tea, Missus Casey?" Duncan asked.

"That would be lovely. You can stay for tea, can't you, Mark?"

Mark's eyes flicked toward her, and back to James. "Yes, thank you."

"Please, have a seat," Kate said, indicating the chair where she'd been sitting next to James. She took a seat on the other side of the garden table.

Mark sank into the chair, eyes never leaving James's face. "I know you're having a rough time of it right now," he said to James. "But I want you to be assured that your old job will be waiting for you, whenever you're ready to come back."

James never budged.

The butler returned with tea, set the cups on the table, and poured.

"Thank you," Kate said.

"Yes, thank you," Mark added.

"Perhaps now would be a good time for a little exercise for Mister Casey?" Duncan asked.

"I think he would enjoy that," Kate said.

Duncan disappeared, and returned a moment later with the crutch. He pulled James up from the wheelchair, planted the crutch beneath his arm, and the two started off around the courtyard.

Kate and Mark sipped their tea, eyes on James and the butler.

"He's worse off than I imagined," Mark said at last.

"He's improving," said Kate. "Duncan takes him walking every day, and although the slate of the courtyard is uneven, he's never even stumbled."

They both watched as James leaned on the crutch and took a step, leaned and stepped, with Duncan close by, ready to catch him if he faltered.

"Does he talk?"

"Yes! He said American when I told him we were going to read a novel by an American author." She paused. "Or rather, he said something very close to American. What's important is he knew what I was talking about."

"I meant it when I said his job would be waiting for him whenever he's ready. Or you, Kate. When you're ready to get back to it, your job will be there for you. We've had to hire someone in your absence, but Des has probably told you already."

"No," she said quickly. "He did not."

Mark seemed about to speak, the muscles of his jaw clenched.

"Anyone but Des," he blurted out at last. "I've known him all my life, and he's not a good man. Even as a boy, he had a bad streak. The truth is, I don't like him at all."

Kate hesitated only a heartbeat. "I don't like him, either."

"Then why are you here?" Mark asked too loudly, too abruptly.

Kate gazed over at James and Duncan. "We won't be here much longer. James needs me to help him heal, but soon I'll return to work. I'll get us a flat and we'll move out on our own."

"Get out now, Kate. You can live in my house. I'm never there. I'm living in a flat near—" He nearly said Room 40, but stopped himself.

"—near where I work. You can move into my house today. You can work as much or as little as you like back at the office."

"*He* goes to the office," she said, and they both knew whom she meant. "I can't risk having him pop in on me anytime he wants. No, I need a fresh start, a new job."

A voice from the house startled them both.

"A garden party? And no one invited me?" Des's voice boomed from behind them, and Kate and Mark both flinched and turned to look. Des stood in front of the French doors, arms crossed, expression displeased.

Kate and Mark glanced at one another, the first time Mark had looked her straight in the eye since he arrived. Neither knew how much of their conversation Des might have overheard.

"Hello, Des." Mark stood. "I came by to see how James is getting along."

"Ah, yes, James," Des said. "Our very important guest. Our wounded war hero." He glanced at Duncan and James, expression sour. "Brandy, anyone?" He turned and went back inside the house.

Mark turned to Kate. "Pride be damned," he whispered. "You need to get out of here now."

Chapter 40

That very night, a scream awoke Kate from a fitful sleep. In the inky blackness of her room, she fumbled to find her robe and slip it on, then hurried downstairs to find Hilly sobbing on Duncan's shoulder.

Duncan looked up. "I'm afraid there's been an accident," he said, voice uncharacteristically shaky. "We've already called for the constable."

Kate held onto the banister, wondering if Des had fallen down the stairs in a drunken stupor. "Has Des hurt himself?"

"I'm afraid not," Duncan said, struggling to utter his next words. "It's Mister Casey."

"No," Kate choked.

She started toward the sitting room, toward James's makeshift bedroom, but Duncan stopped her.

"He's near the library, Madam, but please don't go. There's nothing to be done."

She stared at Duncan, then walked on wooden legs toward the library. She stopped cold when she spotted him.

Her husband lay sprawled on the floor in front of the library door, his head cocked at an unnatural angle, a pool of blood fanning out from beneath. His crutch lay by his side.

The strength left her legs and she dropped down beside him.

He stared at her with blank, lifeless eyes.

The sobbing started deep inside, followed by the shaking as she knelt there, next to her dead husband, and wept for him — for the future they would never have together. There were so many things she wanted to say to him, but they would never be said. So many things she wanted to do for him, but they would never be done. She wept for him, and for Vanessa, overwhelmed with anguish and loss once again.

How can I bear it? A knock sounded at the front door. *The constables, no doubt.*

Duncan had come to stand behind her, and in a near-whisper said, "Shall I let them in?"

She nodded. "Duncan," she croaked. "Mark St. John. You must get Mark St. John here."

Duncan nodded and went to let in the constables.

Mark arrived two hours later, talking first to Duncan and to the constables, who were wrapping up their work. He stopped and knelt by the body, studying his old friend.

"Ah, James," he said, voice cracking. "How can this be? You survive the war, and now this?"

He stayed there a long while, half hoping James would answer his questions.

Next, he found Kate in the sitting room—James's bedroom. Still dressed in her robe, she sat staring, dazed.

Mark knelt down in front of her. "Kate, I'm here. Don't worry. I'll take care of everything. My God! I'm so sorry."

"He was getting better," she mumbled. She looked at Mark almost pleading, as if he could figure all this out and fix it.

"The constables said they talked to you already."

She nodded.

They sat in silence awhile, then Kate sat up straight and looked Mark square in the face. "I can't stay here anymore," she said, as if she had just thought of it. "Will you wait while I get dressed? Will you take me somewhere away from here?"

Mark held her hand as she stood. "At last."

She ran upstairs, put on a dress, and threw two others into a pillowcase in lieu of a valise. She started out the bedroom door but stopped, went back, and opened the wardrobe. She reached up for the red purse, and jammed it in with the dresses. She hurried back downstairs, slowing as she reached the bottom steps.

They were carrying James, covered with a sheet, out of the house on a stretcher.

The emotion of it nearly knocked her to the ground. She almost turned and ran upstairs, to open the red purse and deaden the pain, but Mark appeared by her side.

He took the pillowcase, put his arm around her, and pulled her close. Together, they followed the stretcher out the front door, where the warm and fragrant air felt out of place.

So wrong. How dare the day be so beautiful, when another piece of my world has been shattered?

She should have been in the courtyard, reading aloud to James. Instead, she climbed into Mark's Austin, and when he pulled away from the house, she didn't look back.

Mr. and Mrs. Bridger welcomed Kate back into their home like a long-lost daughter. Mrs. Bridger served tea and hot cocoa, and Mark stayed for hours, the four of them sitting in stunned silence, until Mrs. Bridger insisted Kate soak in a hot bath.

"I can call the doctor and see if we can get you something to help you sleep," Mrs. Bridger offered, covering Kate's hand with her own.

"No," Kate said. "No, thank you."

Despite her grief and shock, Kate felt grateful for their care. When she crawled into bed that night, exhausted, she fell fast asleep.

The next morning, Mrs. Bridger made a breakfast of fried fish and bread. The Bridgers ate while Kate picked at her food.

"Tommy Hart is back at work," Mr. Bridger said to break the silence. "He started last week."

A knock sounded at the door and Mr. Bridger jumped up to answer. It was Mark.

Mr. Bridger said his good morning, grabbed his hat and left for work.

Mrs. Bridger fussed around the kitchen, getting Mark a cup of tea, and clearing breakfast dishes. She paused, wiped her hands on her apron, and looked at each one of them. "I'll be in the garden if you need anything." She left them alone.

They sat at the table with their tea. Mark sipped his; Kate stared at hers.

"I don't know what to say," Mark said at last. "I can't fathom what's happened."

"I had been telling him we were getting our own flat," Kate said. "Reading advertisements from the paper. I know he understood."

"I'm sure he did."

Kate stared into her teacup for a while, as if she might find the answer to all of this in there. Finally, she asked in a weary voice, "What did the constables say?"

Mark looked hesitant. "That he fell, and hit his head on the library table so hard, it broke his neck."

Kate winced, waiting to speak until she thought her voice might hold up. "After Vanessa... died." She could barely utter the word. "I didn't want to live. I felt like I was watching the world from under water, drowning, yet waking up day after day. I didn't want to wake up. When James came home—broken—it became my duty to take care of him. He needed me. Somehow, when I saw him helpless in his wheelchair, hope crept in, as irrational as that sounds. Hope for the future. Hope that I could make up for what I had done in the past."

They both knew what she was talking about.

"Now I won't have the chance," she finished.

"You did take care of him." Mark leaned forward. "When your husband needed you, you were there for him."

"Not at the end." She looked at Mark. "Not when it mattered the most. It doesn't seem right that he would fall over in the house. You saw him walking with his crutch in the courtyard, never stumbling at all."

"Perhaps he caught the crutch on a rug."

"There's no rug around where he fell." Kate paused, considering her words carefully. "Des has become even angrier since James came home. He threatened me the other night. He said I'd be sorry, that I would curse the day I crossed him. He was very drunk."

There, I said it out loud.

Mark stared at her. "You think Des had something to do with James's death?"

"I don't know. I'm telling you that he threatened me, and a few days later James died."

"Des is no saint," Mark said, "but a murderer? I don't think he has it in him. He's weak. He's a drinker, and a gambler, but not a killer. Did you mention any of this to the constables?"

"No. Would it do any good? In this mad time, where thousands like James are dying every day? You think they would spend any time investigating a member of the gentry for the death of an invalid?"

Mark considered her. "Why did you tell me?"

"In the event...." She swallowed the lump that had formed in her throat. "...that something should happen to me."

Few mourners attended the hurried funeral. There were so many these days that the clergy and undertakers found it difficult to keep up.

Kate, hidden behind the black lace of a veil, stood between the Bridgers and Mark.

They laid James to rest next to the tiny grave of his daughter. She didn't ask, but Kate guessed that Mark, the organized businessman, had not only bought a gravesite for Vanessa and James, but had probably secured the adjacent grave for her as well.

Mark interrupted her thoughts. "Anne sends her apologies. She wanted to be here, but wasn't up to it."

Kate remembered the last time she'd seen her, and doubted that Anne had wanted to be here at all.

What does it matter now?

"I'd like to come to the office, maybe tomorrow." She glanced from Mr. Bridger to Mark. "To see Tommy Hart, and make sure neither James nor I left anything behind."

"Certainly," Mr. Bridger said.

A fine drizzle began to fall, and the gravediggers were eager to finish the job. They shoveled dirt, and Kate flinched each time the moist earth hit the coffin below with a muffled thud. Mrs. Bridger sniffled loudly, and Kate closed her eyes, swaying on her feet.

Mark put an arm around her shoulder, and led her to his car.

Chapter 41

Kate stood in the office at Lyman & Stonebeck.

My old office. She sighed. *James's office.*

Tommy Hart walked in carrying a cardboard box, eyes squinting behind the thick lenses of his glasses.

"Hello, Tommy."

"Hello, Kate."

He put the box down on a desk and shyly approached her, engulfing her in his gangly arms. They held on to one another.

Kate took a step back. "How are you, Tommy?"

He, too, had a fine smattering of scars on his face, though not as severe as Kate's. He pushed his glasses up self-consciously. "Oh, I'm all right. Can't see quite as well as I could before, but I never have been able to see all that well anyway."

Kate touched her own scars.

"Mister Bridger said you were coming, so I gathered your belongings," Tommy said. "This was all I could find."

"Thank you. How is business?"

"Not good. It's become dangerous—too dangerous. Dundee, Perth & London lost a ship last week. We have clients who are desperate for their cargo, but no one can guarantee safe passage, despite that fact that the navy's sending ships to escort merchant vessels halfway across the Atlantic, where America and Canada take over. Lord McGregor says not to worry. He wants to ship again next week, although it's getting more and more difficult to get a crew together." He paused. "Are you coming back to work?"

The thought of working in a place where Des would be her boss, where he could show up at a moment's notice, filled her with dread. "No, Tommy, I've found a little work as a seamstress. I've already got one client, and I'll get more."

"If you ever need any help with your books, I'll do them. No charge."

Kate smiled. "If I ever make enough money to need someone to do the books, you're my man."

Tommy smiled, hesitated, and said, "That day... I've turned that day over a thousand times in my mind. I wish I had done things differently. I wish I could have gotten you home to get your little girl before...." His voice cracked and he looked at the floor.

She smiled and placed a hand on his shoulder. "You did all that you could. I wish, too, every minute of every day, that I could change what happened. First to Vanessa, and now to James."

"I'm so sorry," Tommy whispered.

"I'm not a brave woman, but I'm not going to give up." Unbidden tears spilled down her cheeks. "Simple as that. I'm going to get up every morning, find some way to make a living, go to bed each night, and do it all again the next day. If I give up, the Germans will have won. But to be honest, Tommy, I don't know that I can make it through even one day."

She swiped away her tears with the back of her hand, and picked up the box of belongings. Together they walked out the back door, climbed to the top of the stairs, and stood looking over the shipping yard.

"I mean it, Kate," he said to her. "I'll help out any way I can."

"You take care of yourself." She stood on her toes and kissed Tommy on the cheek. Then she walked away from the people and the business that had been her life—*their* life—before it all had been taken away.

How to mourn a husband and baby? A family obliterated as if it never existed?

Every day, Kate fought the urge to slip back into the haze of dark comfort that the powders provided. Instead, she doggedly finished the mending for the dress shop she'd taken on before James had died.

The proprietress of the shop gasped when she saw Kate. "I thought you had run off with my dresses, never to be seen again," she said. After she heard Kate's story, her attitude changed. She looked over the mending, and was impressed with Kate's skill. She even insisted on paying Kate for the first batch, which they'd agreed Kate would do for free.

"Instead of paying me," Kate said to the older, well-dressed woman, "will you write a letter of recommendation so I can get more work?"

"I'll pay you and write the letter," the woman replied, "if you agree to do my work first. And before you go, I have a few more items."

With her recommendation, along with Mr. Bridger's letter, she approached shop after shop, until she had a dozen clients.

She needed the money to rent a place of her own. When James was still alive, she'd begun shopping for a place for them to live, and had spotted an ad for a first-floor flat on Pitfield Street in Hoxton. On the shirttails of the East End, the neighborhood was shabby and crowded, but the price was right, and the first floor would have been necessary for James. Perhaps it was still available.

She found the neighborhood and the building, and the landlord, who said the first-floor flat had been taken, but he had a cheaper walk-up available on the fifth floor, the top floor of the old building. Kate dipped into the money she had saved, and rented the walk-up.

The building wasn't far from where James had lived when he first arrived in London. Like his old flat, it consisted of one room with a bed, wardrobe, and tiny kitchen. A well-used table with two chairs sat next to a window, which looked out onto the rooftop of the neighboring building.

The mending jobs paid for rent and food, but with nothing left over, and she needed to save money for a sewing machine. Mending was fine for now, but her goal was dressmaking, and for that, she must have a machine. She took her letters of recommendation to a company with a military contract to repair uniforms, and they hired her.

The company mended uniforms, handkerchiefs, shirts, socks—anything with enough material left to patch together. Cold air blew in through the slats of the wood building, the one cavernous room packed with sewing machines, hard chairs, and wood plank floors that were nearly as drafty as the walls.

As she mended gashes in the brown wool of winter trousers, she wondered if the young man who had worn them still lived. Who would wear the trousers next? Probably some poor boy, shivering through cold, miserable nights in a trench.

The other women, mostly cockney, glanced at her face with its fading scars, gazes darting away if she returned their stares. Her emotions numbed, their stares and whispering did nothing to cause her to feel one way or another—no embarrassment, no awkwardness... nothing. She worked long days in a cold room filled with women hunched over sewing machines, much like the one James had bought her. Then, one day, a woman stood in front of her sewing machine.

"Katie?" the woman asked.

Kate looked up.

A tall and gangly woman with acne-scarred cheeks and pale hair stared down at her. "It *is* you. Kate MacLaren. It's me, Lily Pickering... from the McGregor's house."

"Lily!" Kate stood, stepped around her sewing machine, and embraced Lily. She could feel the woman's bones through her thin dress and sparse flesh, and Kate felt absurdly happy to see her old compatriot. "Lily," she said again, stupidly. "How did you come to be working here?"

"I left the McGregors when the war broke out." Lily smiled, and couldn't seem to stop. "I heard they needed workers here in London, with all the men gone off to war, and I thought, now's the time for me to see something of the world besides the McGregor's kitchen."

"Get back to work, ladies!" One of the overseers, an old man with threads of gray hair combed back over his bald pate, walked up to them. "We're not paying you to start a social club."

"You're paying us by the piece, so what's a short break going to hurt?" Lily said, smile fading, and uncharacteristically outspoken.

"There's plenty more who'll take your place if you don't get back to it," the man snapped.

"Don't go getting all high and mighty on us," Lily said. "I haven't seen my friend for years."

The old man uttered a syllable of disgust. "Make it quick," he said, and walked away.

Lily looked back to Kate, studying her face. "What are you doing here, in a job like this? Things haven't gone so well for you as you hoped?"

"Let's talk after work, maybe see if we can find a cup of tea?"

"I'll wait for you as soon as work's finished today." The smile returned to Lily's face and she squeezed Kate's hand.

It was late when the final whistle of the day blew. Kate and Lily hurried outside and walked down the street arm in arm.

"Let's splurge on dinner," Kate said, happy to spend some of her precious earnings, just this once, on a meal.

They found an inn serving mutton stew without mutton in it, nor many vegetables for that matter, but the tea was hot, and the room was warm.

"What happened to you after you left?" Lily spooned the watery stew into her mouth.

"No, you go first." Kate didn't think she could talk about the past, about everything that had happened.

Lily launched into long tales of mishaps at the McGregor house, followed by all the troubles she had upon arriving in London. "I found a boarding house run by a fair woman, and this job, and I feel like I'm doing something important—mending these uniforms, helping out with the war."

"I feel that way too," Kate said, and sipped her tea. "You made it out of the McGregor house, Lily. That's an achievement."

"Even laboring away in London is better than working for Missus Shaunessy and the old McGregors." Lily laughed. "Your turn now. What's you been doing all this time in London."

Kate looked down at the table, then back up to face Lily. "I'm a widow, Lily." Kate couldn't bring herself to mention Vanessa. The mere thought of her daughter was too painful. "I married James Casey from Kirken, but he died."

Lily reached out a bony hand and touched Kate's hand. "You poor thing."

"And now I work. I catch a bus every day at six in the morning to come to the factory. And you know how it is there—sometimes we work ten-hour days, sometimes less, sometimes up to twelve hours. I mend for some shops, too. I bring my mending to work in a burlap bag, and during lunch, I drop off jobs at nearby shops, and pick up more. I do the same after work. Then home to a dinner of soup and bread, followed by more mending, finishing about midnight or later."

"Sounds dreary."

"I've saved enough to rent a flat all to myself." Kate couldn't help but brag a little.

"No!" Lily squealed.

Kate smiled. "In fact, I had better get going or I'll be up all night."

She paid for the meal over Lily's protest.

"I'm happy to see you, Lily," she said as the two walked out into the night. "We've found each other again, and now we'll have a friend at work to look forward to."

Lily squeezed Kate's hand. "Yes, friends—two independent women in London."

"That we are." Kate smiled. "That we are."

Chapter 42

On the morning of January 17, 1917, Mark peeked into the office of Commander Hope, but the small space sat dark and empty. He noticed a light coming from beneath the door at the end of the corridor — Captain Hall's office. Normally, Mark would be reluctant to bother him, but this news couldn't wait.

He rapped quietly on the door.

"Come in," the officer's voice called without hesitation.

Mark peeked his head in. "May I have a moment, sir. I have some news I think you'll want to hear."

"Come in, come in. Have a seat." The Captain half stood and swept Mark in with a wave of his hand. "What can I do for you, Lieutenant St. John?"

Mark sat on the edge of the chair, and stared across the modest desk at the captain. "Do you want to bring America into the war?"

Hall barked a laugh. "That's a big question with a simple answer. Yes. Why do you ask?"

"I just deciphered a rather astounding message, sir, which might encourage the Americans, if we can use it." Mark placed the handwritten, deciphered message on Hall's desk and pushed it toward the captain.

Hall slipped on reading glasses and studied the message. His face began to twitch. "Good heavens!" He peered at Mark over the top of his glasses.

"Quite so. It was sent yesterday by the German foreign minister, Arthur Zimmerman, to the German ambassador to Washington—" Mark excitedly repeated what Hall had just read. "—telling the ambassador to contact the Mexican government with a deal. If Mexico were to join any war against America, it would be rewarded with the territories of Arizona, New Mexico, and Texas. Quite a tempting offer, wouldn't you say?"

"Those cheeky bastards."

"Joining the war isn't popular with Americans," Mark said. "Or so I've read in the newspapers. I thought the Americans would join after the bloody Germans started attacking civilian merchant ships, including my own."

"But this," Hall said. "If the Americans were to discover the Germans bribing their neighbors, offering up bits and pieces of America... well, that's something else altogether. Where did this message originate? Surely not ship to ship? And since German cables through the English Channel have been cut, it couldn't have been a telegraph."

"That's the tricky part. The coded message was given by the Germans to the American Embassy in Berlin at 15:00 on Tuesday, January 16. The message passed through our London Embassy before being sent on to the State Department in America. A fellow from the embassy brought us a copy to decipher. We don't think there's been time yet to deliver it to Mexico."

"We got the message before the Mexicans?"

"Yes sir."

Hall's twitch picked up from allegro to prestissimo. "How in the devil can we share this with the Americans? We'll have to reveal the fact that we were spying on a private message, sent to their State Department."

"That's the conundrum, sir, and I've been thinking about it." Mark leaned forward. "What if we wait until the message has been delivered to Mexico? Then we can ask Western Union for copies of anything sent to the German embassy in Mexico from our allies—Russia, France, Italy—and America. We are spying on the Germans, not our allies or America."

"If we can convince Western Union," Hall said, picking up the thread, "we could send one of you to decode the message here in London at the US Embassy, and decode it in front of the Americans. Then we could say it had been decoded on American territory."

"Brilliant idea," Mark said.

Hall stood, Mark stood, and the two shook hands. "Mum's the word for now," said Hall. "I'll talk it over with the men upstairs."

"If you need one of us to decipher the message at the US Embassy, I'm your man."

"Yes you are, Lieutenant. You certainly are."

Two days later, Commander Hope stood at Mark's desk. "Captain Hall wants to see you right away."

"Yes sir." Mark walked down the hall to the Captain's door, and knocked.

"Come," said the booming voice.

Mark walked in.

Blinker was twitching and grinning. "Lieutenant, there's a coded message at the American Embassy. Can you head over there now and see what you can do?"

Mark grinned back. "On my way, sir."

Chapter 43

By January, Kate had saved enough money to buy herself a sewing machine—a used Sheeler & Wilson treadle—and, although not nearly as nice as her old Singer, it got the mending done in less than half the time that it took by hand.

She began toying with new designs. Where she used to go to Harrods, or watch the women on the street, and go home to copy and create those dresses, now, late at night when she couldn't sleep and the powders screamed at her from the red purse, she sketched out dress designs. She scrimped to buy fabric, and by the time spring rolled around, she had sewn four original designs. To create them was one thing, to sell them, another. She convinced a couple of her most loyal shop-keeps to sell her dresses on consignment at a fifty-fifty split.

When they agreed, she longed to run home and tell James of her success. She would have thrown a party for the two of them, to celebrate.

Instead, she confided to Lily her plan to grow a business. "When my business is a success, I'll hire you," she told her friend one day.

"Go on with you." Lily had laughed. "That'll be the day!"

Even with the war, the dresses sold quickly. Somewhere in London, women still had money to spend, and although there were no balls or coming-out parties now, the war had to end sometime soon, didn't it? So, she redoubled her efforts. The next batch went faster, and while she continued at her uniform-mending job, she spent all her spare time designing and sewing dresses. She reduced her clients to a few specialized shops who still gave her mending, but also sold her creations. It not only cut down on the time it took to pick up and deliver, but it streamlined the volume of clothes to carry.

On one cool spring evening, Kate stepped out of one of her client's shops onto the busy sidewalk, having dropped off the last of her new dresses. Feeling a nudge of optimism, she anticipated the short bus ride, followed by a brisk walk home in fresh air. She wore a blue cotton coat she had picked up secondhand and in need of repair. It looked better than new by the time she finished with it, and wearing it made her feel good.

She melded into the steady stream of people on the sidewalk, and hadn't gone far when she noticed a man with wire-rimmed glasses walking ahead of her. She stopped dead in her tracks.

It was Des's friend, Langdon Hughes. He looked rather dapper, strolling along the busy sidewalk with an impressive-looking cane, topped with an ornate brass handle.

Kate did an about-face and walked away. He was a friend to Des, and she wanted nothing to do with either one of them. She hadn't gone far when she stopped and turned to look.

He had vanished.

She stood a moment to make sure he was gone, and started back in her original direction. She soon spotted Hughes again, ahead in the distance. She slowed to allow the gap between them to lengthen, when something odd occurred.

Hughes stopped at a bench where a man sat reading a newspaper at one end. Hughes sat at the other end, and propped the cane against the side of the bench.

Kate stopped and faced a shop window, turning her head just enough to watch Hughes.

He pulled a handkerchief from his pocket, dabbed his forehead, refolded the hanky, and tucked it back into his jacket pocket, arranging it carefully. He then stood and resumed walking, leaving his cane behind.

The other man folded the newspaper, stood, and tucked the paper beneath his arm. He reached down, picked up the cane, and walked in the opposite direction from Hughes.

Kate blinked. If she hadn't been watching Hughes so closely, she might never have noticed.

The man who picked up the cane now moved toward her. Tall, blond, and muscular beneath his business suit, he stared straight ahead until they were nearly abreast with one another. Then his eyes flicked to her—cold eyes—sizing her up in a fraction of a second before snapping back to dead ahead.

She stared stupidly at him as he passed, close enough that she could feel the wake of breeze he created with his bulk and stride. She instinctively took a step backward, and watched as he walked away. His head remained fixed forward, never turning back, until he disappeared from her sight.

She stood rooted to the spot, perplexed, trying to sort out what she had just seen. She needed to catch a bus, so she resumed walking, and once again caught sight of Hughes in the distance. She reached the corner where she usually waited for the bus, but instead of stopping, she kept walking, following Hughes on a whim—an *irrational* whim, she admitted to herself.

She hung back a long way, far enough that she only caught a glimpse of him now and again. After a while, she lost sight of him. At first, she panicked: *Oh no, I've lost him!* Then came the relief: *Thank God, I've lost him!*

She caught sight of him again through the throng of people, cars, and horses, and followed as he walked farther and farther away from downtown. She nearly turned back at least a half dozen times.

What in the world am I doing? I don't know anything about this man, other than his unsavory friendship with Des.

She recalled the night he'd been there when she tripped on the stairs, his expression of disgust when he got a close look at her.

She felt compelled to continue her surveillance.

After nearly an hour of following him, the London she knew disappeared. The evening light had faded to dark, and the road had run out of streetlights several blocks back. Traffic thinned, and even the sounds changed. She could hear babies crying and, farther on, men's raucous laughter. Several times, she considered abandoning the endeavor, but each time, the sight of the little man ahead enticed her, and she continued.

At last, Hughes stopped in front of a large, old hotel. The fading paint over the front door read Wilshire. Kate ducked inside a doorway as he turned, looked over his shoulder, and disappeared inside.

She waited before following, trying to stay in the shadows as she moved around to the side of the hotel and edged up to a window. Standing on her tiptoes, she grasped the ledge and pulled herself up until she could see into what looked to be the lobby, sparsely furnished with dowdy settees and shabby lamps. She knew in an instant that Langdon Hughes must not be the well-to-do gentleman he'd seemed when in the company of Des. What business would he have in this cheap hotel?

Kate watched as inside, with his back toward her, Hughes stood at the lobby desk, ringing a service bell. After a long moment, an old man shuffled out of a doorway, a sour expression on his face. The man groped into one of the cubicles on the wall behind the desk, and handed an envelope to Hughes from a box numbered 26.

Hughes glanced at the envelope and, without any acknowledgment to the hotel clerk, disappeared up a dimly lit flight of stairs.

Kate, who'd been absorbed in the scene, suddenly realized she wasn't alone. She let go of the sill and stepped back.

"What would it cost to knock one off with you, sweetheart?" A man with a dirty face and a frayed black cap pulled low over his forehead stood grinning at her. Several of his teeth had gone missing.

Kate faced him, and he winced. "Bloody hell. Looks like someone took the knife to you," he said. "I'm not like that, darlin'. I only want a tumble."

His breath reeked of alcohol.

Kate panicked, but only for a moment, then got ahold of herself. "That's right. My man took a knife to me." She traced a fingertip down the red line on the side of her face. "As a matter of fact, he's inside," she said, nodding toward the hotel. "And if you don't disappear, he's like as not to do the same to you."

The man's grin faded. He pulled his cap lower over his forehead and hurried off.

Kate grabbed the sill again, and peeked back inside at the empty lobby. She didn't know what to do next. She hadn't thought this far ahead. What could she do? From around the corner, she heard the front door of the hotel creak open and close. She pressed herself against the building, peered around the side, and spotted Hughes again, hurrying up the street, back in the direction from which they'd come.

Kate waited until he disappeared, then walked around the corner and let herself in the front door of the hotel, wincing as the door squeaked open. She quick-stepped to the desk and scanned behind it for the cubicle numbered 26. Empty.

She listened, eyeing the door from which the old man had entered, and heard nothing. She skirted the desk and ducked behind it, facing out, as the old man would have when he helped guests. She bent down and examined two shelves beneath the counter—the top one piled with papers and a half-smoked, chewed-up cigar; the bottom shelf, a cluttered mixture of more papers next to a box filled with keys—keys, each engraved with a number. She rifled through the box until she found number 26.

She hesitated, figuring that if she got caught stealing the key, the old man would kick her out, and that would be the end of it. Or, maybe he'd have her arrested.

She weighed her options, took the key, and walked quietly toward the stairs.

She crept down the narrow second-floor hallway, lined with dingy gray wallpaper of faded and colorless flowers. The bare wood floor squeaked as she walked.

She found room 26, slipped the key into the lock, and felt the gentle click of the tumbler. With one last glance down the long hallway, she let herself in.

Inside, she leaned her back against the door and waited until her eyes adjusted to the dim light. The room held only a bed, a dresser, and a wardrobe, and still she couldn't decide where to begin.

What do I expect to find, anyway?

She started with the dresser, opening each drawer, poking and probing through the sparse contents of socks, underwear, and undershirts, and recoiling at the touch of Langdon Hughes's personal belongings.

She turned to the wardrobe. Inside hung two shirts and two pairs of trousers. She looked at the narrow bed, and bent down to reach under the thin mattress. Nothing.

She walked over to the one window in the room, pulled aside the threadbare curtains, and peered out at the dark streets. Fog was rolling in.

Foolishness. What would Hughes possibly keep in this room that would be of interest to me?

At least she knew something of the man that she hadn't before. He wasn't the fine gentleman he pretended to be with Des, and the exchange of the cane with the sizeable blond man was... well, odd enough to entice her into frittering away a precious evening on a wild goose chase. And she would have a long walk back to her flat.

Kate dropped the curtain, turned back to the room, and started toward the door. The next thing she knew she was sprawling headlong, hitting the floor full on and getting the breath knocked from her. After a long minute, she gasped, pulling air back into her lungs. Once she could think again, she glanced down the length of the floor toward her feet. A floorboard stuck up a fraction, and it had caught the toe of her shoe.

She sat up, crawled to the board on hands and knees, and felt the narrow edge of it with her fingertips. It felt solid, but she pulled and pushed until it gave a little, then jockeyed it back and forth until it eased up and pulled free.

In the gray light, she couldn't see down inside. Heart racing, she reached into the hole, felt an object, touched the edges with her fingers, and pried it out. She held it up before her eyes.

It was a book, but she couldn't make out the title in the dim light. She opened it and feathered the pages.

She felt back in the hole to make sure there was nothing more, and it was empty. Replacing the board, she clutched the book and stood.

It probably isn't even his book. It could have been put there by anyone and forgotten long ago.

The faint sound of squeaking floorboards came from the hallway, and Kate panicked. She slipped the book inside her coat pocket, crept toward the door, and listened. She didn't think she had locked the door, and must have put the key down somewhere, but she had no time to look.

She moved over to the window, pushed the curtains aside, unlatched the lock, and slid the window open. Heart hammering, she leaned out. She saw no foothold, only the vertical outside wall. From the second floor, the ground looked a long way down, but she had no choice. She put one leg out the window, straddled the sill, and turned to face the inside as she pulled the other leg out. She lay on her stomach, legs dangling toward the ground, and grabbed the sill with both hands, easing herself down until she hung there. At last, she let go.

She dropped to the soft ground below with a bone-jarring thud. She stood, checked herself to make sure she wasn't injured, and took off running.

Much later, she remembered she had left the window wide open. Nothing she could have done about that, but now he would know someone had been in his room. When she got home, she found his room key in her coat pocket. She hadn't left it behind after all. From the other pocket came the book.

She turned it over in her hands, but still didn't know the title of the book.

It was written in German.

Chapter 44 – London, March 1917

Two months after Mark had deciphered the message regarding Mexico at the American Embassy in London, Hall summoned him to his office. "Come in," Blinker boomed when Mark knocked. "Close the door behind you. Sit."

Mark did as ordered.

The captain fidgeted. His face twitched and he made a tent with his fingers, tapping them together while peering at Mark with an expression that could only be described as glee. "President Wilson was quite astounded when he read the message you deciphered regarding Mexico. His exact words were, *"Good Lord,"* according to Sir Cecil Spring Rice, our ambassador who delivered the information."

"Good," said Mark. "That's got to help him consider entering the war."

"He's going to lay a little groundwork first. Beginning in a few days, they'll leak the details of the telegram to the American press, credited to the American Secret Service, to save the messy details of British involvement. I venture a guess that the American people won't look upon the offer with indifference."

"Giving the president the support he needs to join the war," said Mark.

"That's the plan. Lieutenant, I commend you for your work on this crucial matter."

"I'm just the lucky bloke who happened to be available when the message was delivered," Mark said.

"And you deciphered it, recognized the importance of it, and passed it along to me, all within a matter of hours. You deserve the recognition, Mark. Well done."

The two men stood and shook hands.

A month later, the news of Germany doling out their states to Mexico had turned public opinion. The plan had worked. Whatever skepticism the Americans held about entering the war had evaporated when they learned of the German's ploy. Additionally, Zimmerman himself unexpectedly confirmed he had sent the memo.

Then the Germans declared a war zone around Great Britain, and the Imperial German Navy started sinking all ships within the zone, even those of the supposedly neutral United States. That was the last straw for the Americans, and on April 6, 1917, they entered the war.

Most European allies greeted the news of America joining in the war effort with relief. They felt American participation had been a long time coming.

The day after the Americans entered the war, Mark received a message from his butler saying that Kate Casey had called and needed to see him. She requested he meet her by the gazebo in St. James Park, at two o'clock that afternoon—terrible timing with the hectic schedule of Room 40. The Germans had gone nuts with the news, and interceptions of German naval messages were pouring in, each requiring decoding and translation. Still, he didn't hesitate a moment.

Kate left work at noon, knowing she wouldn't make it back in time to finish her shift, and not caring. She arrived at St. James Park and waited behind an ancient elm, watching the gazebo until she saw Mark arrive.

She stepped out. "Hello, Mark." Kate faced him, dark hair pulled back into a knot, revealing for all to see the scars left by the flying glass. She knew that the largest looked pink in the sun, but the finer scars were fading.

"Kate," Mark said. "Is something wrong? What's this all about?"

"Let's walk, shall we?" She took off at a brisk pace, and he fell into step beside her.

She glanced behind them as they proceeded farther into the gardens. When the people thinned out, she turned to him.

"I've found something." She stopped, glanced around, pulled the book from her coat pocket, and handed it to him. "It's probably nothing."

He took the book, looked at her curiously, and gazed at the volume in his hands, and read the title on the cover: *Verkehrsbuch*. His eyes widened, and as he flipped through the pages, the color rose in his face. "My God, Kate."

He, too, glanced around them, and together they fell into step once again. He tucked the book inside his own jacket.

"All I know is that it's in German," she said. "I figured it might be something important."

"Where in the devil did you get it?"

"From Langdon Hughes's hotel room."

"Who?" He stopped and peered at her. "Please, start from the beginning. Tell me everything."

As they walked, she told him all she knew of Langdon Hughes and the book, that she had followed him to a run-down hotel, searched his room and stumbled upon it.

Mark stared at her, incredulous. After a long silence, he found his voice. "What were you thinking? You could have been killed, going into that part of town at night. In fact, it's a miracle you weren't, doing a foolish thing like that. What made you follow him?"

"I spotted Hughes on the street downtown, and while I watched, he sat at a bench next to a man reading a newspaper. Hughes leaned his cane against the bench and walked away. He left the cane behind. I thought he must have forgotten it, but the other man—a big, blond man—picked the cane up and walked away with it. They never looked at one another. I thought it quite strange, and decided to follow Hughes."

Mark stopped again and stared at her. "Did he ever see you? Did anyone see you at his hotel?"

An image of the man with the dirty face and frayed black cap flashed through her mind, but she ignored it. The man had been drunk, and had probably forgotten their brief encounter. "No, he never saw me. Oh, I almost forgot." She pulled key number 26 from her pocket. "Here's the key to his room. The hotel is the Wilshire, in the East End."

"Good Lord, Kate." He took the key and stuffed it inside his jacket. "I'll look into this. Meanwhile, you may be in danger. I want you to go to Stonebeck Hall and stay with my family."

Kate remembered the last time she had seen Anne and Winifred St. James, and could imagine the treatment she would receive, showing up on the doorstep at Stonebeck. They'd have her scrubbing the kitchen floor and sleeping in the stables.

"Thanks, but I'm not going anywhere."

"This is serious, Kate." He stepped close, facing her. "Who knows who this Hughes character is?"

"It may not even be his book," Kate said. "It's a hotel. Anyone could have put it there."

Mark gently took her by the upper arms, bent down, and looked her square in the eye. He said very quietly, so no one else could hear, "Kate, this is a German codebook, a current codebook. Do you have any idea what you're dealing with here? If this book is his, this Langdon Hughes may be working for the Germans. If he finds out you were in his hotel room, he'll be after you."

Kate blinked, stunned at this revelation. It seemed impossible. Then she jutted out her chin and stared straight back into Mark's eyes. "What could he do to me that's any worse than losing Vanessa and James?"

"He could kill you, that's what." Mark sounded angry. "Be reasonable."

She pulled out of his grip and stepped back. "This man came into the house where James died," she said. "He saw me. He saw James. You say he could be a killer, and you say Des is not. What if Langdon Hughes murdered my husband?"

Mark exhaled. "I don't think anyone murdered James. He fell and hit his head on the table. It's devastating, I know, but why would anyone want to kill him? He was harmless."

"I can't get it out of my head. He was also on the mend, getting stronger every day."

They began walking back through the park. "Be careful," Mark said quietly. "Don't go out at night, keep your flat locked, and for heaven's sake, don't follow anyone else, no matter what."

She glanced up and gave him a half smile. "I'll do my best."

Chapter 45

Langdon Hughes entered a pub near the hotel. The war had taken its toll on pubs, reducing their hours as the price of ale skyrocketed. Still, a number of men sat in the smoky shadows as Hughes ordered ale from the barkeep. When he paid a shilling for a pint, he made a show of digging through a pocketful of coins.

"I'm interested in talking to anyone who might have been around the Wilshire Hotel last night," he said loudly, and looked around the room.

He moved away from the bar to a table in the corner. It took all of five minutes for a man wearing a frayed black cap to come join him.

"I might have been at the Wilshire last night." With the man's thick cockney accent, it came out, *Oy moit a 'bin 't Wlshir.* "But it's hard to remember, being so thirsty, and all."

Hughes flipped a shilling onto the table. The man snatched it up and went to the bar to get his pint, returned to the table, and gulped a foamy mouthful.

"You were at the Wilshire last night?" Hughes asked.

"The King's truth. I live nearby, I do." The man took a swallow, wiping the foam from his chin with a dirty shirtsleeve. "I walk by it every day."

"I was robbed last night," Hughes said. "Money stolen from my room there."

"'Tis a bad neighborhood, sir."

Hughes squinted at the man. "Did you see anything unusual there last night? Anyone unusual?"

The man chuckled. "You wouldn't expect a man to turn in his mates, now would ye?"

When Hughes didn't laugh, didn't even crack a smile, the man drained his glass. "One more, sir, and I may remember someone who did catch my eye."

Hughes's eyes narrowed, and he placed another shilling on the table.

The man returned to the bar then back again, sat down, and beckoned Hughes forward with a crooked finger.

Hughes's expression tightened in impatience, but he complied, leaning forward.

"I saw a woman, sir. Dark hair, pretty face, like an angel—except for a cut on it that didn't look so good. At first, I thought she might be a new girl around town, if you take my meaning. And I think she were, but she like to scare me to death with her scar, and her mean disposition. But she were hanging about the place last night after dark."

Hughes leaned back.

Dark hair... a cut on her face... the woman staying at Des's house.

He had to give her credit. The last time he'd seen her, she looked a mess. He hadn't given her a second thought. Now he realized his mistake.

He flipped a couple more shillings to the man, stood, and left the pub.

Chapter 46

Mark returned to Room 40 with the codebook, and had a long talk with Commander Hope. He told him everything, from how Kate had first met Langdon Hughes at Des's townhouse, to how sometime later she followed him to a ramshackle hotel, and stumbled, literally, on the codebook. It became apparent, as his narrative wore on, that Des must be mixed up in some very bad business.

The Commander placed a call to the Royal Military Police, and to a superior, to get permission to search Des's Hampshire Boulevard house.

It took all day to make arrangements, and Mark, dreading what they might find, asked to go along.

Dusk had fallen by the time Duncan opened the door to Mark and several military policemen.

Duncan looked over the men without a change to his sober expression. "Lord McGregor is out for the evening."

"I'm afraid we have to come in anyway, Duncan," Mark said to the butler.

Duncan eyed the policemen, then opened the door wide and stood back.

The police began in Des's study and bedroom. They went through each desk drawer, each wardrobe, each cupboard, tore apart beds, and meticulously searched for something—anything—that would be a link to the code book.

While they searched, Mark gravitated to the door to the library, the place where James had died. He stared at the floor where his friend had lain, life trickling out in a pool of blood.

A policeman walked past him into the library and began to rifle through the drawers of the desk there. After an exhaustive examination of the desk, the man turned his attention to the bookshelves, pulled out book after book, and fanned through each one.

Mark wandered around the room, restless, hand gliding along the substantial library table, then over to the corner near the now-ransacked desk. A polished wood box sat on a corner table near the desk. Mark ran his finger along the top, flipped the brass clasp to the side, and lifted the lid. He stared.

The policeman stopped his searching, came over and looked over Mark's shoulder. "A wireless radio?" he asked.

"A wireless," Mark confirmed. "What in heavens name would Des be doing with a wireless?"

The two men looked at one another.

"What, indeed?" said the policeman.

Mark stepped out of Des's townhouse before the police finished their work. The night air was pregnant with rain, a fresh, earthy smell, so at odds with the unsavory discoveries inside the house. A fine drizzle fell as he drove back to Room 40.

A pile of intercepted messages waited on his desk. He decided to tackle a few to get his mind off Des, but the code blurred on the page, and his thoughts returned to Des. They had known one another since they were children. The man was no saint, not by a long shot, but a traitor to his country? It didn't mesh with Des's self-absorbed personality. He suspected Des had sunk into debt with his gambling and extravagant lifestyle, but to cooperate with the enemy, even for a great sum of money, seemed like the last resort of a desperate man. Des hadn't appeared to be in such dire straits. Surely, he would have exhausted all other avenues of funding before sinking to such depths, and he'd never approached Mark, never asked for a personal loan from him, or from the business.

Des *had* begun drawing a salary in Mark's absence — that much he knew — and Mark made a mental note to go over the company's books carefully. Perhaps Des had been skimming off the Lyman and Stonebeck accounts after all.

Mark returned to the work at hand.

Just two. Knock off two messages, and then go try to get some sleep.

Trying to focus, he methodically translated the first message code to German, and from German to English. It took him an hour to get through it, and then he picked up the second message and began what was usually a laborious task, but part of this code he knew already. He had deciphered the name before — *Spazierstock.* Walking Stick.

It took him some time to figure out the rest of the code:

Spazierstock, nach hause kommen.

Walking Stick, return home.

A walking stick could be another name for a cane. The implication of the message punched him in the solar plexus, rendering him breathless. He stood, knocking over his chair, and ran toward the door.

Chapter 47

Langdon Hughes sat at Kate's kitchen table, staring up at her, eyes flat. Before him sat two items: a red purse and a plate.

Kate's vision widened out to take in the flat. Drawers and cupboard doors yawned open, spilling out their contents. Clothes lay scattered across the bed and floor.

Hughes indicated the chair across the table with a gloved hand. "Please, sit down. You must be exhausted after your long day."

Kate wavered, then collapsed into the chair on legs gone watery.

He watched her, and she stared back at him, eyes wide.

He sat forward. "I believe you have something of mine. I want it back. *Now.*"

She had to stall for time, had to think. Her voice eluded her, then snapped back into place, sounding surprisingly casual — conversational even. "Whatever could I possibly have of yours?"

He exhaled, a brief, sarcastic hiss of air, and picked up the red purse, reached inside, and pulled out a brown bottle. Removing the cork, he held the bottle over the plate, tipped it, and with one finger tapped out cream-colored powder into a little hill.

With one gloved finger, he pushed the plate across the table until it sat directly in front of Kate. "For you."

She tried to look nonchalant.

His lips twitched on one side. "I know you like it. It would be a shame to waste. In fact, I think you'll take all of it — tonight."

She knew how a modest portion of the powders affected her. The entire amount before her would put her into a sleep from which she would never awaken. "I don't think I can drink that much."

"Why don't you sniff it?" He breathed in, an exaggerated, noisy inhalation through his nose. "It's quicker to work, and far more potent that way."

They both knew it was enough to kill her regardless of how she took it.

Self-pity swept over her, and her lower lip trembled. To have gone through so much and have it end like this. Unthinkable.

She didn't know how he could have discovered that she had found the codebook. Indeed, she hadn't been sure until now that the book belonged to him.

"The codebook was yours," she said matter-of-factly.

He said nothing.

"You're working for the Germans?" she said with surprise. "I was convinced that you were merely a drunken gambling friend of Des's."

His lips pursed together at the unflattering characterization.

"You're more than that, aren't you?"

He remained silent.

"Is the codebook worth money? Are you running an errand for Des? Did he stumble upon this German codebook, and you're trying to sell it to —"

"Enough!" Hughes's fist came down on the table, causing the plate of morphine to jump and scatter powder.

Kate's blood ran cold, but she persisted. "How will I ever know, Mister Hughes? You can pretend to be anyone you want, but I've watched you for a long time now, carousing all night at the clubs, gambling your money away, drinking. This..." She indicated the hill of powder. "Des likes it. Do you like it, Mister Hughes? The sweet euphoria of morphine?"

"You're a foolish woman." He talked in a low growl, teeth gritted. "You know nothing—nothing of discipline and dedication, of sacrifice to something greater than yourself. You and your Des are birds of a feather. That's an English saying, is it not? Birds of a feather flock together? You're birds—tiny-brained and weak."

Beads of sweat popped out on Hughes's upper lip as he spoke. "Ich bin Deutsche. I am German."

A cold river of fear trickled through her veins at his words. "My compliments, Mister Hughes. You speak English impeccably, with no trace whatsoever of an accent."

"I spent years in an English boarding school as a young man, away from my family, for the sole purpose of attaining the speech of an Englishman, and learning their ways. The fatherland plans ahead, unlike Des McGregor—spoiled, self-indulgent, wealthy, and privileged, not by hard work, but by circumstance of birth."

"Will you answer a question first?" she asked, desperate to stall for time.

His eyebrows rose, gaze never leaving hers, and he nodded slightly.

She took a deep breath, and asked the question only he could answer. "Why did you kill him?"

No need to say the name; they both knew who she meant.

"Tell me," she persisted, trying to hold herself together. "What happened the night he died? I need to know. At least leave me with that."

He paused, shrugged. "If you wish."

Hughes didn't pretend ignorance, but answered in an even tone. "The imbecile? War, pure and simple. It was nothing personal. He became a liability. But you...." He leaned forward. "You're an entirely different matter altogether. You've caused me a lot of trouble, and I will handle your death personally, and with great pleasure."

"Tell me," she persisted, trying to hold her emotions together, to appear calm. "What happened the night James died? I need to know. At least leave me with that."

"It's no wonder you English are about to lose the war. Years of self-indulgence and inbreeding have created a soft, inferior race. James Casey was nothing—a leftover shell of a man who got in my way. You want to hear the details of how your husband died?" He cocked his head.

"Yes." Kate could hardly breathe.

"It's irrelevant, but I'll tell you. I'll grant the last wish of a dying woman."

He began to talk.

Chapter 48

Langdon Hughes stood with his back to the library door, hunched over, a headset covering his ears, speaking his native tongue into the microphone of the wireless radio.

Des had finally stumbled into bed after midnight, an hour earlier. The man had been despondent all evening, and the more brandy he drank, the more pathetic he grew. Hughes thought he would never retire, and by the time Des staggered upstairs, the servants had been in bed for hours, the woman was undoubtedly intoxicated with morphine, and the man with one leg lingered in bed in his usual mental haze.

Hughes finished, took off the headphones, and pulled out his matches to burn the paper on which he had written out the coded message. A movement caught his eye and he looked up.

The man with one leg stood in the library door, pajama-clad, singular pajama leg fluttering empty, crutch beneath his arm.

Hughes stared at the man, whose eyes did not stare back.

"Germ," the imbecile said.

Hughes's eyes narrowed.

"Man."

Hughes waited.

"Germ. Man," the imbecile said.

Hughes sucked in his breath. This wounded idiot had just become a risk he couldn't take. He stood and closed the distance between them in seconds, then reached up, put his hands on either side of the man's head, and with one swift and brutal twist, broke the man's neck with a loud crack.

The man dropped to the floor with a thud, crutch clattering.

Hughes reached down and grabbed the man's head again, this time dragging him to the library table. He was in luck. While many library tables had elaborately carved or rounded edges, the thick, heavy mahogany of Des's library table had been edged with a simple ninety-degree angle, making it sharp yet sturdy. He pulled James up by his head, no small feat for a man Hughes's size, but muscle tough as steel ran through his wiry body. He bashed James's head down hard on the edge of the table. The sickening crunch of his skull fracturing signaled success. Whoever examined the body would think James had fallen and hit his head so hard on the edge of the table, that it fractured his skull and broke his neck. After all, the cripple had only one leg.

He dropped the man to the floor, walked back to the wireless, packed the headphones and microphone back into the case, and returned the Lyman & Stonebeck shipping schedule papers to the top of the desk in the corner—the spot where Des left them each Tuesday evening.

Hughes decided to risk carrying the coded message in his pocket instead of burning it. Best to get out of the house now, and he wouldn't be coming back. Too bad, as it had been the perfect setup.

He skirted the man's body as he left the library. A pool of blood oozed across the floor from behind the man's head. He stopped to examine the scene one last time, and listened hard, but heard nothing save his own accelerated breathing. Satisfied, he turned, let himself out the front door, and disappeared into the night.

Chapter 49

Kate stared in shock at the description of the brutal death of her husband.

"Your turn to talk," Hughes said. "How did you find the book?"

Kate couldn't breathe, but somehow, she managed to speak. "I tripped over a loose floorboard in your hotel room. I pried it up."

"Ah, yes, I remember. You're not the most graceful woman, are you? How did you find my room?"

"I saw you on the street," she said, her voice almost a whisper. "I followed you."

"Why?"

Her lips twitched, and she almost smiled. "Because of the bad company you keep."

Hughes did not look amused. "What did you do with the book?"

She took a deep breath. "I gave it to the authorities."

His eyes narrowed and face reddened. "That explains it," he muttered to himself, then to Kate. "You have caused me a great deal of trouble, more trouble than you can imagine. It's bad enough that the book has fallen into the wrong hands, but this is humiliating. I have a reputation to maintain in certain circles, you see, and this type of thing is unacceptable."

"Maybe they don't need to find out," she ventured.

He laughed, a dry, bitter sound. "They already know."

He reached inside his jacket, pulled out a stag handle, and held it, eye level, between them. One gloved thumb pushed a brass trigger, and a blade snapped out from the handle, a four-inch steel blade.

He stood and moved behind her in an instant, and bent down to her, his lips brushing her ear. "I'm not a monster," he whispered, his breath heavy on her neck. "I want you to have one last bit of pleasure before you... go."

He grabbed a handful of her hair, gripped it firmly with his free hand, reached out with the knife, and shoveled it into the morphine. He held the powder-laden knife next to her nose, and pressed the cold steel of the blade to her nostril.

"Sniff," he hissed.

Kate turned to ice, frozen between his grip on her hair, and the terrifying pressure of the knife.

He increased the pressure, pushing the knife more firmly, until the powder touched her nose and the sharp edge of the knife felt cold on her flesh.

Kate trembled and tried not to cry as she closed her mouth, and sniffed.

The morphine burned its way in. She had only drunk the powder before—never taken it like this, and the familiar rush hit her with an unexpected speed and intensity. It had been so long.

Hughes scooped another serving and pressed it beneath her nose. "Sniff," he commanded.

She did.

Minutes ticked past, and fear glided away. Her muscles relaxed, as did Hughes's grip on her hair. She felt herself slipping out to sea.

Death might prove welcome.

Vanessa's image took shape before her, but without the blow of grief that usually followed. James's face materialized.

This man killed James.

"There's more here. Take all of it," he whispered.

Tears sprang forth and ran down her face, salty on her lips. "Please, I'm thirsty," she croaked, and her voice sounded as if it came from a long way away. "Allow me one drink first."

He scowled, but let go of her hair.

When she stood, her chair fell to the floor with a crash that seemed muffled and distant. She drifted to the kitchen sink, picked up a glass she'd left there that morning—a lifetime ago—filled it with water, drank, and filled it again.

Hughes waved the knife at her, watching with malevolent amusement. "Now, come back and sit down."

She set sail back toward the chair. Then an image of Tommy flashed before her—Tommy the day of the bombing, his glasses shattered, face bleeding. *"One good turn deserves another,"* the image of Tommy whispered.

Of course. Why didn't I think of that?

As she neared the table, expression slack, she staggered to the side, toward Langdon Hughes and his knife, glass gripped tightly in her right hand. With all the strength she could gather, she swung her right arm, stiff and stretched out as far as it would go, and slammed the glass into Hughes's face. The glass shattered, as did his spectacles, and a geyser of water, blood, and glass exploded into the air.

Then her world went dark.

Chapter 50

Mark slid open the bottom right drawer of his desk—a drawer he hadn't open since his initial Naval Intelligence training. He reached inside and pulled out a leather holster that held a revolver—a Webley Mk V, double action that held six powerful nitrocellulose propellant cartridges—the latest in ammunition technology. With a maximum effective range of 45 meters, the gun had proven to be reliable, and able to cope with the mud and water of the trenches on the Western Front, as well as resistant to the sand and grit.

Holster in hand, Mark ran straight to the garage where he'd parked the Austin, climbed in, dropped the holster onto the passenger seat, and pushed the ignition switch. The moment the motor purred to life, he jammed it into gear and gassed it, speeding out into the streets of London. The drizzle had turned into a hard and steady rain, turning the night black and the streets slippery. He gripped the wheel, tense with worry, and turned east toward Hoxton, to Kate's flat.

Driving at night under blackout conditions required light guards on his headlights, and nerves of steel, but he had to stop and remove the guards. No worries, as no German Albatross fighters would be flying the skies on a night like this. Driving was difficult at best even if you knew where you were going, but although he knew Kate's address, he'd never visited her new flat. He peered through his windshield as the wipers weakly fought off the rain, and found his way to Hoxton.

He began searching for Pitfield Street, driving by braille, expecting to be stopped at any moment by military police on patrol. He finally spotted the street sign for Pitfield and turned onto it. It was deserted, no people walking about at this late hour, and the only other vehicle on the road was an ambulance, in no particular hurry, cruising in the opposite direction, tires splashing through the rain.

Mark found the address, pulled up in front of the building, and jumped out. The front door was unlocked, and he took the stairs two at a time to the fifth floor. It didn't take long to find the door with Kate's flat number. It stood ajar. He froze, and listened.

Nothing. Silence.

He walked inside. Rain pounded on the roof, and a soft drip somewhere in a corner betrayed a leaky roof. A single bare bulb illuminated the room—clothes were strewn about, cupboard doors open, and the kitchen table beneath the light sat covered in flour or sugar. He picked up a brown bottle that lay on its side in the mess.

Morphine.

He could barely breathe. "My God," he said out loud to the empty room.

He ran out and down the five flights of stairs as fast as he could go. When he hit the first floor, about to rush outside, a side door opened.

"Officer," a woman's voice, thin and high pitched, called after him. "Sir?" An old woman peeked out of the open door, wide-eyed, pulling a robe about her neck, gray hair falling to her shoulders. "Are you looking for the young woman? The one they took away?"

Mark backtracked to her door. "Yes. Yes, that's exactly who I'm looking for."

"She looked dead, that's the God's truth. And one of the gents didn't look so good, neither. The ambulance took her not five minutes ago."

Mark's mind stopped at the word dead. "Ambulance," he repeated. The single vehicle he had passed on the street had been an ambulance that was....

In no particular hurry.

"That's right," the woman said, and pulled her robe tighter about her neck. "I try to mind my own business, but I couldn't help but see what was going on. What with all the tramping up and down the stairs, two men carrying the stretcher, one big blond bloke, the other a little man who looked beat up, he did." She paused with a look of concentration on her face. "There was something else."

"What else?" Mark grew impatient.

"My hearing ain't quite what it used to be, but I heard somethin' queer when they were carrying the poor dear out the door. The blond bloke said *snail*."

"Snail?" Mark repeated, walking toward the door, eager to follow the ambulance. Halfway out the door he stopped, and turned back to the woman. "*Schnell?* Did he say *schnell?*"

"That's it," the woman said, brightening.

Mark ran out the door and jumped into his Austin.

Chapter 51

Kate listened to the hum of a car engine, and wondered if she had fallen asleep in Mark's automobile as he took a drive in the country. How funny that she would fall asleep with James, Vanessa, and Anne riding along. A thrumming on the roof of the car seemed odd, until she realized it must have been raining — *pouring* by the sounds of it.

As the car jostled her, she felt sick to her stomach, and realized she was lying on her back. She tried to open her eyes, but her eyelids felt like cement. Willing the contents of her stomach to stay down, she tried to pry her eyes open by sheer willpower. At last, they fluttered open and she looked around, blinking, trying to make sense of it all.

She lay stretched out on a bed of sorts in the back of an enclosed lorry. Large cotton bags with the word "bandages" written on them hung nearby, swaying next to a couple of bolted-on leather loops. A box marked with a red cross sat on the floor, secured by canvas straps.

An ambulance.

Her mind raced, probing for an explanation.

Why am I in an ambulance? How did I get here?

She came up blank. The last she thing remembered was arriving home after a long day's work, reaching up to pull the cord to the light, and....

It all rushed back — the morphine, the knife, Langdon Hughes.

I survived! I must have been unconscious, and someone found me and called an ambulance. They must be taking me to a hospital.

She turned her head. Another bed lay opposite hers, with a narrow space between them, and on that bed sat an injured man. A bloodied bandage covered one side of his face, tied on with a white strip of fabric, looped over his head and beneath his chin. The man stared at her with his one, exposed eye.

She tried to sit up, but only her head and shoulders lifted, and she felt lightheaded and sick again. She lay her head back down until the wave of nausea passed, then glanced down at herself. Three straps secured her to the bed — one across her chest, one at the waist, and a third near her ankles. Her arms were tucked beneath the top two straps, and her hands were tied together.

She glanced at the man again, and that's when she spotted the pistol he gripped in his lap, barrel pointed straight at her. He touched the bandage on the side of his face, and frowned, and she finally understood.

"Hughes," she croaked, staring at him through a hazy state of shock and dismay.

A voice came from the cab of the lorry. "*Sie muss ruhig bleiben, wir müssen noch über mehrere Grenzen gehen.*"

Kate craned her neck to peer through the window into the cab of the lorry. A blond man swiveled to glance at her, and she recognized those cold eyes instantly—the man Hughes had handed off the cane to on the downtown sidewalk.

"He wants me to keep you quiet," Hughes said. "We're approaching checkpoints. Can you keep quiet, Kate? Or would you like more powders?"

She stared at him, mute.

"*Kein problem,*" Hughes replied to the driver. "*Ich gebe ihr Beruhigungsmittel in ein paar Minuten.*"

Hughes spoke to her. "I have been called back to the fatherland... because of you. It only seems fair that you accompany me."

Fog muddled her head and she struggled, thick tongued, to speak. "Did Des know about you? Did he help you?"

Hughes smirked at her, seeming amused. "Your benefactor, Des McGregor, knew nothing. His bad habits—drinking to excess and gambling away his family fortune—made him an easy accomplice. It's easy to help a drunkard lose money to his gentlemen friends. After one particularly devastating loss, I lent him enough to pay off the debt. He saved face with his friends, and I became his new—how do you English say it?—his chum. Until you arrived, and then your pathetic husband, the situation was ideal. I was trusted by his acquaintances, important gentlemen. None of them had ever met me before. We hadn't attended Oxford together. Our families didn't go back hundreds of years. Yet they let me into their midst, allowed me to listen to their conversations. Des proved to be most accommodating—unexpectedly helpful. He regularly brought home paperwork from his shipping business and left it lying around in the library. Nothing like a time schedule to help sink ships."

Kate thought back to compiling the weekly reports for Des, and felt sick to think she might have helped the Germans learn the routes of merchant ships.

Seeing the look on her face, Hughes smiled, then winced and touched the bandage on his face. "Our driver—" He nodded toward the cab of the ambulance. "—is a trained killer who won't hesitate to break your neck in an instant, if you should be considering escape, which I assure you, is impossible. He is taking us directly to Saint-Gilles, a prison where a cell is waiting for you. There will be a trial, naturally, for your crimes against Germany. I will be the star witness, and will do my best to make sure you get *todesstrafe*. You know German?"

She shook her head gingerly.

"*Todesstrafe* is the death penalty." He prattled on as if discussing the weather, looking quite pleased with himself. "You do know how they carry out the death penalty in Deutschland, don't you? Firing squad. And don't think being female will do you any good. You won't be the first woman from England to be executed."

The few times she had encountered Hughes, she'd never seen him look so cheerful, despite the bloodied bandage on his face.

"At my trial," she said, working hard to enunciate her words, and to speak loud enough to be heard over the deafening rain, "I'll tell them I'm a simple woman, with no training in the ways of war. Yet I found you, and your codebook, as simply as locating a book in a library." She licked her parched lips, swallowed, and continued. "I'll suggest that they do a better job of training their spies, to make it more difficult for common citizens, a woman no less, to find them out."

The smile evaporated from Hughes's face.

"Perhaps," she continued, "you'll be the one on trial, Mister Hughes. Maybe we can face the firing squad together—me for espionage, you for incompetence."

Hughes's expression turned ugly.

Suddenly, the ambulance jerked sharply to the side. "*Verdammter die idiot!*" the driver shouted, as the ambulance swerved.

There was an explosion of sound like a thunderclap, followed by a tremendous jolt. The ambulance recoiled in the opposite direction, and rolled to the side.

The straps dug into Kate's flesh, as her body pressed first toward the side of the ambulance, and then toward Hughes. The blast of his gun reverberated in the cramped space, and pain seared Kate's thigh. The vehicle rolled a complete revolution, and a shower of objects peppered her body and face. She tucked her head down toward her shoulder until the vehicle slowed in its rotation, went up on one side, paused, and settled back, rocking to a stop.

Silence. Her own breathing came hard and fast, and her heart hammered in her chest. She blinked and looked over toward Hughes.

He lay perfectly still, his bandaged head at an odd angle against the side of the lorry, his body lying across the ambulance bed. His unbandaged eye was wide open, glassy, and lifeless.

A stream of hammering heartbeats passed, then a pounding on the back door of the ambulance. The handle twisted one way, then the other, and the door heaved as it was pushed and pulled.

When the metal door groaned open, the sound and smell of the rain flooded into the ambulance, unleashed to its full intensity.

Kate blinked, steeling herself to confront the driver, the blond killer, who was surely coming to finish her off.

Mark St. John's face appeared in the open door, his eyes searching wildly. He crawled inside without a word, glanced at Kate, then went to Hughes and placed two fingers on the man's neck. He opened Hughes's one good eye with thumb and forefinger, peered into the glassy, dead orb, and nodded.

He turned to Kate, unbuckled each strap, gathered her up in his arms, and carried her out the back door of the ambulance.

The rain bathed her face unmercifully, washing away the cobwebs in her brain. She tried to cover her face with her hands, but they were apparently still bound together and secured around her waist, because she couldn't budge them. She strained to see around her.

The blond driver lay sprawled outside the driver's door, face down in the grass and dirt of the field where the vehicle had come to rest on its side. The side of his face was streaked with blood, dirt, and rainwater, his arms outstretched. A gun lay a meter beyond his reach.

They appeared to be at an intersection of two roads. Mark's black Austin Defiance sat at a ninety-degree angle to the ambulance, back end crushed. Kate gazed up at Mark as he laid her gently on her back in the grassy field.

He leaned down until his face was inches from hers, water dripping from his hair, a dark stream trickling down from a cut on the side of his head. He started to say something, but abruptly jerked his head up and leaped away from her.

She lay there, paralyzed, and listened to a scuffle full of grunting and panting. A gunshot rang out, and then the sounds began to fade, seeming to come from very far away. After more faint scuffling sounds, another muffled shot sounded. Even as the rain begged her to stay awake, the night grew darker, and her world faded to black.

Chapter 52

Kate's mind swam upwards from the depths of unconsciousness, seeking the light. Her eyelids fluttered open and she blinked at her surroundings, a room devoid of color—white walls, white ceiling, and a white sheet covering her, pulled up to her chest. Beneath the sheet, her torso and legs lay straight. Her arms lay outside of the sheets and down to her sides. She felt a soft pillow behind her head. A hospital, she thought, and then her mind recoiled. She remembered that, upon her last awakening, she'd thought herself safe in an ambulance, on her way to a hospital, only to find herself a captive of Langdon Hughes and his thug companion.

I won't be fooled twice. Is this a hospital room or a prison infirmary? Where did Hughes say he was taking me? Saint-Gilles—the German prison where they would hold me until a sham trial, which would result in my execution by firing squad.

She couldn't allow herself to hope.

Then she saw him, asleep on a chair beneath an open window, hair ruffling in a soft breeze, one shoulder wrapped in a white bandage. His mouth hung slightly open and his head lolled to the side, but the unseemly pose did little to tarnish the handsomeness of his face.

Perhaps I'm dead, and so is he. Could this be heaven?

Mark's eyes opened—those hazel eyes, green flecked with brown— and he sat up abruptly and looked at her hard. "Kate?"

He jumped up and covered the distance between the chair and the bed in three strides, then leaned down, a frown furrowing his brow. "Kate?" He reached out and picked up her limp hand, and cocooned it between his own two hands. They felt warm.

She smiled.

"Kate," he said for the third time, only this time his voice sounded relieved, sure of itself with that one, happy syllable.

He released her hand, picked up a glass from a bedside table, and held it to her lips as his other hand cradled the back of her head, lifted it up, and helped her to drink.

She sipped, and sipped more, and then her own right hand came up to hold the glass so she could drink even more. Water had never tasted sweeter.

"Help me sit up, please?" Her voice came out a whisper.

He piled another pillow behind her and helped ease her up to a sitting position. He returned to the chair beneath the window, carried it to her bedside, and sat. For a moment, they stared at one another, smiling.

"Can I get you anything?"

Kate shook her head, a small gesture, still lying back on the pillow. "All I want is to know what happened. How did you find me? How did you know?"

"I should have known earlier. I should never have let you go after you gave me *Der Verkehrsbuch*, the codebook."

"How did you find the ambulance?" she whispered. "Tell me."

He frowned. "It began with Des," he said, watching Kate's face for a reaction. She stared back at him, unflinching. "After I told my superiors about the codebook, how you found it, and about Langdon Hughes, they knew Des had to be investigated. I went with them to his townhouse. We found a wireless radio, Kate. Hughes must have been transmitting to the Germans using the wireless from the library."

Kate nodded weakly. "Shipping schedules. Hughes said Des brought the company's shipping schedules home, and he used them to sink ships."

Mark flinched. *Des responsible for killing their own employees?*

He continued. "After I left Des's house that night, I went back to the office and found a clue that made me realize who Langdon Hughes really was, and I knew in an instant that you were in danger. I drove to your flat, but it was too late. The place was in a shambles, and you were gone. I had passed an ambulance on the way, and the woman downstairs told me they took you away in an ambulance. I drove as fast as I could, searching for it—for you—but I couldn't find you. I knew Hughes had been called back to Germany, and—"

"How?" Kate asked. "How did you know that?"

"War secrets—can't tell you everything." He gave a rueful smile. "I had several routes I thought they might take, and decided on the most direct route I could think of. Then I drove as fast as I could through a bloody downpour. I thought I would be stopped by the police at any moment, but I made it through, and when I spotted the ambulance, I knew I had to stop it."

He stopped, looked down at his hands, then back up at Kate. "I knew what I had to do. I had to stop the ambulance any way I could, but I was afraid I...." He fell silent for a moment. "I was afraid I might hurt you. I had no choice. I had to risk it, rather than have them take you away. I turned out the headlights, and as the ambulance approached an intersection, I drove in front of it. It hit the side of the Austin, and spun me around, and the ambulance rolled."

"Oh, yes, I remember that," Kate said.

"Thank God they strapped you in. I thought the driver was dead, cast half out of the lorry as he was. I kicked his gun away, and went looking in the back for you. I had a devil of a time getting those doors open, but there you were. I made sure Hughes was dead before I pulled you out, but I hadn't made sure the driver was dead. That was my mistake."

"I heard gunshots," Kate whispered, and licked her lips. Mark poured more water from a pitcher into her glass, held the glass to her lips, and she drank.

When she finished, he put the glass on the table, and sat back down. "He wasn't dead, the driver, whose name was Wolfgang Schirmer, by the way—a very bad chap. He took a shot at me, and grazed me, here." He touched the bandage on his left shoulder. "Luckily, I got the final shot."

"You could have been killed," she whispered.

"And so could you."

They stared at one another in silence, pondering their fates.

Mark broke the silence. "Another thing... that cane you saw Hughes pass off to Wolfgang? They passed messages by hiding them in the handle. I'm sure there were more than just the two of them communicating that way."

"How do you know all this?" Kate gaped at him.

Just then, the door opened and a nurse walked in, middle aged, dressed in white from head to toe, a smart cap perched on gray hair. "You're awake," she pronounced. "We were worried about you. I see your gentleman friend has got you sitting up. How are you feeling?"

"Hungry," Kate said.

"That's good. Let's take a look at you." The nurse laid the back of her hand on Kate's forehead, then took Kate's hand, found her wrist and a pulse, pulled a watch on a chain from a deep recess in her dress, and began counting. Satisfied, she placed Kate's hand back on the bed.

"How is that leg feeling? The doctor got the bullet out, but if you're in pain I can get you a shot of morphine."

"No," Kate said loudly and too quickly. "No, thank you. It doesn't hurt much."

"I need to change the bandage." The nurse raised her eyebrows at Mark.

"If you'll excuse me," he said, and stood. "I'll go in search of tea."

"There's a café just down the street to the south," the nurse said.

Mark stepped from the hospital, with its astringent odors and stuffy air, into the coolness of the afternoon, and began to walk. He quickly found the small café, where patrons sat at small tables on the sidewalk.

He was about to walk inside when he heard a familiar voice say, "Wait here. I shan't be long."

He turned and spotted a tall woman leaning over one of the small tables. "Muriel?"

The woman spun around.

"It *is* you. What in heavens name are you doing here?" Mark walked toward his sister.

She stared at him with an odd expression, and when he embraced her, she held him stiffly.

He looked over her shoulder at the young man she'd been talking to, who looked like the butler's son. "Christopher?"

"Christopher drove me," Muriel said quickly.

"He drove you?" Mark repeated, studying his sister, who looked guilty as hell. "How did he pry the steering wheel out of your hands?"

"She drove me, actually," Christopher said, looking and sounding tired. Gray peppered his dark hair, which hadn't been there the last time Mark had seen the young man.

"Christopher's just home from the front," Muriel said quietly. "On leave."

"I hear it's bad," Mark said.

Christopher's face turned to stone. "Hellish.".

Muriel glanced at him with a look of concern, then turned back to Mark. "The hospital sent a telegram to let us know your wound was superficial and there was no need to worry."

Mark touched his shoulder. "They sent a telegram?"

"Yes, a nurse recognized your name and thought we would want to know."

"I should have gone to the Naval hospital," Mark said. "They're better at keeping secrets."

"What kind of secrets? What happened to your shoulder?"

"It's just a scratch from a run-in with an ambulance."

"How ironic."

"How did you ever get Mother to allow you to come to London?"

Muriel looked even guiltier. "She doesn't know. I was home when the telegram arrived, and wicked child that I am, I didn't give it to her. I wanted to come see you, but I knew she would insist on coming, and I wanted to come alone. She thinks I'm... somewhere else."

"I see. At least I won't have to explain this—" Mark touched his shoulder. " —to Mother. If you can keep a secret."

"Oh, I can keep a secret." Muriel nearly smiled.

Mark contemplated first Muriel, then Christopher. "I came to get some tea while the nurse is changing Kate's bandages."

"Kate is here, too? Is she hurt?"

"She's on the mend."

"Dear God, I do need to hear all the details."

"Let's step inside and order some tea." He held the door open for his sister.

Once inside, they ordered a pot of tea and three cups. Mark glanced at Muriel as they waited, and said quietly, "It looks like you've stopped listening to Mother."

"Be careful of the advice you give, brother. Someone just might listen to you."

"I hope you know what you're doing."

"I certainly *don't* know what I'm doing," she said, sounding vexed. "What I do know is that Christopher is home on leave, staying with his mother and father for ten days. I've visited him there twice, or rather, I go collect him and we go riding. When I got the telegram about you, I asked him to come with me to see you, and he said yes. So here we are. In a couple of hours, I'll drive him home, and be back at Stonebeck just past the time Mother thinks I've been gone too long."

He studied her stubborn expression, and sighed. "You've got a good head on your shoulders. I'm not worried about you."

"Good, because I'm worried about me enough for the both of us. Now, let's get our tea, and then I want to hear everything."

Chapter 53 – November 11, 1918

Mark joined the Room 40 staff, assembled in the center of the offices, called together by Captain Blinker Hall. A year and seven months had passed since the night he had raced after the ambulance to save Kate. His wound had long since healed, and he'd missed only three days of duty.

Hall looked out over the group of men, face twitching subtly. They were all older and decidedly more haggard looking than when they'd first arrived in Room 40 nearly four years earlier. The men suspected what Hall was about to tell them, and he didn't disappoint.

"I am happy to announce that today at eleven in the morning, on the eleventh day of the eleventh month," his voice boomed, "an armistice will go into effect, ending the war."

The men cheered.

He let the noise go on for a short while, then held his hands out for silence. "We shall continue operations without change, business as usual, until further notice. Good job, fellows." He looked around the room. "Your dedication and expertise has been indispensable in helping put an end to this war."

The news was not unexpected, as events had been building up to this conclusion for some time, and although they shared a few moments of boisterous celebration, the men of Room 40 took it all with cautious optimism. After all, just two days earlier, as peace supposedly hovered on the horizon, a senior officer in charge of airship message decoding discovered that the Zeppelin Station at Nordholz had reported to its commanding unit that it was still functional and on alert for orders.

Nonetheless, the announcement called for drinks all around, although the hour was early. They hovered near their desks, keeping an eye out for one more message to decode, one more sign that things were not as they should be.

Mark chatted with his associates until the hour of eleven struck. A cheer went up again, as the armistice went into effect, followed by more back slapping, and then Mark drifted back to his desk, picked up a message he'd been working on earlier, and soon sunk down into his chair to resume where he'd left off.

Early in the morning on the eleventh of November, Christopher sat on a wooden box and leaned back against the dirt wall of the trench, helmet shifted down over his eyes, and tried to catch a few precious minutes of sleep. He was filthy, his uniform barely discernible beneath layers of dried mud. He hadn't had a bath, or shower, for weeks. His socks were so full of holes, they barely separated his bare feet from his boots.

His attempt at sleep proved futile. He squinted out of one eye at the soldier next to him, who sat on the mud floor of the trench trying to light a cigarette. The man's hands shook so badly that he couldn't get the cigarette and the flame to meet. Christopher sighed, pushed his helmet back up where it belonged, leaned down, took the match from the man's trembling hand, and held it to the cigarette. The flame took hold.

The distinct whine of a bullet in flight hissed so close to Christopher's ear that the hair on the back of his neck stood up, and the dirt wall where he had just rested his head exploded into a geyser of dirt. Christopher fell off the box face-first, down into the mud, and flung his arms over his helmet.

When it seemed no more bullets would follow the first, he peeked up at the soldier, who was blissfully drawing on the hand-rolled cigarette, inhaling the tobacco smoke, a contented look on his face, oblivious to the near calamity.

Christopher, figured sleep was out of the question for the foreseeable future, or at least the next few hours, so he crawled down the trench on hands and knees in search of breakfast.

Kate's eyes burned. She fed the fabric beneath the needle of the sewing machine doggedly in the dismal light of the factory. Her long hours were taking their toll, working all day mending uniforms and all night sewing for her department store clients, but she had no choice. She didn't want to move into a boarding house, like Lily, so she had to work to afford the rent on the flat, and to put money aside for the future.

After her encounter with Langdon Hughes, she had convalesced in the hospital for a week, after which Mark had insisted on sending a nurse to Kate's flat to look after her for another week. Finally, she'd returned to work at the uniform factory. The gray-haired, sorehead of a manager at first refused to allow her back. She never tried to tell him the truth—that she'd been kidnapped and shot by a German spy—but said her mother had been sick and died, which was true, although the timing was a bit off.

While she'd lain in bed healing, she developed a plan that she wanted to discuss with Mark, but she couldn't talk to him unless she had some contribution, besides her skill and labor, to make toward the plan. Thus, she worked and saved money, scrimping on food just like everyone else during this time of rationing.

There was talk that the war was nearly over. Turkey had surrendered, as had Austria. The Kaiser had abdicated, and Germany had sent its representatives to General Foch, Supreme Commander of the Allied Armies, to arrange for a suspension of hostilities. But so far, it was all talk. Men were still fighting and dying, each and every day.

Over the hum of her sewing machine, Kate heard a distant rumbling, along with gunshots—another German air raid, no doubt. She stopped sewing and prepared to head to the basement for shelter.

Someone in the factory began screaming. "It's over! It's over! It's over!"

"What?" She looked at the girl next to her.

Then Lily came running over. "It's true," she squawked.

"What's true?" Kate asked.

"The war is over!" Lily jumped up and down, and pulled Kate out of her chair and hugged her hard, then began jumping up and down again.

Kate grabbed Lily's hand. Every seamstress was up out of her seat and running toward the door, cramming themselves into the aisles. Kate and Lily fell into the swarm and were carried along until they found themselves ejected out onto the street. It was nearly noon, and although the day outside was misty and bleak, the streets were filled with people cheering.

A group of soldiers, home on leave, swarmed down the thoroughfare. When they reached the glut of women coming out of the uniform factory, they towed them along. One young man took Lily and Kate by the hand, then linked arms with them, and they joined the others marching down the street. The soldiers began singing, "Rule Britannia," and soon the entire throng joined in. People waved flags, and gunshots fired up into the air. The rain now fell in earnest, but it did nothing to dampen the triumphant celebration.

Then, through the ruckus, came the deep toll of a great bell ringing. "It's Big Ben," someone shouted. "They're ringing the bells of Big Ben for the first time since war broke out!"

Lily laughed and looked over at Kate as they marched through the crowd.

Kate turned her face up to the sky, allowing her tears to blend with rain, and smiled.

Afternoon had come by the time Muriel neared home on horseback. As the stallion trotted toward the stable, a car sped past her, skidding on the pebbles of the sweeping driveway, causing her horse to snort and prance.

The car came to a sliding stop in front of the main steps of Stonebeck Hall, and the family's barrister from the village jumped from the car and took the steps two at a time.

Muriel nudged her horse closer.

The man pounded on the door until Stephens appeared, and then held a telegram out in front of Stephens's face so he could read the words, although his hands were trembling so badly that the paper fluttered.

Muriel stopped at the bottom of the front steps and called up to them. "What's going on?"

The barrister turned to her. "It's real this time. They stopped the war at eleven this morning! It's over!"

Lady Winifred appeared behind Stephens. "The war is over?" She reached out and snatched the telegram.

Anne crowded in beside her, looking over her mother-in-law's shoulder.

"It's over!" the barrister said. "Our boys are coming home!"

Anne's hand flew to her mouth, and even Winifred gasped. "Mark's coming home," they said in unison.

Muriel focused on Stephens, who was staring at her, eyes glistening. He gave her a small nod with a trembling smile. Muriel gazed back at him, stunned.

"A party... we must throw a party," Winifred said. "Stephens, we'll need to make a menu."

"This isn't the time for a dinner party, Mother," Muriel said, collecting her wits. "It's the time for a celebration. I propose champagne for all, family and staff alike. This is a day like no other."

Winifred hesitated for a moment, then announced, "Splendid idea. Champagne, then... for all."

Chapter 54 – Stonebeck Hall, December 1918

The rough handle of the ax felt good in Mark's gloved hands, though his muscles tired quickly as he swung over and over again.

Christopher chopped at the tree from the other side, until at last it groaned and fell to the ground. "That one took some effort," the young man said.

Mark set the ax down and rubbed the fatigued muscles in his arms. "I'm afraid I've pushed pencils too much in the last several years. I'm out of practice."

"Won't take long until it comes back."

Mark started to make a flip remark, something about being an optimistic twenty-year-old, but stopped short. Both men had been in the war, but Christopher had been in the infantry, and suffered greatly in the trenches. Instead, Mark leaned against the sled. "Awfully nice of you to help out."

Christopher shrugged. "I was visiting Father, and happy to lend a hand."

"What are you going to do now that the war's over?"

"I was assigned for a time to a bridge building detail during the war, and one of the engineers said I had the right kind of mind for it." Christopher snapped his ax into its leather sheath. "I have the potential, he said, to become an engineer. It would require training, and he said he'd help me."

"Admirable ambition," Mark said. "In the meantime, would you consider coming to work at Lyman and Stonebeck? The salary will be quite reasonable, and perhaps we can find a way to accommodate your engineering training at the same time."

Christopher regarded him solemnly. "I would be most grateful," he said at last.

"Good. It's settled." Mark considered the tree they'd fallen. "Now, shall we batten this monstrous tree down to the sled, and see if it's too tall for the ballroom?"

"It won't be too tall for *that* room."

Two horses pulled the sled with the tree, while Christopher rode ahead, reins in hand, and Mark rode behind.

When they pulled up in front of Stonebeck Hall, Muriel flew outside and down the steps in a loose wool coat and scarf. "It's a beauty." She admired the tree, then walked up to Christopher's horse, rubbed the animal's muzzle, and gazed up at Christopher. "I wanted to come with you, but Mother wouldn't allow it. How long did it take to cut down?"

"Long enough to wear me out," Mark said, riding up alongside his sister. "But it didn't seem to tire Christopher."

"It wore me out, plenty." Christopher dismounted next to Muriel, and the two of them stood face to face, eyes locked.

"Muriel!" Lady Winifred appeared on the top step, frowning. "I need your assistance inside."

"See what I mean?" Muriel whispered, then smiled, and walked slowly back toward the house.

It took four men to haul the tree into the grand room at Stonebeck Hall, hoist it to its full twenty-foot height, and secure it.

Mark stood and admired it. Christmas felt authentic this year, for the first time since war had been declared.

After over four years of bloody conflict, the Great War had cost some nine million lives.

For Mark and his colleagues in Room 40, the war didn't end until ten days after the armistice, when the entire British Grand Fleet escorted the Hochseeflotte, the battle fleet of the German Imperial Navy, to Scapa Flow, a body of water in Scotland, where the ships would be interred and eventually scuttled.

One month later Room 40 had held its own farewell party.

Mark had stood, drink in hand, exhausted and stunned as he listened to speeches, poems, and songs sung by the commanding officers and his colleagues.

Toward the end of the party, Captain Blinker Hall sauntered up and handed him a glass of scotch, then clinked his own glass with Mark's. "To the end of bloody thing."

"Here, here." Mark took a sip.

The captain glanced around them and, seeing no one close by, lowered his voice and leaned in to Mark. "The war is over, but keeping an eye on the enemy goes on."

Mark regarded Hall, whose face, for once, was devoid of movement—not a twitch to be seen.

"This is an excellent scotch," Mark answered, sipping.

"You've served your country well," Hall went on. "You're the kind of man we need to keep an eye on things, even in peace time."

It occurred to Mark, as the scotch began to warm his blood, that the long hours, the all-consuming vortex of Room 40, had come to an end. The work that had consumed him was finished.

He took a deep breath. "I'm eager to return to my life, to be home with my family, and I need to see what remains of my company."

"Of course," said Hall. "Sometimes a man can have it all—a family, a business—and still find means to serve his country. Quiet ways." He paused. "Hush hush."

Mark digested the meaning of the captain's words. "I appreciate your confidence in me, but you've got the wrong man. Thanks for the scotch. Now, if you'll excuse me."

"Never say never," Hall said, as Mark walked away.

"Father." Charles walked into the ballroom where Mark stood admiring the tree.

Mark turned to his son. "Come along. I'm covered in needles and pitch." He smiled. "If I pick you up, Mother will make us both sleep outside tonight."

"Will it be cold?" The boy looked up at his father.

Mark laughed and tousled the boy's flaxen hair.

"The tree is perfect," Lady Winifred announced as she floated into the room. She stopped briefly by Mark's side to lay a hand on his shoulder, and continued on to examine the tree. "Norway Spruce. Exactly what I wanted."

"As you requested at breakfast." Mark scooped Charles up in his arms and stood. "Which is exactly why it's here, Mother."

She turned and grinned. "It's so good to have you home."

"Good to be here," he said, returning the grin.

"Moo Moo." Charles wiggled out of Mark's embrace, dropped to the floor, and ran toward the ballroom entrance and smack into Muriel's arms.

"Hello, my little man." Muriel picked him up and kissed him on the forehead with an exaggerated smack.

"Muriel, please, that's vulgar." Winifred sighed. "And it's Aunt Muriel, not Moo Moo, Charles."

Anne trailed behind Muriel. "Here's Mum," she whispered, patting Charles on the head, but not attempting to uproot him from Muriel's arms.

"Ready to put decorations on the tree?" Muriel asked the boy.

"Yes," he shouted.

"Okay. We have our work cut out for us."

"We don't want to tire him," Winifred said, and frowned. "He should nap."

"I'm too big," Charles protested, holding up three fingers. Then he added, "Almost," and held up four fingers.

"He's right," Mark said. "Far too big for a nap."

"You'll regret that later when he gets cranky," Winifred said. "Christopher, you'll do the decorating on the upper tree. You'll need the ladder."

"Certainly, Lady St. John."

Decorating the tree with his family felt both odd and wonderful to Mark, as if he'd traveled back in time to his childhood, with the whole family together and excited for the festivities of the season. Now, however, the role of father fell to him. He watched as Charles hung an ornament on a low limb, with help from Muriel, while Anne stood off to the side and rustled through the box of ornaments. He walked over to her, reached into the box, touched her hand, and smiled.

She looked up at him, and didn't pull away.

Stephens quietly entered the room and walked up to Winifred. "A moment, my lady?"

"What is it?" She turned to the butler.

"A final count for Christmas dinner?"

"I believe I've heard back from everyone. Forty-two at last count."

"Very well," Stephens said. "You've seen the menu. Any other special requests for the kitchen staff?"

"Pigs in a blanket!" shouted Muriel.

"A goose!" Mark squeezed Anne's hand, never taking his eyes off her, as he called out to the butler.

Anne hesitated. "Christmas pudding," she said timidly, then louder, "with plenty of raisins and cherries."

Stephens regarded them all with an expression of somber amusement, eyebrows rising. "Your requests have been duly noted," he said drily.

Chapter 55

With a festive mood in the house and the promise of much company, games to be played, and prodigious amounts of food to be consumed on Christmas day, Christmas Eve was devoted to a servants' dinner. While the St. Johns ate a modest meal upstairs, the servants enjoyed a more lavish supper downstairs, knowing they wouldn't have a moment's rest once the guests began to arrive the next day.

After their supper, the servants filed upstairs to enjoy the spectacle of the tree, with its candles and glittering baubles of colored glass. They fell into line, in hierarchical order, to receive their gifts.

"Merry Christmas, Stephens," Winifred said to the butler, and presented him with fifteen shillings and a bottle of port.

The butler took the gifts. "Thank you, and Merry Christmas, Lady St. John."

"Your son," Winifred began, eyeing the butler.

"Christopher, my lady."

"Yes, Christopher... will he be going away to find work, now that the war is over?"

Mark stepped up beside is mother. "Christopher is coming to work for me at the company, and he'll soon be training to be an engineer." He turned and glanced at Muriel, who broke into a smile.

"Thank you, sir," said Stephens. "That's very kind."

Winifred uttered a kind of *harrumph*, and continued down the line.

For the housekeepers, cooks, housemaids, and ladies' maids, she gave a length of cloth for dressmaking, along with chocolates. After many a thank you, bows, and curtsies, the staff returned downstairs, everyone dismissed of further duties until the next day.

Since the servants were dismissed, Muriel put Charles to bed herself—over his loud protests—and returned for one last glass of wine with the family in the ballroom, in front of the Christmas tree.

"I'm enjoying our peace and quiet while it lasts," Mark said, sitting next to Anne. "It's going to be a madhouse around here before we know it."

"How many people are staying?" Muriel sat on the divan, with a deliberate space between herself and her mother.

"Every guest room will be full until after Boxing Day," said Lady Winifred. "Only the nearest neighbors are going home after Christmas dinner. It's wonderful to be able to truly entertain once again."

"It tires me to imagine it," Mark said, smiling at Anne. "I'd like to give you each your gift tonight, if you don't mind."

"Will I get another on Christmas morning?" Muriel winked.

Mark left the room for a minute, and returned with three identical rectangular boxes festooned with large red bows. He handed one to his mother, one to Muriel, and one to Anne.

"What's this?" Winifred loosened the ribbon and opened the box. She pulled out a silk dress of Egyptian blue. She stood and held it up, examining its narrow skirt and ribboned bodice. "It's quite chic."

"Mine's teal, and modern, and beautiful," Muriel said. She pulled the dress from the box, held it to her chest, and twirled around. "I didn't know you had such grand taste in women's clothing, brother."

"I had some assistance," Mark said, and turned to Anne. "Do you like yours?"

Anne's dress was sleek, the palest yellow with white lace trim. "It's lovely," she said.

"What's this?" asked Winifred. "There's some type of writing stitched inside, but I can't read it without my glasses."

Muriel looked inside her gown. "It's a piece of cloth stitched inside that says Vanessa."

Mark grinned. "These dresses are originals, made for you by a new designer."

"Why bother with a label?" Winifred asked. "One has a dress made, one knows who makes it."

"The Vanessa label will be sold in the best shops," Mark said. "Original designs, but available at a moment's notice, already fashioned. Or you can visit the shop, and have a dress created the old-fashioned way. It's a new business I'm funding."

Winifred frowned. "Isn't Vanessa the name of the Caseys' little girl, the one killed in the bombings?"

"Yes. The designer of these dresses is Kate Casey."

Winifred gasped and dropped the dress, and the silk slid off the divan to the floor. "I prefer to buy my dresses from a skilled dressmaker, not a maid."

"Kate *is* a skilled dressmaker, or rather designer." Mark's holiday spirit faded. "She's hired seamstresses for the actual stitching." He plucked his mother's dress from the floor and folded it back into its box.

"I love mine," said Muriel. "She picked my favorite color."

Anne folded her lemon-colored creation, and placed it carefully back into the box. "I'm rather tired," she said. "I'm off to bed."

A round of goodnights followed as she stood. "I think I'll look in on Charles first."

"Mind if I join you?" Mark asked.

"Promise you won't wake him? It takes forever to get him back to sleep."

"Quiet as a church mouse," he said.

Upstairs in Charles's room, they stood side by side, staring at their sleeping son.

"Isn't he a bit old for a crib?" Mark whispered.

"I suppose so. Your mother wants to make sure he doesn't fall out of bed."

"She's a bit overprotective, I'd say," a tad louder than necessary.

Anne faced Mark and put a finger to his lips to shush him.

He took her hand in his, and looked over at his sleeping son, then back to his wife as she gazed up at him, there in the shadows of the nursery, beautiful as a porcelain doll. He leaned down and kissed her gently. "Do you like your Christmas gift?"

She didn't answer. Instead, much to his surprise, she kissed him again.

Hand in hand, they looked at their son one more time, and then walked to Anne's room. Instead of turning him away at the door, she held his hand and led him inside.

Chapter 56

Mark's eyelids felt heavy and refused to budge at first. Finally, with much effort, they fluttered open. His head felt dull and he couldn't remember where he was. Then it all came rushing back to him. Bewildered, he turned to look, to make sure his mind wasn't playing tricks on him, and there, by his side, lay Anne, tucked securely beneath the covers and sound asleep. She looked so lovely and innocent, all fear and shyness erased from her features.

He winced as his head began to pound.

I didn't drink much wine at dinner, so where did this bloody headache come from?

He swung his legs over the side of the bed and sat up, and his head pounded doubly hard. He stood and realized his whole body ached. "What the devil," he muttered. Never one to catch so much as a cold, he felt sick.

He let himself out of his wife's room and returned to his own boyhood bedroom to dress, but ended up crawling back into bed.

By noon, it became obvious that Mark had fallen ill, and a slow unease pervaded the family and staff. There had been talk of influenza, first sickening soldiers in the trenches, but soon everybody seemed to be getting sick. At first, no one had paid much notice, until people began to die—not only soldiers exhausted from years of fighting, but healthy young people in their twenties and thirties.

Winifred called for the doctor right away, and by evening, the diagnosis had been made. Influenza had come to Stonebeck Hall.

The guests began to arrive, but when they learned that Mark was ill, the festive air deflated. Dinner conversation remained subdued, and a few guests who'd planned to stay for days, decided to return home, even at the late hour.

By Boxing Day, the last of the guests left, and Winifred allowed most of the servants to go home to their families if they desired.

Winifred hired two nurses, women in their fifties, who said they had each already recovered from the influenza, to look after Mark, who grew increasingly feverish as the days passed. Then he sunk into delirium. Winifred and Muriel tried to help with his care, but the nurses insisted that the women keep their distance. The best thing the family and servants could do, they said, was keep away.

Anne never attempted to visit her husband, but remained in the shadows, watching.

Five days after Mark fell ill, however, Anne ventured to the doorway of his bedroom. Wide-eyed, a glossy sheen on her pale skin, she watched as Mark lay perspiring and thrashing beneath the sheets, while one of the nurses blotted his face with a damp towel.

"My head hurts," Anne whimpered to the nurse after a long while. "I don't feel well. I fear my husband has infected me."

Tears coursed down her cheeks as she first sank to her knees and then crumpled to the floor.

The nurse left Mark's bedside in alarm, and called out the door to her colleague to help, as she rushed to Anne's side.

"There, there, let's get you off to your own bed," the nurse murmured.

"I should have known better," Anne said as the second nurse arrived. "He's trying to kill me again."

"I think she's delirious already," the first nurse whispered to the second. "Help me get her up."

"Don't let me die," she implored as the women, one on either side of her, pulled her to her feet.

"There, there, dearie, let's get you to your own room."

"Murderer!" Anne sobbed and pointed a finger at her husband. "You'll never touch me again!"

The nurses frowned at one another, and gently coerced the agitated woman out the door.

Chapter 57 – London, Spring 1920

Mark stood on the sidewalk at 178 Regent Street. The writing on the shop window read, *Vanessa's,* and underneath, in elegant lettering, *Original Designs.* The display window held two mannequins made of hardwood, dressed in elegant gowns.

While commerce slowly returned to London, a pall still hung over the city, an aftershock of the war, followed by the influenza epidemic. However, genteel women seemed most inclined to resume prewar life, and that included refreshing a wardrobe that had fallen years behind.

Mark removed his hat, raked his fingers through his blond hair, and stepped inside.

A woman sitting behind a mahogany desk looked up and smiled when he entered. "Hello, Lord St. John."

"Miss Pickering," he answered.

A slender man with thick glasses emerged from a door in the back of the room. "Lord St. John. Welcome."

Mark smiled. "Hello, Tommy."

"Good to see you, sir." Tommy stepped forward and shook Mark's hand.

"We're sorry to have lost you from the company," Mark said, "but I can see you've made a very good business decision for yourself."

"I promised her a long time ago that if her business ever grew, I'd be there along with her." Tommy turned to the receptionist. "Lily, would you mind getting us some tea?"

"Don't bother," Mark said. "I'm going to see if Kate will go for a walk." He glanced around at the tasteful decorations, the furniture, the lighting. "The place looks elegant, yet comfortable. You've done a great job."

"Our clients seem to like it," Tommy said. "Fitting and dressing rooms are in the back, and the dresses are made off-site. We've rented a portion of the factory where Kate and Lily mended uniforms during the war, and hired some of the best seamstresses. Most of our sales are coming from Harrods. They signed Kate exclusively for their designer clothing."

"I haven't heard Tommy talk this much the entire time I've known him." Kate emerged from the back room dressed in a navy blue skirt, straight and long, and a white blouse tucked in at the waist. A brooch was pinned at her throat, and her dark hair was swept up and twisted into a French roll. The pale skin of her face betrayed only faint traces of tiny white scars. Even the long cut that ran down her cheek had faded to a fine line, nearly invisible beneath discreet makeup.

Mark smiled. "Hello, Kate."

"Mark." She held her hand out to greet him. "Is this business? You've received our monthly reports, as usual?"

"Tommy is most efficient. Yes, we've received all the necessary paperwork." He took her hand, holding it for a beat too long before letting go.

"And our payments are arriving on schedule, I trust? Tommy is astonishingly punctual."

"That goes without saying. Your business has been one of the best investments Lyman & Stonebeck has made."

She acknowledged the compliment with a dip of her head. "What brings you to our neighborhood?"

"I was nearby and thought I'd drop in. Can you take a walk, get some fresh air?"

"That would be lovely." She turned to Tommy and Lily. "I shan't be long."

"Enjoy the sunshine." Lily smiled and touched a hand to her wispy hair, tucked smartly into a clip, and glanced shyly at Tommy.

Mark held the door and they walked out into the sunshine, falling into step, side by side. They strolled past dress shops, haberdasheries, and cafés. Pots of spring flowers lined the sidewalk, spilling over with early hydrangeas, rhododendrons, and azaleas, each sweetening the breeze with its own perfume.

Kate glanced at him as they walked, and said at last, "Did you get my letter? About Anne, that is? I'm so sorry."

Mark's expression turned dark. "Yes, thank you. The influenza, you know, took her, like so many others. To be honest, it was bloody awful. I was sick with it myself when I visited home for Christmas, but I didn't know until I got there. I'm afraid she caught it from me. Anne's dying words accused me of murder."

"What?"

"She kept saying I had tried to kill her before, and this time I intentionally infected her, that I was trying to murder her. I can't tell you how dreadful it was."

"She must have been delirious with fever."

"That's what the nurses said, and what I tell myself."

"How is the baby?" Kate asked at last.

"Charles is no baby," Mark said, voice relaxing, warming. "He's already a bookworm—picture books, that is."

Kate remembered with an ache that Vanessa would be beyond reading nursery books by now, had she lived.

"Luckily," Mark continued, "Muriel and Charles are very close. She's always been a mother to him. He misses his mother, but he has Muriel, and his grandmother dotes on him."

Ah yes, Lady Winifred.

They left the sidewalk and followed a path into the park, winding their way farther and farther into the cool shelter of trees, flowers, and shrubs. They came to a huge oak tree, its branches thick with new green and glossy leaves, and stepped under its canopy. Kate leaned her back against the thick trunk, and Mark stood facing her.

"You'll be testifying in Des's trial next week," Mark said.

"Yes, and I'm not looking forward to it."

"It doesn't look good for him. His friendship with Hughes, the wireless in the library that Hughes must have used to send his intelligence to Germany—it's all quite serious. The prosecution wants him hanged for treason."

"I can only tell them what Hughes said to me that night," she said. "That Des was an innocent dupe Hughes used to ingratiate himself into society. Des unwittingly brought Lyman & Stonebeck's shipping schedules home, never knowing Hughes was looking at them, much less relaying the information on to the Germans. I'll tell them how I overheard Hughes give the wireless to Des as a gift."

Without thinking, Kate smoothed a hand along her thigh, where the bullet from Hughes's gun had penetrated the night the ambulance flipped over—one of her many scars from the war that was still healing.

"Your testimony may save Des's life."

She looked Mark full in the face. "Ironic, isn't it?"

"Kate," Mark said tentatively. "In the past, things happened that were... that is to say, perhaps we behaved in a manner that we're not proud of." He looked down. "Behaved out of character."

"By we, you mean me, and you're talking about what I did with Des," she said frankly.

He looked embarrassed. "Yes, but I'm talking about me, too. Despite my best attempts at total independence, it seems I've done exactly what my mother wanted all along, including marrying Anne." He looked away. "She was easy to marry—so shy and quiet and eminently acceptable. It pleased Mother...."

"And you loved her," Kate said.

Mark paused. "Yes, for a while, I believed I did." He took Kate's hand, eyes locked on hers. "Here we are, the two of us," he said, voice low. "A widow and a widower. The war is over and we have our lives to live. I want a future, Kate. I don't want to live in the past."

"It's a new world now, after the war," she said. "For those of us who made it through."

"What I mean to say is...." His eyes riveted onto hers. "I want a future with you."

Kate's heart thudded in her chest. When she spoke, it came out a whisper. "But how can you forgive what I've done? What I did with Des?"

"It's not my place to forgive you. It's only my place to love you."

She wanted to believe him. "Words are easy, but to forget such a thing... may be beyond your ability."

His eyes never left hers. "The past is past. I'm a very different man than before. My marriage was dismal, except for becoming a father, and the war—it all changes the way one looks at life."

Tears sprang to Kate's eyes. "What about your mother? She won't be happy."

"It's you I want to make happy, my darling. Not Mother."

He pulled her close and kissed her, and then, lips barely apart, murmured, "I think I've loved you since the day we met, but I couldn't admit it, even to myself, because you belonged to someone else."

Kate, very gently, stepped out of his embrace and walked away from him, her head swimming. She went a short distance, stopped, and turned back to see his somber expression.

"It's been a long time since I've been in the country," she said. "What do you think of a picnic?"

Mark looked confused. "A picnic?"

"Yes." Then, with more confidence, she said, "I fancy going on a picnic. You do still own an automobile, I'd wager."

Mark managed to appear pleased and sheepish all at the same time. "As a matter of fact, I recently purchased a sporty little number—an Alfa Romeo. I rather think you'll like it."

She began to walk backward, unable to take her eyes off him. "I must get back to the shop. Sunday might be a good day for a pic—"

"Sunday," he blurted out, not even letting her finish.

"Will you pick me up at my new flat, around noon?"

"Yes, I'll be there," he said, gazing at her hard, as if she might evaporate. "I'll bring the food and drink and everything we need."

Kate nodded, forced herself to turn around, and walked away from him. Twice, she nearly stopped and called the whole thing off. Nearly... but she kept on, and then, after she'd walked a while, she realized she was smiling.

When she neared the shop, she stayed on the opposite side of the street, stopping on the sidewalk to take in the view before her—the steady stream of gleaming motorcars and dusty buses, people walking briskly, as if late for an important meeting. Two women, smartly dressed and topped with stylish hats, peered into *Vanessa's* window, leaning into one another, talking and pointing.

The shop—*her* shop—stood proudly, one of a long line of upscale storefronts on a popular street, in a prosperous neighborhood of London.

Kate's mind flashed back to her days in Scotland, plodding through a monotone existence, until a handsome stranger arrived one day and changed everything. Des was no hero, but if it hadn't been for him, she might still be peeling potatoes in the kitchen of the McGregor house alongside Lily, both of them squandering their lives, with no hope for the future.

The greatest gifts in her life had been Vanessa—love incarnate— and James, the most trustworthy and honorable husband a woman could ask for. Yet their presence had been oh, so brief, vanishing in the blink of an eye.

Now there was Mark, and here she stood, on the precipice of a new life, the old world gone.

It dawned on her, as she watched the busy street life in front of her, that she wasn't afraid of the future. In fact, she welcomed it, excited by the prospects that lay before her.

The door to the shop opened, and Tommy came out. He must have seen her standing there. He pantomimed a phone call waiting.

She smiled and nodded.

The phone call could be the largest order from Harrods they had received yet, bringing more money in one day than James had earned in a year. Or it might be Lady Winifred threatening Kate to stay away from Mark, Stonebeck Hall's only son and heir.

It didn't matter a wit to Kate which scenario it might be, because at that moment, the future shone before her like a night sky filled with brilliant stars — full of wonder, beauty, and hope.

Book Club Guide

1. In the early 1900's, Kate lives in the Scottish Highlands and works at a noble household as a young girl. What opportunities does she have for her future?

2. Desmond, nephew of a noble family, becomes interested in, and then obsessed, with Kate. What were the social norms at the time for relationships between members of different social classes?

3. James works as a clerk at Lyman & Stonebeck. How was he able to secure the position, and what kind of life can he provide for a wife and family?

4. Kate invites her neighbors to tea, trying to fit into her new role in society. What happens and why?

5. Desmond McGregor and Mark St. John own Lyman & Stonebeck, yet are British upper class. How do their positions in life affect the story?

6. When World War I breaks out, what military opportunities and limitations are there for Mark St. John, James Casey, and Muriel's friend Christopher?

7. Mark's wife Anne lives with her mother-in-law Winifred at Stonebeck Hall. What was life like for Anne on the estate?

8. As an officer in the Royal Navy, Mark joins secretive Room 40. What was Room 40, and what activities were its staff involved in?

9. Mark's sister Muriel is expected to marry a wealthy widower. Where do her true affections lie, and what are the consequences of those affections?

10. What happens to Kate after the dirigible attack in London, and how did she survive the physical and mental hardships?

11. James returns home from the war maimed and shell-shocked, with a very unusual friend. How did that friend help both James and Kate, and how did Kate's life change as a result?

12. Kate unwittingly stumbles upon a German spy. What were his spy tactics, and why did he come to find Kate the ultimate enemy?

13. How did British society change after the end of World War I, and how did those changes affect the characters in the book?

14. What was the relationship between Muriel and Christopher after the war, and how would they be accepted into British society?

15. The end of the story finds Kate filled with hope for the first time in a very long time. Why is she so optimistic?

Interview with the Author

Q. Why do you write?

A. I'm a reader and a movie buff, so I love stories told in different ways, both written and visually. I love being moved emotionally by a story, and I appreciate beautiful language.

Q. How long did it take you to write *Invisible by Day*?

A. I finished the first draft writing part time over a couple of years. I shopped it around some, and then put it away for almost twenty years. At a writer's conference, I was pitching a non-fiction book to a publisher. On a whim, I told her about *Invisible by Day*, and she wanted to see it. By this time, Downton Abbey was a big hit on PBS, and interest in the time and place of my book was high. I edited the book for another year, and they published it. The novel was in print for a short while, and then the publisher closed its doors. I worked on the book again, expanding the story and fleshing out some secondary characters, and then Evolved Publishing took me on within a year.

Q. What's your writing process?

A. I don't use an outline or have any pre-conceived idea of where the story will go. I have a big idea, and a setting, but other than that, I'm open. I've read that Stephen King writes this way—he is curious to find out how the story unfolds as he writes. That's the model I use. That wasn't a decision I made consciously; it was simply how the process unfolded when I sat down to write my first novel. I try to write at the same time each day, with a goal of writing for three hours or so. On a good day, I get so involved in the story that four or five hours will go by before I realize it. When everything is going well, I truly am in a "flow"—the concept that Hungarian psychologist Mihaly Csikszentmihalyi studied, defined as a highly focused mental state where time ceases to exist.

Q. How does it feel when you sit down to begin a book?

A. It depends. If I feel a sense of obligation and deadlines, it can be daunting. If I have a story idea that's been rolling around in my mind for a while, and no external pressures, I'm excited to sit down and get it started—to bring the idea to life.

Q. How does it feel to finish a book?
A. Nirvana!

Q. Why did you write historical fiction?
A. Because I was too young and inexperienced to know that you're supposed to write about something you know about. As a young reader, I enjoyed teenage mysteries by authors Phyllis Whitney and Eleanor Hibbert, so when I sat down to write my first novel, that's the general idea I had in mind—Scottish moors and mysterious castles. A short way into the novel, I realized I didn't know the year, the technology, or the culture. I'd set the story in Scotland and England, neither of which I had ever visited, so I had a lot of research to do.

Q. How did you conduct your research?
A. I wrote the first draft of the book in the 1990s, before the internet was pervasive. Luckily, I was a librarian, so I had all the books I needed at my fingertips. As I continued to develop the book years later, the vast online resources available helped me to find more details about the time period, including the specific activities of Room 40, which I incorporated into the book.

Q. Do you have a favorite author and book?
A. I have too many favorites to list, but some recent examples include *A Gentleman in Moscow* by Amor Towles, *All the Light We Cannot See* by Anthony Doerr, *Expats* by Chris Pavone, and *Beautiful Ruins* by Jess Walter. That's just a drop in the bucket, believe me.

Q. What are you working on next?
A. A novel set in Central Washington State called *The Clovis Dig*. The book was inspired by true events, when a Clovis cache was discovered in an apple orchard in East Wenatchee in the late 1980's. There was conflict between the archaeologists involved, and the price of apples had just plummeted after the Alar scare. In the novel, the main character, Claire, inherited the orchard from her family, but hard times are putting her livelihood in financial jeopardy. When the artifacts are unearthed, her livelihood is interrupted by the dig, putting her finances at further risk, but also introducing her to local archaeologist Joe Running, and Chicago archaeologist Spencer Grant, two ambitious and very different men. There's peril and mystery—some in the past, some in the present.

Acknowledgements

Many people helped me to make this book a reality. Among them is writer and poet Lauren Fink Shea. Sharing our writing with one another has been a joy, and made me a better writer. Thanks to writers A.C. Fuller, Cathie West, Jon Magnus, Lloyd Smith, and Grant Byington for your editorial wisdom. Tracy Fitzwater, Maureen Bryant, KC Heywood, Karen Kneadler, Susan Cox, Laura Fulbright—thanks for reading early versions of the novel and offering encouragement.

I am grateful to the Pacific Northwest Writers Association for providing the many opportunities for writers, including workshops, literary contests, and the annual conference that brings writers, publishers, and agents together.

Thanks to Dave Lane (aka Lane Diamond) of Evolved Publishing for taking on this project.

And to my husband Don Fink—thanks for your steadfast belief and encouragement.

About the Author

Teri spent her early childhood years in Redondo Beach, California before her family traded the beaches of the Pacific Coast for the apple orchards of Wenatchee, Washington. Her career has taken her from librarian, to corporate writer, and communications officer before becoming a novelist. Her writing has won literary awards for both fiction and nonfiction, and she's a member of the Pacific Northwest Writers Association. Teri and her husband live on beautiful Lake Chelan in central Washington State.

What's Next from Teri Fink?

THE CLOVIS DIG

Watch for this literary/women's fiction to release in the spring of 2020. Please stay tuned to the Evolved Publishing website for updates.

www.EvolvedPub.com/TFink

Amidst the beauty of the Wenatchee Valley at the feet of the Cascade Mountains, orchardist Claire Courtney struggles to make a living from her apple orchard. It's the late eighties, and an environmental health scare over a chemical used in apple production has dropped the bottom out of the market.

When strange and ancient artifacts are discovered beneath her orchard, Claire wonders whether the ensuing architectural dig will bring her the funds she so desperately needs, or force her to lose the home and livelihood that has been in her family for generations. An antagonistic relationship between the archaeologists on the dig—Joe Running from the west, and Spencer Grant from the east—threaten the entire project.

When a shocking discovery is found among the primeval relics, an investigation of a different kind begins, as Claire tries desperately to salvage what's left of the orchard and her life.

More from Evolved Publishing

We offer great books across multiple genres, featuring hiqh-quality editing (which we believe is second-to-none) and fantastic covers.

As a hybrid small press, your support as loyal readers is so important to us, and we have strived, with tireless dedication and sheer determination, to deliver on the promise of our motto: **QUALITY IS PRIORITY #1!**

Please check out all of our great books, which you can find at this link:

www.EvolvedPub.com/Catalog/

Thank you!